Kingdom
of the
Hill Country

Henry Melton

Kingdom of the Hill Country

Henry Melton

Wire Rim Books
Hutto, Texas

WRB

Kingdom of the Hill Country © 2012 by Henry Melton
All Rights Reserved

Printing History
First Edition: May 2012
ISBN 978-1-935236-36-8

ePub ISBN 978-1-935236-37-5
Kindle ISBN 978-1-935236-38-2

Website of Henry Melton
www.HenryMelton.com

Cover art © 2012 Henry and Mary Ann Melton

Printed in the United States of America

Wire Rim Books
www.wirerimbooks.com

Acknowledgements

My beta readers do more to build a novel than they probably realize. So I want do give particular thanks to Debra and Jonathan Andrews, Matt Borgard, Jim Dunn, Linda Elliott, Mike Lynch, Alan McConnell, Mary Ann Melton, Jim Reader, Mary Solomon, Tom Stock, and Nick Wall.

Bettye Baldwin, the author of "Horses for Writers", was always ready to give me good advice on the horses.

Special thanks to Kristina Gavit for her help with the cover image.

Back before this novel was even much of an idea, Kim Young, co-owner of the Falkenstein Castle in Burnet County, Texas was gracious enough to give me a tour of the inspirational site and those images stayed with me for years, shaping certain parts of this story. Thanks for the tour, and thanks showing how dreams can be come reality.

Contents

Prologue

After thousands of years being nothing more than the 'arm-pit' of the constellation Orion, Betelgeuse had the last say. It was getting old, as stars go. For all of human history and more, it had been a red giant, bloated up and puffing off gas clouds, just hanging on.

It was those clouds that made the difference. The star collapsed and exploded into a supernova. Not a tidy one. There were lobes and flares in this gigantic eruption. One of those flares just happened to be aimed at a much smaller star, Sol, and its little collection of planets.

Normally, at that distance, the brightness in the sky would have been spectacular, worthy of parties and short-lived end of the world panics. There would have been some gamma radiation, but most of it would have never made it through the atmosphere. Scientists would have have become media stars of the moment, and then the world would have gone back to normal as the star faded.

But there were those gas clouds. When the explosion ripped atoms and the star itself apart, first in line to get the untamed brunt of the blast were the bands of gas, smashed to plasma. What continued on towards Earth was more than just pretty lights and gamma radiation. The tortured remnants of the gas clouds had spawned electromagnetic pulses with power beyond anything created by puny hydrogen bombs. Spread out over long enough time to bathe the entire rotating planet with EMP spikes, the star fried everything made out of semiconductors.

Surely, some rural villages might not have noticed the sudden failure of all radio, all Internet, all computerized engine controllers—basically all the infrastructure of the Techno civilization. Unfortunately, even those villagers couldn't escape what came next.

Astronomers had taken pictures of many supernova remnants. With their spectroscopes and historical records, they had a very good idea of just how fast the expanding envelope of a ruptured star could travel. There was certainly no worry that anything from Betelgeuse could arrive at Earth for a long, long time. That confidence, unfortunately, was based only on what their telescopes could see. They couldn't see those EMP spikes, and they couldn't see the shock wave of ruptured atoms speeding away from the main envelope at nearly the speed of light.

Like ions from a particle accelerator, those came a bit later than the EMP and smashed into the upper reaches of the atmosphere like cosmic rays and bathed the planet in high energy fragments. Even the isolated villagers couldn't ignore livestock collapsing, at least those exposed for too long to the evil looking light in the sky.

By the time the light began to fade, Betelgeuse had made an indelible impression on the surviving human race, it had become the Star. With no long distance transportation nor communication, nations fragmented into small, isolated communities. The global Techno civilization was gone. It wasn't about to reboot. It would have to be rebuilt, piece by painful piece.

Eleven years later, a turning point was reached.

Bandits at Bell Springs

Enchanted Rock glistened. The flat top of the granite-dome mountain was transformed by the hard rain, and everywhere the ancient moss-rimmed pools were full and overflowing. Ed Morgan slipped down into the protective cave opening and wedged himself tightly between the granite walls. Being able to foresee a lightning strike coming down on top of you didn't make it any less frightening. His old, frayed white robe was damp and heavy as he hid in a crack between stone slabs.

Only one more strike.

It was not long coming. He quickly put his hands up over his ears and the bolt flashed. The air snapped around him, forceful even at the edges of the strike. His head rang from the explosion.

That's it. He edged out from under the boulder just as the lightning-inspired rain increased its fury.

Ed smiled, even as he blinked to keep his eyes clear. The trip here had been a good idea. This was a holy place again.

Before the Texans, before the Germans, and before the Spanish, this had been a sacred site for the Indians. Ghosts walked up here, a lost tribe gone extinct. The Tonkawas who came later feared them, holding their sacrifices at the base, not up on the peak.

He strode across the broad expanse of the dome until he could see the long abandoned State Park buildings below. The creek was up from the rain, but he had no doubt he could ford it by the time he made it to the base. With the granite wet, he would have to move slowly down the steep trail.

For now, he just stood and absorbed the trailing edge of the storm that was even then venting its lightning strikes on the next mountain to the north. The Hill Country was green and alive. Even when he had been a young man, and the Techno civilization was in full swing, this land had never really been conquered.

Remnants of the old highway curved around the regolith down below, and he was grateful for its easy grade, but how many more seasons before not even the ox-drawn wagons would be able to pass that way? Young bold trees grew up among the broken slabs of asphalt. Bridges were broken and shoulders eroded. Roads between towns survived, cut-offs and shortcuts that made sense before the collapse now had to prove their worth anew.

If he wished, he could go ask the road what its future would be, but he had no such wish. The future was spiteful. It was always best to let events unfold at their own pace. Too much curiosity had brought him here, and he'd have given anything to forget what he'd learned.

He adjusted his robe closer about him, and tried to ignore the sense of decay and dirt that was in store for the garment. He could see the future, it was his curse, but nearly two decades of practice and discipline let him ignore the question of whether his robe would be wrapped around his body as it rotted.

It was a great joy that even now, with his whitish hair and weathered skin making him look prematurely old, instead of only thirty-five, he did not know the time nor place of his own death. He intended to keep it that way.

He sighed as he felt the future edging into his thoughts again. It was going to be hard, very shortly. He had a death to oversee, a dynasty to bless, and a war to suffer through. He was grateful for this retreat; he would need the peace it had given him.

As another echo of a distant lightning strike, softer and more complex, caressed him, he turned downward, walking the trail millions of tourists had traveled before, feeling their lives every time he put out his hand to touch the rock.

...

Helen Black whistled. Snowcap perked his ears and looked up the valley to where she was was resting in DeeBee2's saddle. It was time to move on and she had made the mistake of leaving the young horse in the near pasture.

When he'd noticed she'd left on one of her house calls, he must have jumped the rail fence and come looking for her. He was too restless to follow meekly on a rope, and while he would let her ride occasionally, he was not yet trained to be comfortable carrying baggage.

DeeBee2 snorted as well, giving her opinion of the young one. She knew she was Helen's favorite.

Helen would have dismounted and rested more comfortably if it hadn't been for her long black dress. With her brown hair tightly combed, and in her best clothes, getting on and off the saddle was a little more trouble than it was worth. She clicked her tongue and DeeBee2 moved up to the ridge. Snowcap would follow. It was his nature. He hadn't drifted far out of eyesight since she'd delivered him, bloody and weak, from his dying mother.

The bandits weren't new this year. And it hadn't been the first time the roving thieves had seen a horse and considered it just another animal to be hunted and eaten. She would need to secure him in the tall fenced pastures to keep him home when she was out and about.

When she had been a little girl, horses had been common in Texas. But the radiation that had nearly killed her had taken Dadbert. It had been hard enough to keep people out of the Starlight and protected from the evil rays from the sky, much less their livestock. Even the native white-tail deer had nearly been wiped out. But there must have been some deer that had found canyons in the Hill Country to hide out the worst of it, because after about a decade, they started coming back in numbers great enough to hunt. Only a handful of horses had been given enough protection. Anyone younger than fifteen had likely never seen one.

If I find another one of my babies injured, I swear I'll start carrying a gun myself.

Snowcap's mother had been just the first horse she'd lost to hunting wounds. The mare had gotten free of the attacker and his blade, but by the time her owner had found her and called for the girl who treated horses, it was too late.

She looked back over her shoulder. Snowcap was dancing across the grass, climbing the slope after her. She smiled.

DeeBee2 halted unexpectedly, and she grabbed the pommel. "What?"

But her mount hadn't liked what she'd seen. Down near the creek, scruffy dark figures were walking among the trees. There were maybe a half-dozen of them. Helen eyeballed the distance between the group and the ford in the creek. Rains had soaked the ground over the past few weeks and there was only one place ahead to cross over to where she lived in Bell Springs. The only other choice was to head back south to Dripping Springs.

I can make it. She needed to get home and warn her family that bandits were in the area. Plus, her penned up horses were nothing more then easy prey to these scavengers.

Snowcap was playfully taking his time behind her. If they hadn't seen her and her brown mount yet, they would the instant the white horse crested the ridge line.

"Come on Dee, let's make a run for it." She kicked her flanks and leaned forward as her experienced horse shifted into a gallop. There was a whinny behind them as Snowcap suddenly discovered himself in a race.

There were shouts off to the left as the bandits saw them making their run.

We'll make it. Nothing could catch a horse.

Except another horse. Snowcap galloped past the loaded-down Dee-Bee2 and slowed as he splashed into the water. He knew where home was.

Crack! She gasped and looked off into the trees. A puff of white showed their location. They had guns! Her heart sank. Most of the bandits were barely more than beasts themselves, traveling in packs with knives and sharp sticks to encircle and trap their prey. These were running towards her.

Stumble and fall, she cursed silently. She'd never been able to hit something while moving. Hopefully, they wouldn't either. *And I'm a moving target!* Helen stood in the stirrups as her horse moved unevenly into the churning waters. There was another gunshot behind her, and then another, but she had her eyes on the far shore and Snowcap still running on a trail that he knew well.

DeeBee2 stumbled at the edge of the water. "Come on girl. We've made it. Solid ground and we can easily outrun them." She patted her neck.

And then hooves slipped on the mud and they were both in the water. Helen frantically grabbed for the reins that had torn loose when she fell.

And then she saw the blood, bubbling out of her faithful horse's side. And there was red foam in her mouth. Big dark eyes were wide with panic, looking at her to make it better.

On the other shore, there were shouts of triumph. Helen looked back, with a growing panic in her chest. Bandits raped every woman they caught.

It killed her to have to wade up the muddy bank. "Dee! I'll be back for you."

If they leave me alive after they're done with me.

Splashing water and shouts were behind her. Too close. It'd be nearly impossible to outrun them in her water-soaked dress. *We'll see about that.* Being a horse doctor included a fair amount of running. The only trained horses around were the ones she taught.

She was up on dry ground and staggered into a run. She glanced back and locked eyes with one of the bandits. He only had eyes for her. They wouldn't stop for the injured horse.

Wet and heavy, her long skirt threatened to trip her up. She'd dressed up for the visit into town. Vanity might just have gotten her killed.

The leader of the pack reached the bank and gave a roar. He was first in line.

She couldn't help it. No matter how independent and self-reliant she'd been, she screamed "Help!" louder than she'd ever shouted before. The only people who could hear her were the predators behind her.

But Snowcap heard. When she concentrated on the trail ahead of her, she saw the white bundle of motion heading her way. *Don't get shot! Don't get shot!* She couldn't bear to lose him, too.

As he closed the distance, she could tell he knew this was more than another game. There was a shot, and she could see him flinch, but he didn't falter.

He pulled to a stop in a cloud of dust. No stirrups, no halter, but she was up on his back effortlessly, shaking with her own adrenaline.

"Go! Home! Go!"

There were two more sharp cracks from behind, but Snowcap never missed a step. They flew down the trail and crossed the old Bell Springs road and across the field, taking the direct route. Her father Will, and neighbor John Lamar, were working on the old dam on the creek.

"Bandits!" she shouted. They took one look at her muddy dress and bareback ride, dropped their shovels and came running.

Ten minutes later, they had five horses saddled. Will Black, Mr. Lamar and his two dark-headed sons all had rifles. Helen carried an uncomfortably large pistol. She had elected to ride Snowcap, now bridled and under control. All the other women and the smaller children were barricaded in the Black's house and there was no one to take care of a horse.

The bandits scattered, moving back into the trees when the first couple of rifle shots landed came close. The farmers chased after them, confident in the greater range of their guns and the mobility of their horses.

Helen pulled up to the brown body in the water. Snowcap was uneasy and she had to keep a firm hand on the reins.

DeeBee2 must have survived a bit longer after she left, because the deep slash on her neck had bled heavily. But the gunshot into her lungs wasn't something Helen could have cured even under the best of conditions.

When her father rode up a few minutes later, she was still knee deep in the water shaking with rage, her hand stroking the warm, but motionless side.

"Helen! I want you to go back to the house. Some of them got away."

She looked up, barely able to focus on him through the tears in her eyes. "I abandoned her."

"Girl, the bandits killed her. You can't blame yourself. You're just lucky you got away. Now I'm not joking! Get back to the house now. I'll take care of her."

She nodded. But it just made it harder. Eleven years ago, during the Star, he'd had to dispose of her first horse. And now she was making him do it again. But she was older now, and Daddy had to deal with murderers. She didn't argue. Even if the men took care of this pack of bandits, there could be others. Her pistol needed to be back at the house, protecting Momma and Billy and Jenny.

She scavenged as much as she could of her bags and her medical tools. Some of her drugs were ruined by the creek water. She would have to make more. Her books were okay. Once again, the scarce, waterproof wrapping had paid off.

Snowcap didn't like the bags as Helen slung them across his back, but he didn't like what he saw in the water either.

Helen rode him back to the house at a walking pace. She needed time to think.

The families of Bell Springs could handle an occasional raiding party, as long as their ammunition held out. But they were coming more frequently, and in larger numbers. Five little families made a comfortable little community, but they couldn't fight forever. They needed help. Where were Austin's fabled Guards? Hadn't they promised to extend their patrols out this far years ago? Someone needed to make that happen.

Little Africa

Ed hesitated as he stepped into the wide grassland of Buchanan Valley. This used to be a lake, one of a string of man-made lakes to the west of Austin, and he could feel remnants of the cold and dark with every step. To his physical eyes, it was very different. The mud flats of the former lake had left a soil where trees didn't grow. Grasses waved in the wind, like waves on the sea. Something that looked like a deer with tall, spiraled antlers watched him across the distance.

Back before the Star, many of the ranches in the Texas Hill Country raised exotic animals, some imported from Africa. When everything fell apart, the zoo owners and exotic ranch operators had other, more pressing issues to deal with, and the imported gnus, zebras and the like were butchered or escaped. Now they were on a level playing field with the native deer, roaming the country, seeking favorable habitat.

It appeared that the Buchanan Valley, with no fences and endless grasses was like a little Africa for several of the exotic species, especially the ones that needed to see predators coming in the distance.

Ed kept walking deeper into the valley until he reached the river, brown and thick from the recent rains. There was a wagon trail following the river. In dry weather, there was a ford near where he stood, but with the water so high, travelers like him needed to follow the muddy ruts to the next ford a ways downstream. He fished into his tote bag, but there was nothing left but an apple. It had lost its crispness, but he nibbled it down to the seeds. He didn't worry. Food would happen.

The dam stretched across the horizon, except where the water had broken through—a line of concrete, white above the waving grass. The far horizon was rolling green hills, with a castle riding the top of the ridge—an old European design made real by a wealthy couple before the world collapsed.

The sight of the castle reminded him of something—either in the past or the future, he wasn't sure.

Off to the left of his trail, there was a limestone outcropping. He turned. A hundred paces later, he found a clear pool of water, dammed up by the rock. A great blue heron stepped cautiously in the shallows on the far side, watching him. He carefully dipped his canteen in to refill it with the clean, mud-free water, then sat on the edge of the stone to wait.

...

James Fuller raised his arm, and the dozen Mounted Guards, men on motorcycles, slowed with him. He pulled to a stop on a relatively bare stretch of the old Highway 290, a few hours east of Austin. The engines eased down to silence.

"Men, Brenham is just five miles ahead. We're here to make a show, not to fight. So riding formation is much more important than your guns. Shiny chrome is more important than bullets. We know Houston is moving into this area and we need the locals to think highly of Austin. Make your last minute adjustments and move out, in formation."

The soldiers, most of them older than he was, checked their bikes, their guns, and their recently laundered uniforms. During the Star Time, the old Texas National Guard units based in the city had been absorbed into the Austin City government and were officially renamed the City Guard. Most spent their days watching the streets, catching minor thieves and making the city dwellers feel safe.

James had struggled for more than a year to organize a motorcycle patrol for the outlying communities. He had made his place in the Guard, gaining respect in spite of his family connection, but the City Council hadn't paid any attention to his requests until a trading convoy from Navasota reported that they had to pay a toll to Houston troops before they could return to Austin. James had taken his own bike out, scouting the cities to the east. When the Council saw his list of towns, from Hempstead to Sealy under

Houston control and with Houston's own National Guard remnant troops having been reported seen in La Grange, his father, Mayor George Fuller, gave him official permission to tour the borderland towns with a show of force.

He just hoped it was enough.

...

Ed had seen enough television before the Star to remember what ox drawn wagons used to look like—wooden boats with large iron-rimmed spoked wheels. Today's versions were a bit different, with most built on the framework of old cars and trucks. Coming down the muddy trail behind him, this wagon had a white cotton canopy like the old ones he remembered from westerns, but with big tractor tires. The driver's bench was down in the gap where the engine had been. There was only one ox, but it showed its Brahman lineage in its size and the hump on its back.

He waved as soon as the driver noticed him. When he got closer, Ed yelled, "Clear water!"

The wagon slowed and pulled up to the rock were he'd been waiting.

"Hello! Taylors here out of Brady. Did you say 'clear water'?"

"Yep. Nice pool here. Tastes clean and sweet." He held up his canteen and took another sip. "I'm Ed."

Mr. Taylor glanced around, but there was no place for bandits to be hiding other than in the grass. A woman's voice came from inside the canopy. "Cal, I could use a break."

Ed smiled and showed the family, Mary and Cal and their ten-year-old son Simon, where they could fill their bowls without stirring up the mud.

"We've drunk enough mud this past week." Mary shook her head.

Simon was fascinated by his strange white clothes. "Are you a wise man?"

Ed chuckled. "Probably not."

"We're going to see a wise man."

"Oh?"

Mary was watching him as she worked, washing out several water barrels and replacing the brown water with clear.

She nodded. "Simon has fainting spells. We've heard tell of a wise man in Austin that can heal people."

Ed shook his head. "I know the rumors, but most of them are exaggerations."

Cal Taylor asked, "We've been looking for a ford. It's supposed to be near here, but I haven't been able to find it."

Ed pointed. "In dry weather, it's right over there. But with the rains, your rig would be bogged down in the mud so badly it'd take an extra team of cattle to haul you through. You're hoping to hook up with old Highway 29?"

Cal sighed. "Yes. That's the route I was given."

"You should follow me to Inks Dam. It's a toll path, but your rig would fit on the new bridge they built over the shoals about a mile below the dam. There's passable routes from there back to 29. It's a popular way ever since the Buchanan Dam broke and took out the two bridges downstream from it."

He shook his head. "That would be too far out my way. The trucker I talked to said there's another ford below this dam."

Ed nodded. "It's rocky, and you could probably make it through, but there are bandits in the area."

He looked at his wife. "Yes. We've seen the signs. That's part of the reason we're moving to Austin. It seems the bandits are all through this area. We need to stick to the main road."

Ed shrugged. "If I can't change your mind, then I can't." He already knew the man was set on his course.

"Have you seen bandits, Mister?"

He looked down at the boy. "Yes. I've seen quite a few, especially since the winter. They seem to be on the move."

"Don't they fight you?"

"No. Not me."

"Why not?"

He shrugged. "Maybe because they can see I don't have anything to steal. No money. No food. And I'm much too skinny to be much of a threat to them."

Simon smiled. "Daddy scared the bandits off with his rifle."

Ed nodded, with a sad look. "They'll definitely choose the weak prey to attack."

Cal looked at the sun. "We'll probably spend the night here and find the lower ford in the morning. Ed, would you care to have supper with us?"

"Thank you. I would appreciate that."

...

Ed chatted with the boy as they ate. The parents watched and talked quietly to themselves.

"Mister, do you know anything about the wise man in Austin?"

He smiled. "Quite a bit, actually. First thing to know is that he's not very wise."

Simon frowned. "But people say..."

"It's just a trick."

"What is?"

"What he does. You see, he can see the future a little bit. Sometimes he can see enough to let people know what to do to avoid their sickness. But that doesn't make him wise, and it doesn't let him heal people. He doesn't tell many people that, because people would want him to tell their future all the time, and that isn't a good thing."

Simon looked at his parents. "They're not going to be happy. They wanted him to heal me."

"They're not the only ones. That man who can see the future, he has started taking long walks through the countryside so that he can avoid all the people who want to take advantage of his gifts. It's easier to hide than to tell all those parents that he can't really heal their precious child."

The boy frowned at him. "He walks around the countryside?"

"Yes."

"Just walking? No wagon or anything?"

"Nope. No money. No food. No change of clothes. Just a canteen sometimes."

"How can he survive?"

Ed chuckled. "He can tell the future. Suppose he knows some nice people will be coming along the trail in a couple of hours that would be happy to feed him. All he'd have to do is sit down on a rock and wait for them."

Simon's eyes were wide. "So...so... " He swallowed. "So you knew we'd feed you so you waited for us."

He nodded. "For a couple of hours. But it was actually more than that. I'd seen you several days ago. I knew I had to be here to take your hand and see your future and to talk to your parents." Ed shrugged. "Some things I just don't have any choice about." He held out his hand.

Simon hesitated and then reached out his own.

For a moment, Ed closed his eyes and felt the little boy's life. Then he smiled.

"Simon, go tell your mother that you won't have any more spells. Would you do that for me?"

He nodded and ran over to where his parents sat. Ed could hear a few words as he energetically convinced them.

After a few moments the parents came.

"You are him?" Cal asked.

Ed nodded.

Mary asked, "And Simon? You healed him?"

Ed sighed. "It's not that. I just know his future. You have to do your part. If you go put Simon to bed and tell him a bed time story and let him know just how much you love him, the spells won't come back. Your worries have been a part of the problem. I can guarantee that with just a tiny little change, his brain won't act up anymore." He smiled at her. "You love your son. Let him know that. Let him know that every day, and it will be enough."

He looked at Cal. "And you too. He idolizes you and you have to let him know you're proud of him. Go now, share a story about you as a boy. Bond with him."

Cal stood. "I can do that." He helped his wife to her feet. "You know, I do think you're a wise man, no matter what you said."

Ed watched them go. *But I know better.*

. . .

In the morning, he helped the Taylors get back on their trail. Three happy travelers waved him good travels as he parted with them at the broken arch. The old Buchanan Dam had crumbled away during a bad flood when the inactive flood gates let the lake overtop the main span. The whole region was lucky the surging waters hadn't taken out the lower dams as well. The family navigated the narrow path around the dam and down into the rocky canyon below.

Ed took a side path to the old walkway that crowned the remaining arches.

There was a gunshot in the distance. A moment later the canyon echoed with the absolute despair of a mother's loss, cut short by a sword thrust. The bandits shouts were like crows in the distance. Ed's knees gave away and he knelt on the old concrete and let the grief flow over him. It was grief he'd felt coming for days. His visions of the future were fragmentary, but some things were unchangeable. Cal Taylor's path had been fixed, no matter what the advice of a chance-met stranger. The bandits, who waited in hiding for travelers struggling in the current before attacking, were the Taylors' fate, and the only thing he could have done for them was to let them have that one perfect night before their deaths.

A Visit to Austin

"Something has to be done about the bandits." Helen argued.

Her father nodded, cutting his rabbit and chewing thoughtfully. He said, "The Mayor promised great things, but it's been a long time since we've seen City Guards out this far. Maybe we should never have moved."

When he saw his daughter wince, he shook his head. "No. I didn't mean that." They'd moved because he could never deny his daughter's calling. They needed this place, farther out from the city, where she could raise her horses. He knew he was a doting old fool, but since that day years ago when that Morgan boy somehow healed her radiation sickness, he'd somehow known that she was destined for a path more grand than he could ever give her.

Helen thought a bit. "Maybe the Mayor needs reminding. I've got to deliver that Arabian back to the Gregersons in Pace Bend. I could take a side trip to Austin and tell the Mayor just how bad the bandits are getting out here."

"Oh, no, Helen! You can't think of going out again, after what's just happened," Karen Black said.

"Mom. This is what I do. I have a business. I'm twenty three, and I'm not going to just sit here and wait for the Lamar boys to grow up and get interested in me. You have Billy and Jenny to take care of, but I just can't hide behind your skirts anymore."

Will chuckled, and his wife glared at him.

"Hey, what did I do? It's funny, is all. When did Helen ever hide behind your skirts? At that age, she was agitating to get a cell phone of her own and badgering me into paying for her riding lessons. Helen, where did you get that phrase anyway–out of one of your books?"

Helen blushed a bit. Collecting historical romances was her biggest vice, and more than once she'd taken her vet fees in old books.

Her mother wasn't done. "Honey, promise me you won't do anything foolish right now! It's dangerous out there."

"Mom, it's dangerous here! Those men were just over the ridge line. I'll be safer going into the city than I will be here. And that's got to stop! We three are the only people in this place who have actually met the Mayor. It may not be much, but we did talk to him back then, and he did make promises. You and Dad have to stay and protect this place, but I have to go anyway. Why not take an extra few days and try to get help?"

...

It was a long argument, but when Joshua Lamar came over to return some tools and heard what was being discussed, he volunteered to go along with her.

Helen was furious that a boy five years younger than her made the trip more reasonable for her parents, but Joshua was big for his eighteen years and there was no doubt that he was much better with a rifle than she was. He was even cute too, but they'd been neighbors for too many years and she'd been his babysitter for some of them. Shelly, his mother, had mentioned from time to time how much she'd love to have Helen in her family, but she couldn't see Joshua that way. And certainly not his younger brother Carl.

I don't know why I can't seem to get interested in anyone. Mom was expecting grandkids by now. She shook her head. She patted Snowcap again. Maybe it was the horses. Nobody seemed as interested in them as she was. Even Dad only put up with her herd as a favor to her. *Maybe if I could make more money at it, other people would see them as valuable, not just an obsolete plaything of the Techno civilization.*

It had been just bad luck, as far as she was concerned, that so many horses died under the peak radiation times of the Star. By the time it had passed, there was barely any livestock of any kind in the Austin area. Most of the cattle since then had come from herds protected by ranchers from around Mason and Fredericksburg. People hungry for beef and for animals that could be trained to pull loads imported them as fast as they could be bred.

Cattle were trained to be oxen. Horses had just been forgotten.

...

Joshua put his boot in the stirrups. "Ready to go?"

She nodded, and mounted Snowcap. She wore her jeans and had her 'business lady' dress washed and packed in her travel bag. She wouldn't make the same mistake again. If she had to run, she wanted to be able to run fast. Her father led Tawny, the Arabian, over and tied the lead rope to Sandy's saddle. Joshua could handle both horses fine, and she wasn't ready to give Snowcap the distraction, not yet. Tawny was walking well, now that the ugly cut on her foreleg had healed. It had taken some doing, but Helen was proud of the work she'd done saving the mare. From her seat on Snowcap, Tawny looked decidedly small. It was going to be much easier to return her. When she was injured, Tawny been delivered in an ox-drawn horse trailer, with a sling to carry her weight.

And then, waving goodbye, they were off. Joshua led the way, eager to get on the road. She hoped he was as responsible as he seemed. Right now, his face had a great big grin and he seemed like a kid off on a joy ride.

...

Angela Morgan raced down the stairway, startling her maid, and opened the front door herself.

She startled the bicycle messenger, and her disappointment was plain on her face. "Yes? What can I do for you?"

The youngster, barely in his teens and wearing an official cap too big for him, held out an envelope. "A Net request for Edward Morgan."

"I'll sign for it." She barely gave it a glance and scribbled her name on the clipboard. He was startled when she handed him a quarter as a tip.

"Thanks!"

Angela smiled at the boy's reaction. Back before the Star, she'd given up on pennies. They weren't worth the bother of picking them up. How things had changed! Paper money had started to fade out of use, as the government that backed it was no more, but the coins were still valuable. Big contracts still listed 'dollars' but they no longer referred to Federal Reserve Notes. Banks were now arbiters of an elaborate barter system and backed their own script.

Once he pedaled away, she glanced at the envelope. The computerized printing was a novelty. Only the IIS had computers and printers. She picked up an ornate silver letter opener from the table by the door and slit the envelope.

Request 908435 received at the International Informa-tion Service in North Austin:

REQUEST FOR READING ON ...

She stuffed the unread letter back into the envelope and put it on the stack of others just like it. Here in Austin, her husband was well known, but it surprised her when fortune telling requests came in from France or Australia. How in the world had his reputation spread so far? She knew he ignored most of the requests. His job was to advise the Austin City Council, in particular the Mayor. But even then, he vanished, sometimes for two or three months at a time.

He didn't even tell her where he was going. She suspected he didn't know either. She sighed and started the climb back upstairs where she was working on the invitations to the Lakeside Restoration Benefit.

Everything seemed so much harder than back in the Techno age when you could just print out address labels instead of writing each card and hand addressing everything. But at least her cursive handwriting had gotten so much more elegant and legible. Back in the old days before the Star, she hardly wrote anything. It'd all been keyboard and tapping the cell phone.

...

Sam Mason pedaled back to the office, pleased with his tip. Normally customers tipped him a penny or so; sometimes nothing at all. That was why he kept a mental list of the good tippers and moved their deliveries to the top of the pile. Normally, he'd wait until there were a half-dozen or so letters to go out, but not when he saw Ed Morgan's name. The man himself sometimes forgot to tip, but the lady was at the door most of the time.

He rested the bike against the wall and then went in. April was only eleven, but she was his boss. "No reply?"

He shook his head. "Nope. I don't think he's back yet." He checked the to-be-delivered slot, and there were only four.

She smiled. "Randall came by while you were gone and took all the government addresses."

Sam grumbled. All of those could be delivered with nearly one stop, and yet his quota was based on numbers delivered, not numbers of stops. Tips were nice, but if he didn't keep up his quota, Hodges would be hunting for a new courier. He scooped up the remaining envelopes. There was no guarantee there would be more. Some days there were dozens, with more every hour. Other days, there was just a trickle.

He glanced at the names. They were familiar. Most were businesses with contacts in Houston or Dallas. There used to be an IIS station in San Antonio, but it had dropped off the Net, and no one knew why.

April turned her head to the printer as it began spitting out paper. "Hold on." She pulled the single sheet and used her ruler to strip the addressing label from the first couple of lines. She pasted that to a blank envelope and folded the message and inserted it inside. She handed it to him. "Looks like Randall left a little early. One more for the Driskill."

He raised his eyebrows when he saw the name. He slapped it onto the top of the stack and yelled, "Thanks!" as he dashed out the door.

...

Tawny was so eager to get back home that she broke free of the lead rope when the house came into view. Joshua was embarrassed that he'd let it slip free, but Helen wasn't going to make a fuss. The Gregersons were pleased with how well she had healed, and although it was expensive for the farmers, Axel wrote out the bank draft for her services with a smile.

"That's a good-looking stallion you've got there. You gonna put him out to stud?"

She patted Snowcap's neck. "Sooner or later."

I ought to ride out more often. People were interested in horses, once they saw people riding them. Lots of little kids had never seen one before. A lot of adults thought they were extinct.

It was so obvious to her that horses were the future, but even though people thought nothing of hitching a wagon up to a steer, there were only a few people, like the Gregersons who thought the way she did.

Joshua was watering their horses and chatting with Axel when she finished packing away her money. Getting paid was more important than the actual money. She'd been thinking of her vet services as a 'business' long before she began charging. Maybe some day, she could think her efforts as a business without the mental quote-marks.

"Are we going to spend the night here?" Joshua asked.

Axel nodded toward his house. "You're welcome to stay."

Helen shook her head. "We have to go to the city."

Joshua pointed out into the lake. "We could take the ferry."

The open-air barge was docked a quarter mile away, and she could see some people loading. She put her foot in the stirrup. "Let's check it out."

...

The ferryman's bare arms looked like they'd long ago burned to dark leather. He shook his head. "No. Livestock takes up space. If you can't pay the price, I have other people who can. With the bandit attacks, I've had to double my trips, and these old Mercuries drink gasoline like nobody's business. I have to keep raising the price, or get you people to row for me."

Helen shook her head. "We'll find another way. We can ride our horses."

He shrugged and moved to the next group. There were waiting lines to get to the safer side of the lake.

Helen moved back. She could have paid, but with all the cross-lake traffic, the ferry no longer took the long run down to Hippie Hollow near the dam. She watched a mother corral a rebellious little girl, the ordeal plain on both their faces. They had seen bandits or heard a story, and they needed to reach safety, no matter what it cost.

I understand. There was raw place in her heart that no amount of grateful customer checks could heal. And on top of grief was fear. She really didn't want to see bandits again.

"We'll ride. We'll ride all night if that's what it takes. We need to get to Austin as soon as we can."

Joshua winced. "Okay, but I'm not used to being in the saddle as much as you."

She pulled out a well-used roadmap, a prized family heirloom, printed before the Star. She traced routes with her finger and estimated distances.

"If we stick to 71, it's about 30 miles to West Lake Hills. We can cross at Red Bud Isles. Both Snowcap and Sandy are sturdy. If we take it at an even pace, on a flat road, we should have no problems."

"Why did we even bring camping gear if we're not going to use it?" he grumbled.

She gestured towards the people. "Those folks are scared to death of bandits. It's not just around our little valley. The attacks are happening all over the place. I'd rather keep moving. I couldn't sleep out in the open. Could you?"

"I guess you're right."

"Then let's move, but at a easy pace. We'll need the horses rested enough to run for it if we see trouble."

Special Delivery

"You've got to do it." The scar on Pete's face just made his grim determination that much more unrelenting. He held out the scissors and a razor.

Hek took them with distaste. He felt his beard tentatively. It was part of him. He'd sooner cut off a finger. He hadn't shaved since the battle of Fort Sam.

But, they had a farmer's clean clothes. If he were going to sneak into the city, he'd need be bathed and shaved to look the part. But it would be a year or more before he'd be able to sit around the fire without the other Hunters laughing at him.

Pete tapped the pot with warm water in it. "Get started. And don't cut yourself doing it."

"Yeah, I'd hate to look like you!"

He took another look around the cave, to make sure the other guys weren't watching, then started.

...

Sam walked into the Driskill Hotel lobby with his best official courier face, and straightened his five foot, six inches as the receptionist looked across at him.

"I have an IIS dispatch for Mr. James Fuller."

She reached for it. "I'll see that he gets it."

He shook his head. "IIS has standing orders that dispatches for Mr. Fuller are to be delivered to him only."

She frowned. "I'm not sure if he's back in town yet."

"I'm familiar with the building. I can check. I've delivered to his office before."

She nodded. "Go ahead then." She gestured to the guard at the stair well, and Sam headed up to the third floor. The City offices had relocated to the Driskill a couple of years before, after a fire had gutted the old City Hall on 2nd Street. Built long before the Techno age, the grand old hotel was less dependent on air conditioning and elevators than the remaining glass towers downtown.

Sam reached the office, hoping that the climb wasn't in vain. He wasn't joking about hand delivery.

He knocked on the door, marked only with a number. If you didn't know where he worked, the man wasn't going to tell you.

"Enter." The voice inside sounded tired.

When the door opened, it was clear he'd just arrived, still in his leather riding clothes and still dusty. He nodded. "Sam. You have something for me?"

He presented the sealed envelope and turned his back. Mr. Fuller needed his privacy. There was the sound of tearing paper, then the scratch of a pen.

"Here." James handed him the folded sheet he'd written. "See that it gets out promptly."

Sam grinned and removed an empty envelope from his pouch and secured the package. "Always, Mr. Fuller." He turned to go. The man never tipped, but somehow, a bonus tended to show up in Sam's weekly pay whenever he made deliveries to this office. Not that he'd care. James Fuller was his hero.

"One other thing, Sam. Is April on duty?"

"Yes, sir."

"Could you give her this for me?"

. . .

April's eyes were bright as he handed over the two items. She let the novel sit out the countertop, untouched. But her hands were shaking until she composed herself and took the outgoing message over to the computer and keyed it in. She even used the privacy shade, although there was no one in the office but the two of them.

Sam had been shown a glimpse of one of James Fuller's secret messages once before. It was random looking 'words', all five letters long. He had even explained.

"Sam, some government messages are so important that people would steal to get a look at them. Now, I trust you and the IIS, but just so no one gets the idea that they could knock you out and steal a message you're carrying, just about all of the messages I'm sending and receiving will be coded like this, so it won't do them any good to try."

It was just like what Hodges had said when he was hired. All the IIS messages on the radio waves were all coded so they could only be read by the person they were addressed to.

April typed quickly and carefully, then pressed the button to send the text off on its way. She dropped the sheet into a shredder and cranked the handle twice before she zipped back on her wheeled office chair to the book on the counter top. Sam could see the title, *Harriet the Spy*, but it just looked like any old beat-up book to him.

"James Fuller said he found it in a little store in Giddings and thought you might like it."

"Oh, yes. Oh, yes! I've heard about it, but I could never find a copy. If he were here, I'd kiss him."

He smiled. She'd have to get in line. When Mr. Fuller had been in the crowd on Congress Avenue during the Survivor's Day parade, with him riding on his motorcycle at a walking pace with his Mounted Guard soldiers riding behind him, he'd heard quite enough girly squeals.

All the girls in the crowd had been excited to see him. He was the hero of the city, especially after he'd led a volunteer army to quell the Taylor Rebellion. And then again, when he personally led the fire-fighting efforts during the blaze that had taken City Hall. His efforts kept it from spreading throughout the tent and shack community that had built up on the north shore of Lady Bird Lake. Thousands of people owed him. The whole city loved him.

But the girls wondered why, in his mid-twenties, he wasn't married yet.

...

The guard stationed at the bridge at Red Bud Isles, just downstream of Tom Miller Dam, peered at Helen's document.

"Just how old is this thing?"

Helen didn't immediately answer. She'd been standing in line since dawn, waiting her turn. Joshua stood slightly to the side, talking in a low voice to the horses. Sandy was patient, but Snowcap had never seen this many people before this trip and he didn't like it.

"I don't remember exactly. I just recall George Fuller–Mayor George Fuller–saying that this document should get me through any city checkpoints, and that if I had any trouble at all, to get back to him in person to take care of it."

She didn't care to add that she was a little girl at the time and that he was actually speaking to her parents. She'd spent some time in the hospital, being treated for radiation exposure from the Star. Also, she didn't want to mention that the pass was to allow her family to exit the city with no problems, not get back in. Still, none of that was mentioned on the sheet of paper. And George Fuller was still the most powerful man in the city.

Helen tried to look bored and impatient, and to ignore the fact that the guards were turning most of the people away, sending them to the bigger entrances at Mansfield Dam or the Mopac bridge.

Rumor had it that all the entrances across the Colorado River were being well-guarded and restricted. The bandit activity had been increasing lately, and the City Guard's first priority was to protect Austin, even if that meant turning away refugees. The river, especially now with the rains, made a formidable barrier to the south.

Even South Austin had become a second-class community, though Austin still claimed its borders.

"Okay," the guard glanced at Joshua and the horses, then decided it wasn't worth it. He handed back her pass. "Go on across."

Once on the other side, Joshua sighed deeply. "I'm glad we're past that–and we didn't even have to pay."

She didn't comment. Although they'd gotten a few strange looks because of their horses, she'd heard a few comments that left a sour taste. The soldiers were apparently a little tired of all the 'goat-herders' and wished they'd all go back to their hills.

It matched other things she'd heard. Austin loved the farmers to the north and east. The Black-land Prairie made for fertile croplands that fed the city. They would just as soon abandon the rocky Hill Country where goats and small garden plots made up the bulk of the agriculture. Unfortunately, it made her quest to extend the city's protection to her part of the world seem impossible.

...

Austin looked different. When she was a child, just recovering from the blood transfusions and endless bed rest her radiation sickness had visited upon her, the streets had been relatively wide and yet littered with abandoned cars. Some of the buildings she remembered from their visit had burned, but many were just the same. The most noticeable difference was the buildup of side-to-side sheds and open air booths, many built out onto the pavement. There was still a clear road, but it didn't need as many lanes as it had before the Star.

Snowcap reared the first time a small, yet noisy, gasoline-powered truck met them on the road. From the droppings on the street, ox-drawn wagons probably outnumbered the mechanical beasts by a large margin.

They turned left at Congress Avenue and made their slow progress up towards the Capitol building. It was every bit as massive as she remembered, but by the time they reached the park-like grounds, she could tell it was deserted.

"Oh!"

Joshua looked her way. "What is it?"

"I forgot. This is where the State government was. The City never ruled from here."

They continued up the curvy entrance road and dismounted at the entrance.

Joshua took the reins and walked the horses over to a grassy patch. There were several cows in a nearby pen.

Helen walked into the high-ceilinged building, her every step echoing off the granite. She was surprised that it was relatively clean.

A small, lively, bald-headed man scurried down a stairway. "Excuse me, but you can't stable your horses here without a permit."

Helen put on her best smile. "Of course. I am just new in town. I was looking for the City government and came here first."

He sniffed. "I'm sure they'd take over the Capitol building if they thought they could get away with it. Certainly, they make noises about it every so often. But not on my watch."

She held out her hand. "I'm Helen Black, from Bell Springs, just this side of Dripping Springs."

He shook it, "Nice to meet you. I'm Jake Dennison, Texas State Comptroller. At least until they hold another statewide election."

"So...there is an active state government?"

He looked embarrassed. "So I claim. Nobody pays their taxes, and I have no way to enforce it." He looked up to the top of the dome. "I just hang onto this place and hope things will change for the better. It's more a symbol of better times than anything. I have to rent grazing rights for money to keep it going. You're lucky you came by in the daytime. It's a little spooky at night. I can't afford electricity."

"Well, I don't want Snowcap and Sandy to eat all your grass. I'll be moving on, as soon as I find out where to find the City government. I have a few complaints to make."

He smiled tightly. "They're over at the Driskill Hotel," he pointed, "Sixth and Brazos."

"Thanks. Umm. Could I ask a favor? Is there a ladies' room?"

. . .

Dressed to impress, she walked into the entrance, and then stopped when she realized she had no idea where to go, or who to talk to.

The girl behind the counter asked, "Can I help you?"

Helen tried to throw off her uncertainty. "Yes. I need to speak to George Fuller. He's the Mayor."

A pained smile let her know she was showing her out-of-town roots. "Do you have an appointment card?"

"No, but the last time I talked to him, he said I could come by at any time."

The desk clerk nodded slightly, as if she'd heard that line before. "I still need a card before I can bother any of the city officers."

Helen frowned. "Okay, how can I get an appointment card?"

Speaking slowly, as if she was stupid, "You can get a card from a city officer, or their secretary."

Helen took a deeper breath. "May I speak to the Mayor's secretary?"

"I'm sorry, but you will need an appointment."

"Well, where can I get that appointment?"

She shook her head. "I'm sorry, but the secretarial staff is on the second floor, and without an access pass, the guard won't let you through."

Helen glanced at the guard. He showed a grin, as if he were enjoying the interplay.

Well, she wasn't enjoying it.

"And where can I get a pass?"

"From one of the city officers."

House Guest

Steamed, she admitted defeat after a few more minutes. The receptionist had all the angles covered, and Helen was sure she played the same game on a regular basis. Short of calling in Joshua to wrestle with the guard, she wasn't going to get in.

"Come on," she took comfort in stroking Snowcap's neck, "I can't get in the front door. I'll have to find another way."

Joshua nodded towards a concrete structure down the road. "A man came by to see the horses and he said there's a public stable in the 'parking garage'. Should we check it out?"

"I guess so."

Soon they'd exchanged some Bartlett's Bank script for stalls for the horses, grain, hay and water. Helen dug through her papers.

"What's that?"

She re-read the yellowed note. "It's a letter I received a few years ago. It was an invitation to come visit. I think I need a local to help me get through this maze of snooty city workers. I wonder where Enfield Road is?"

A stable worker, pitching hay into a feeding cage, had been listening. "Do you need a guide? My brother's even got wheels."

...

The wheels were a rickshaw cart hooked to a bicycle, but the horses needed the rest and so did they. Helen fussed at herself for trying to tackle the city offices while she was still dead tired from the trip. They really should find a hotel soon. But in spite of her exhaustion, she was desperate to make some kind of headway in her quest.

As the pair of them rode elbow to elbow through the streets, she was surprised to see just how many of the rickshaw carts there were. Their hard, skinny wheels would never work back in Bell Springs. They needed hard, flat roads.

The house was two stories tall and comfortably filled the large tree-shaded lot, with floweres lining the entrance walkway. Hesitantly, Helen double-checked the numbers on the beside the doorway and knocked. She glanced back at Joshua. He was whispering with their driver, just in case they'd need to ride back to the stable.

A well dressed woman opened the door, panting from racing to answere the knock. Helen recognized her slowly, her face a little older from the last time they'd met, eleven years before.

Angela Morgan was having trouble with her face as well.

"Hello?"

Helen smiled, timidly. "Hello. My name is Helen Black and ..."

She reached out and pulled her in. "Certainly, Helen! I remember you. But my, how mature you've become."

Helen pointed behind her. "And that's Joshua Lamar. He's my babysitter for the trip."

"Both of you, come in! Come in!"

She reached for a bell sitting on a table and rang it. "Jane, we have guests!"

...

Joshua carefully sipped from the cup that looked so delicate that he was afraid he'd snap the handle. "I'm enjoying the trip. I was only seven when the Star happened, and I don't really remember anything about when we lived in the city."

Angela was doing her best to make them comfortable. "So what do you think about Helen's horse business? I rode myself when I was little–oh years before the Star. And it was Helen's other horse that saved me when I had the car accident."

Joshua shrugged. "I always thought she was crazy. But she's making it pay."

"And you, Helen. What brings you to the city? Did you come to visit James?"

Helen looked puzzled. "James?"

"James Fuller. George Fuller's son. Surely you remember him. He pushed you around in a wheelchair. You two spent hours together."

She tilted her head in thought. "Hmm. I do remember someone. But it's been so long, and I was much younger then."

Angela smiled as if she knew some amazing secret.

Helen shook her head. "No, I came to talk the city into sending guards out to Bell Springs, as protection against the bandits. It's getting very dangerous out there. Unfortunately, I can't seem to get in the front door."

She related her battle with the receptionist.

Angela shook her head. "Your problem is that you're still thinking the city is like an old time democracy, where the citizens could complain. That's long gone. Nobody is going to see the Mayor unless he owes her a favor. But you're in luck. Come with me."

Angela led her into a study nook, and inside a tall cabinet, she revealed an old time telephone with a hand crank. "I just happen to know the Mayor personally."

...

James Fuller walked up the steps shaded by massive old pecan trees. Jamison, the butler, let him in with just a nod. His father was resting in the library.

"How did it go, son?"

James plopped down in a large overstuffed chair. "The only way it could have gone worse would have been if the Houston Militia actually fired on us instead of just laughing."

The Mayor grunted, and shook his head.

"It was bad timing all the way around. We rolled into Brenham, all shiny and chrome, and Houston had arrived five hours earlier with more trucks than I had bikes, all of them filled with soldiers and a peace offering of gasoline—two tanker trucks worth. We looked pathetic.

"I said all the proper words–hoping for future trade, et cetera, but really... Brenham was already committed to becoming a Houston protectorate."

George shook his head. "As long as Houston has the refineries and can afford to buy loyalty with gasoline, they'll just keep on expanding. And we're a prime target. They've already reduced our shipments to a trickle."

"I don't know about that. My Houston area spy hasn't seen a single oil tanker in the Gulf Coast harbors for nearly six months. And that one was found drifting out at sea, probably a ghost ship since the Star. They were certainly liberal with their gasoline to buy Brenham, but they can't keep it up forever."

"Do they have any other supplies of crude oil?"

James shrugged. "Certainly nothing significant. Reports from Dallas before they caught on to our Larry Jenkins indicate that they have the East Texas Oil Field locked up tight. And the other massive fields in the Permian Basin are over in the west. Houston just might have to go through us to get it. I don't know."

"Couldn't they go around us? We've got strong trading ties north as far as Waco, but couldn't they go south?"

They both fell silent. Something had happened to San Antonio. As recently as two years previous, the IIS had made a trade deal to ship a fully functioning Net station to act as a communication hub for that city. It had been set up. Various businesses had made contact and it had appeared that Austin and San Antonio would soon be trading regularly.

Then it all stopped. Hodges of the North Austin IIS had contracted to send a investigator south to see what had happened. He never returned.

Solving the mystery of San Antonio was just one of a dozen big questions demanding time and manpower that just didn't exist.

James was about to mention his puzzlement about the two tanker gift to Brenham—especially if Houston was really running short of fuel. There was a piece missing in the picture.

But then there was a loud ringing noise.

"What?"

George pointed to the desk. "A phone call."

James struggled to his feet and picked it up. He expected disaster. That's what phone calls meant.

An effort to reestablish the Austin phone system had been one of the more expensive failures.

The Star had fried the extensive switching devices that allowed any phone to connect to any other one. It was all irreplaceable junk. The wires were still good. Museum piece phones had been found. But making a functioning switchboard for more than a hundred phones was impractical. The city offices, IIS, the fire central, and the hospital all had phones—as well as home phones for a handful of important people. Everyone else just walked their messages, or hired couriers. There was a strong popular sentiment for a real post office.

But who would be calling here?

"Hello, this is the Mayor's home."

After James listened carefully for a moment, he handed the phone to his father with a big grin on his face. Shortly, he discovered that he and his father had been invited to dine at the Morgan house.

George chuckled as he hung up the phone.

"Angela Morgan. She's got an 'old friend' we all know visiting her, but she won't tell me who it is until we arrive. It's a surprise, she says."

James frowned. "Could Ed be back from his walkabout?"

George shook his head, sadly. "No. She managed to squeeze in a question to see if we've heard anything from him. She's in the dark, too.

"Besides...I don't expect to see him again."

"What? You mean *ever* again?"

He nodded, his old lined face grim. "Just before he left this time, he came by to say goodbye. And the way he said it...well, when a fortune teller says goodbye like it's for the last time, it makes you think." He shook his head. "With the medical care the way it is, I don't expect to survive another heart attack."

"Dad, don't talk like that! Don't borrow trouble. We've got enough to worry about."

...

Oak Hill had been killed by the Star. It was one of those Austin satellite communities that grew up along the highway, with gas stations and restaurants to serve the travelers. Later on, a large semiconductor manufacturing facility was built there, just down from the 'Y' where highways 71 and 290 split. Star electromagnetic pulses fried most cars and certainly the semiconductors. Oak Hill had its heart stripped away in the Star's glare.

Three figures moved from tree shadow to tree shadow. There were a few people around, still living in some of the houses, but the spies' job was to scout out the terrain and report back to Red, Chief of the Dragon Hunters.

"Ken," Stu whispered, "what's that building?" He pointed off to a big complex across the old roadway.

He shrugged. "Some kind of factory."

Hal moved closer. "I thought I saw movement through one of the windows."

"You think it's live?"

"No chance. But maybe someone's living in there."

Stu chewed on his lower lip. "You could stage a whole army inside that building, and no one would notice."

Hal nodded. "Let's check it out."

A decade of neglect had let weeds and small trees grow up through the cracks in the parking lot pavement. The place had hundreds of abandoned cars that hadn't moved since the Star. The three had plenty of experience making use of concealment much worse than that. They moved close enough to enter a small parking garage in the sourthern-most building.

The sliding glass doorway between the garage and the lobby had a notice pasted on it: THIS BUILDING AND ALL ITS CONTENTS ARE PROPERTY OF THE CITY. TRESPASSERS WILL BE TREATED AS LOOTERS.

The warning didn't slow them down. Looting was a shoot-on-sight offense everywhere, but the Brotherhood of the Hunter paid no mind to local regulations.

Stu hit the glass with his machete, and it rattled loudly, but the glass was thick. It would take a big rock or something.

"Stand back," Hal moved closer and began pushing sideways, hoping to force the door back into its slot. He struggled, his hands slipping on the glass. Stu moved in to add his weight to the task. There was a click, and then the glass started to sluggishly move. They kept at it until the way was wide enough to slip through, one at a time.

The place was dry and dusty, with the lobby plants shriveled and surrounded with dead leaves. Stu lowered his blade. "It looks like they just dropped everything and left."

Hal shook his head. "There could be someone here. There are probably other entrances. Be on the lookout."

The place was a maze, but someone had bolted most of the doors shut, even the numerous fire escape exits. Ken found a vending machine, with its front glass shattered. He rummaged through the trash, but there were no edible scraps. Previous looters had been thorough.

Stu sighed, holding a handful of pencils. "If we wanted office supplies, this place is a gold mine, but there's nothing usable here." He dropped them and let them spill out over the floor.

Hal pointed to another corridor. It was narrow, and ended at a sealed doorway. While Stu tried prying at the door, Ken checked the wheeled cart, parked in the corridor, but it was tightly closed as well.

"Do you think..." Hal started to ask, then he slumped to the ground.

"Gas!" Stu and Ken were on the ground as well.

A moment later, when the men were motionless save for breathing, the lid on the wheeled cart opened up and a robotic arm came out with a squirt bottle. Wheeling close to the bandits, it squirted their clothes and hands, and then retreated back to its original location and locked itself back up.

Introductions

Helen felt silly, like Angela's dress-up doll, but when she was presented to the Fullers, she felt distinctly pretty, the way the two men smiled and bowed as she entered the room in the white lace dress. She had thought her black dress made her look so professional, but Angela would have none of it. "This is a different world. You aren't knocking on his office door. You're trying to make the social connections that could make all the difference."

Angela made the introductions. "You remember Helen Black from the Star Time. I couldn't have been more pleased when she came knocking at my door."

"My dear, this is George Fuller, and his son James. I'm sure you remember him."

She nodded and smiled. She did remember the elder Fuller, but if James was the same guy as that boy who pushed her around in a wheelchair, he'd changed quite a bit. If anything, from those hospital days, she remembered someone who laughed, and while this upright and formal man had a social smile on his face, didn't look like he'd laughed in years.

"That was a big day for me!" Angela rattled on. Ed had proposed to her at the hospital. "It wasn't a time for elaborate plans. We didn't even have a place to stay in the city. We borrowed clothes from the doctors and married in the St. Edwards Chapel."

Helen remembered some of it. There were a lot of people—a lot of sick people, and the wedding had been almost like a party. She looked at the younger man again, trying to picture him there.

Both were dressed in a style she hadn't seen before—long black coats with white shirts. The Mayor wore some kind of pendant around his neck. It was certainly far different from the celebrations they'd held at the Community Church, where Joshua's father John wore his overalls and a leather apron, even to weddings. She was even a little grateful for Angela's dress-up impulses. It wouldn't do to appear to be a country bumpkin.

George smiled, "Yes, of course I remember Miss Black. You were a bit pale back then, I recall. How are your parents?"

"Still well. We moved out to property at Bell Springs, between Bee Cave and Dripping Springs. We needed grazing land for our horses. Of course, it's a bit dangerous there now, with the bandits."

Miss Jane Gunn appeared in her maid's finery at the doorway, chiming a small bell once.

Angela reached to snag Helen's arm. "Ah! The table is ready. Come with me."

She had the Mayor sit across from her, and James across from Helen. The aroma of beef cooked in a mushroom sauce filled the air. She suspected Joshua had already sampled it. Angela had urged him to join the dinner party, and she was ready to send a runner to get a local girl to make the numbers come out right, but he had chosen to stay out of the finery and to chat with Jane in the kitchen.

As a bowl of soup appeared before her, Helen realized that James Fuller was watching her. His face carried a smile, but there was something about his eyes that didn't match.

"So," she asked, "do you really remember me, or are you just being polite?"

He nodded. "Yes. I remember back then. You were bossy."

"I'll take your word for it. Angela's memories are much more reliable than mine."

"You said you have horses. Tell me about them. They're pretty rare around here."

For the first time that evening, she gave him a real smile. She finally had something to talk about. By the time strawberry tarts were presented, she realized she'd been rattling on for far too long. James really didn't say anything, other than make appropriate admiring sounds when she praised her horses and say "Oh?" and "Then?" at times to keep her going.

The Mayor had been listening too. "Is that why you came to town? To sell your horses?"

It threw her off. "Um. No. Maybe. Not really. I mean, not yet. It's the bandits. I wanted to come talk to you about sending City Guards to help Bell Springs."

Smiles dropped and the men exchanged looks.

The Mayor suggested, "Perhaps it would be better to talk about that at the Driskill, not over Angela's fine meal."

If she could have snorted like her horses, she would have.

"I tried that! But you have guards and secretaries whose sole purpose in life is to keep people from talking to you, and they're having a grand old entertaining time doing their job, too! If it weren't for that guard standing there with a gun, I'd have wiped that smug grin off your lobby lady, *soooo* pleased with herself as she ran me around the loop. No visit without an appointment. No appointment without a city officer. No city officer without a secretary. No secretary because of the guard at the door. No way past the guard without an appointment. Twice, she taunted me through the gamut.

"And now you too! Don't talk here. Go back to the Driskill where I can be insulted and demeaned all over again! Were you even there at the Driskill, or were you at your fine mansion, resting in comfort while your servants took care of you?"

Angela cleared her throat. "Perhaps if we...."

James had a familiar look on his face. His nostrils were wider. His head was back. She'd trained horses enough to recognize all the signs.

He spoke quietly. "No. Angela. We can talk without insults. Miss Black here just doesn't understand the scope of the city's business."

Helen knew better than to back down. "Then please enlighten me." She crossed her arms, glaring at the young man.

James glanced at his father. She didn't follow his eyes. This was between her and him.

He sighed. "It's a matter of resources. I have maps of the area, and I'm very familiar with all the roads and communities a hundred miles around the city, and I know that back at Star Time, there wasn't any town of Bell Springs. It, like so many others, have sprung up as neighbors rely on neighbors and form communities all their own, rather than being just a fringe around Dripping Springs or wherever. There are probably hundreds of places just as important as Bell Springs, and just as impossible to find on the old maps.

"Now your concerns in Bell Springs may seem terribly important, but..."

"Yes, like life and death!"

"...but the City Guards have to pick and choose which areas to protect. It's not a matter of whose life is more important. It's a matter of making the biggest impact, making the most noise if you will. If the City Guards can maintain a reputation that can keep the scavengers at bay, then they can protect people that never see a guard patrol."

"Well, if you're trying to protect the City Guard reputation, then you're doing a bad job of it! Bandits are at large in Bee Caves, and don't tell me Bee Caves isn't on your maps, because I know better! I rode from Pace Bend to Red Bud Isles and the entire population is on the move, trying to find some way to get across the river and out of the bandits' path.

"Your guards are building a reputation all right. A reputation as un-feeling, callous bullies who don't care one bit about the people of the Hill Country and only want those 'goat herders' to go back to where they came from—no matter if there's a raiding party waiting to rape and kill whomever they find!"

James flushed, but kept his jaw clenched as she lashed out at him.

He leaned forward, "It doesn't change the issue one bit. I have a limited number of soldiers. A limited number of motorcycles to mount them on, limited gas, limited guns, and limited bullets. We can't protect everyone."

Angela leaned closer to George as the argument continued. She asked in a low voice, "Have you heard from Ed?"

He shook his head. "Not since he left—oh, six weeks or so ago. He's still out there, from all reports. He warned one family away from their wagon, right before a cooking fire spread and burned it to the ground. There was another story of someone being healed, but it was probably the same old thing—just telling their future. The stories are coming from some of the refugees from Miss Black's area.

"And if you hear from Ed, please tell us immediately. You know how valuable his advice has always been."

She nodded, glancing back at the younger ones, still arguing.

George murmured, "I'm sorry you got caught up in this. A lot of people can't seem to understand that the city can't solve all their problems. It's a shame she tracked you down and used you to get to us."

Angela smiled and shook her head. "You've got that backwards. Ed has seen something in her. We wrote her a letter some time back inviting her to come, and it was only after she failed to make contact through official channels that she came to visit me. This dinner was my idea." She frowned. "Although I hadn't expected fireworks."

George looked at Helen more closely, as she straightened her back for another attack.

"You're stuck in the old Techno mindset! Yes, Austin was a great Techno city back then, but things have changed. You're too dependent on your motorcycles and your gasoline powered trucks."

James spread his hands. "You want us to turn our back on technology? You want us fighting the bandits with rocks, dressed in deer skin?"

"No. I'm just listening to you talk. Your motorcycles are breaking down. You're running out of gas. You have no bullets for your guns. If you can't build a new motorcycles or make new bullets, then the technology isn't yours. You're just using up what the Technos left us.

"I use technology, but it's stuff I can make. I breed horses. My dad can make a saddle and tack from scratch. We cast our own bullets and Nick Moses the next valley over makes a good quality black powder. He's also tinkering with making primers, although his only work half the time.

"We've got technology that's ours. It's not hand-me-downs. It's stuff that we can make and hand on to the next generation even if all the old cities burned to the ground."

James nodded. "I applaud your efforts. And we *can* make our own black powder ammunition. I didn't mean to imply that we couldn't. But as laudable as your efforts are, you can't get much beyond where you already are with village technology. You'll never be able to make good steel. Nitro powder, the stuff your guns were really designed to use, takes more sophisticated chemistry than you can handle in your community. You'll never have electricity. Medicines will never be any better than what could be made two hundred years ago. Papermaking, printing, rubber, plastics—none of that will happen without a city. Not to mention electronics and computers.

"A village can support a certain level of technology, but it takes a city for some industries, and a nation for others. When the Star came, the world had technologies that it took the whole world to support. We'll never see those, not in your lifetime, nor mine.

"I've got a city here, with hand-me-down technology that still works, and I've got to make the best use of it for as long as it lasts. Hopefully, we'll learn what we need to keep it going before it all breaks down."

Helen pointed at his chest. "But you're ignoring older technology at your peril. You wail about your precious motorcycles when you could be using horses and get a much better mobility for your troops, without using a pint of gasoline."

"Ha. You're not the first to try to breed horses around here. The gene pool is too small and every attempt produces ill tempered, flighty animals that can't be used for anything."

She sneered, "Horse training is a technology too. Just because your people don't understand horses doesn't mean a thing!"

Jane Gunn appeared at the door. She looked distressed.

Angela asked, "What is it?"

"There's a messenger at the door. The stables downtown report that Helen's horse is running wild."

City Life

Helen pushed back from the table and was at her feet at the news.

George turned to his son. "Perhaps you'd better take her there in the car. It's fastest."

"Right."

Helen was already moving out the door, yelling, "Give me two minutes to change. And get Joshua."

Three minutes later, Helen in jeans, boots and blouse jumped into the car. Joshua was already in the back seat. George waved them off.

As the car sped away with James at the wheel, the Mayor asked, "Angela, what did Ed say about our hot-headed guest?"

She hesitated. "I'm not sure whether to tell you or not."

"You don't trust me?"

She chuckled. "I've seen your political tactics!"

"Hmm. Point taken. Let me put it another way–if Ed says something will happen, do you think I'd have any chance of stopping it?"

"No. So I think you ought to just let this play itself out. Ed saw this coming a long time ago, before you even met her as a little girl."

George nodded, thinking of his long history with Ed, and his abilities. He rubbed the corner of his mouth thoughtfully with his thumb. He sighed. "Okay, then. Do you have another of those strawberry tarts? I don't think I gave mine the appreciation it deserved."

She laughed. "I think we can find something to satisfy that sweet tooth of yours."

...

The messenger had arrived on a scooter, a nice reliable machine. James bit his tongue to refrain from mentioning it. Yes, it would be a point on his side of the argument, but since she was in obvious agony over the fate of her horse, he'd let it slide.

Hadn't he been saying something about wild, uncontrolled horses before they were interrupted? There was a lot to be said for machines. He hoped Angela would tip the boy well. It was obvious Miss Black didn't know city ways—or horses either.

James knew all the shortcuts. The Guards were on notice that certain streets had to be kept clear of new construction. Anyone who built a shed on the pavement restricting 15th Street from Lamar to the old I-35 would have it torn down immediately. He couldn't spare the effort to enforce any other building codes, but if Austin were ever to regain its status as a transportation hub, then he didn't want to have to clear a major street of someone's brick house.

The girl was kneeling in the seat, facing backward, discussing horsey things with the young man Joshua in seat behind them. If she ever knew about seat belts, she'd forgotten. He kept a toe ready to ease on the brakes if someone walked into his path. It wouldn't do to have her slam her head against the windshield. *It's a pain to get a windshield repaired*, he thought unkindly, still a little agitated after their dinner conversation.

He was tempted to give her rear end a swat and tell her to sit down and buckle up, but perhaps now wasn't the right time.

He took the right turn on San Jacinto slowly, but she reached for a strap anyway, and then sat down properly in the seat.

A few blocks later, he slowed to a crawl in the middle of the lane. A crowd had gathered, surrounding the rearing white horse. Some of the braver men were trying to throw a rope over the stallion.

The girl was out the door before he'd stopped.

"What is going on here?" she shouted.

People looked her way, but it was the horse she was talking to. "Snowcap! You know better than to act up like this!" She elbowed her way through the crowd and walked straight up to him.

The horse was wide-eyed from fear and foaming around the mouth from his exertions. He was wearing a bridle. She reached up and slipped her hand into the straps with no complaint from him. She patted him and spoke soothing words. In less than a minute, he was totally calm and people were beginning to disperse.

But she wasn't done.

"You! People. Who put this bridle on my horse!"

There was no answer. A good percentage probably didn't know what she was talking about.

"I had this horse stabled for the night. He had a long ride to get to this city and he deserved to be well fed, watered, and left alone to rest! Which one of you *dared* to put a bridle on him and try to steal him?"

The stable owner hurried up to the front. "It wasn't any of my people. I'm positive it wasn't any of mine. I'm the one who sent the messenger, and Bill knew where you'd gone. I am so sorry this happened."

James walked up, and a whisper went through the crowd. He spoke quietly, but everyone listened. "Have any of you seen strangers in the stable?"

The owner shrugged. "I'm sorry, but people are in and out of the stable all day long, getting their oxen and such. But people don't steal from here, usually. If I had known, I would have had someone watching the horses." He turned back to her. "You have my sincere apology, Miss Black."

She nodded, still struggling with her fury that someone had tried to steal her horse. "I don't blame you." She shot a baleful look at James. "I had been led to believe that the city was more free of crime than it really is. But as soon as Snowcap cools down, I'll be taking our things. Joshua tells me that the place we're spending the night has a large fenced-in yard, and I would rather keep my horses close by."

The stable man nodded. "I'll make a packet of hay and grain for you, with my compliments."

"Thank you."

He walked back towards his stable. James quickly caught up with him. "Mr. Watkins, a word."

The man looked surprised that James Fuller knew his name. "Yes sir?"

"What do you know about Miss Black?"

He smiled. "A lot more now than I did before. But really, I hear things. People in the know had heard of the Horse Lady long before she arrived. Supposedly, she has a whole herd of horses somewhere off near Dripping

Springs. She's a horse doctor, too. When I saw her horses in the street, as she was in there fighting city hall, I made a point to offer my stable. Hoped to pick up a few pointers, you know. There's no one better than me taking care of oxen, but a horse is a different critter."

James nodded, and then walked back to where Miss Black was still talking in a low voice to the magnificent white horse. She saw him coming. From the look on her face he braced himself for an angry tirade.

But she was mostly polite. "Thank you for driving us here, Mr. Fuller, but Joshua and I will be riding back to Angela's house on our own."

He nodded. "I understand. However, I will be returning to pick up my father. Is there anything I could carry in the car."

"No. Thank you. Joshua and I are used to handling our own gear."

"Good evening then."

She nodded, not really looking his way. "Good evening."

He watched her walk away, making a note to himself to leave her a more current pass to get past the city guards. If she had more trouble, he'd hear about it.

...

Sunlight on the horizon crept in through a high window in the Oak Hill building. Stu woke on the tiled floor, and scrambled to his feet, kicking and waking Hal and Ken.

"Come on! Chemical leak! We've got to get out of here."

Stumbling and blinking their eyes against the tears, they hurried back out the way they came, out into the parking garage.

Hal sniffed. "I still reek of the stuff. What is it?"

"I dunno. We probably broke a seal when we tried to jimmy the door open. We're lucky it didn't kill us. Industrial chemicals are the worst!"

The hurried back to the tree line. The sun was nearly down.

"How long have we been out?"

Stu shuddered. "I hope we don't get cancer from this."

After the bandits hurried off, the wheeled cart went up to the sealed door, and it opened. After it went in, there was the sound of a mechanical drill, as the door was being tightly secured against the next break in.

The glass door at the entrance came to life and closed itself before powering down again.

...

Helen slept long past her normal waking time. The sun was up in the sky and it looked to be a hot day. Snowcap had discovered her window and pressed it with his nose. It was an effort to pull herself out of bed, but she opened the window and gave him some attention. She'd asked for a ground-floor room where she could watch him during the night, but hardly had her head touched the pillow when her long hours had caught up with her.

City life brought back childhood memories. There was an electric clock in the bedroom with glowing numbers. Where had that gadget been hidden when the Star was destroying everything electronic? The bathroom had hot and cold running water, without having to go outside and build a fire under the hot water tank.

For all the complaints James Fuller had about lack of resources, city people had plenty to spare for the creature comforts.

And as long as she was a guest, she didn't mind sharing. But she could only stay another day.

When she and Joshua had ridden up last evening, tired and discouraged, with no hint of progress on her mission, Angela was sympathetic, but would not hear of her leaving.

"You have to stay and be my guest for another day or so! Think of how lonely I'll be without you to liven the place up. You must rest before your long ride. Your horses must rest, think of them. And let me show you around the city."

Helen had brought two dresses and her jeans and blouse. That was packing heavy as it was. With the idea in her head to get a few things washed before starting back, she put on the ordinary dress. Her mother had made it for her twenty-first birthday, and even with a couple of years wear, it looked nice. It was white, short sleeved, with a cluster of spring wildflowers embroidered on the right. The colored threads were starting to fade, but it still was one of her favorites. It was probably terribly rustic for these city folk, but that was their loss.

...

"So, how do you like the city?" Jane Gunn asked, as she kept busy, washing a few dishes that had escaped last night's cleanup.

Joshua sat at the kitchen table, sipping hot honey-sweetened milk she'd prepared for him. She'd learned he liked it last night when he hid in the kitchen during the fancy dinner. "Oh, I like it. There's always something going on, no matter where you look."

"Are you planning to stay?" she asked, smiling his way.

He shrugged. "It all depends on Helen. This is her trip. I'm just along to make sure she's safe."

"I'm not sure she needs protection, as fierce as she was last night. Arguing with the Mayor's son." She shook her head. "People around here don't tend to get on the Mayor's bad side."

"She can get that way sometimes. They must have said something bad about her horses or something."

She finished wiping down the counter top and then sat down at the table with him. "So, any plans of your own?"

He smiled. "Oh, maybe. I certainly want to come back here. We have a nice place in Bell Springs, but you know how it is, I wasn't born to be a farmer, neither was my father. It just happened that way. We were displaced by the Star and ended up there."

"Tell me about it! I was seven when the city caught on fire and we had to live in the basement of an apartment building until the Star stopped being dangerous. Mom was a lawyer before then. She does laundry for the rich people now."

He nodded. "Dad was a computer operator. Big computers, for the State. No call for that job now!"

She chuckled, "Nor for federal tax law either. But it takes money to live. So we find work where we can."

He smiled, looking around at the fixtures decorating the walls. "It would be nice to live in a place like this."

She shook her head. "Now you're talking big money."

"Angela is rich?"

"Her husband. Surely you know about Mr. Ed Morgan?"

He shook his head. "Um, we don't get much of city gossip our where I live."

"He tells the future. And gets it right. He's the Mayor's main advisor. If the ten smartest people in the world told him to go north and Ed Morgan said go south, then the Mayor would start walking south, and be right for it!"

She looked down at the table. "When Angela needed a new maid, Mr. Morgan said I was the right one to get, so I got the job even though the other lady was more experienced."

Joshua frowned. "I think I've heard of him. And Helen knows this guy? Why hasn't she mentioned him before?"

"She may not have known. I've lived in this house with him for over a year now, and most times he doesn't do anything weird. Well, other than go on these walks of his. He's been gone for weeks now, and no one knows where he is."

"That's strange."

"Tell me about it. Angela… Mrs. Morgan, worries about him."

Sensing she had spoken beyond her social position, she hopped up and began rummaging in the pantry. Last night's dinner had been prepared here by Chef Conway, brought in for the event, and she'd just presented at the table, but most meals were her domain.

Joshua watched her working.

So, it takes a lot of money to live in the city. Where could I get enough money? About the only thing I'd be qualified for is working at that stable. It wouldn't be enough.

His eyes followed Jane around the room as he thought.

Deliveries

Angela caught Helen looking over the laundry room.

"There you are. I was looking for you. That's a nice dress, by the way."

Helen smiled. "It's seen some use, but I like it." She pointed. "I vaguely remember a washing machine as a child."

"This one is probably ten years older than you are. Washing machines were one of the things that survived the Star pretty well, at least the older ones. There's no real electronics in it, I'm told. Just spring wound timers, motors and switches. A lot of them have been scavenged to build other things."

"We don't have electricity back at Bell Springs. I was just wondering if I could wash these things before I leave."

Angela looked at her little pile. "Jane, could you come here please?"

She appeared a moment later.

Angela asked, "Do you think you could wash these for Helen?"

"Oh, I was going to do it myself. I don't want to impose."

Jane had already picked at the pile. "I'll have no problem with these, but this black dress has some stains. I'd prefer to get my mother to look at it."

Angela smiled. "Fine." She turned to Helen. "Now don't complain. I want to take you around town today." As she noticed Joshua in the hallway, she added, "And you too, young man, if you'd like."

He glanced at Jane, then nodded. "Yes. I'd like that."

...

The taxi was a strange, home-built beast. There was tight room for the three of them in the back, and the driver drove the three-wheeled vehicle in the front like a motorcycle. He chuckled at Joshua's fumbling questions.

"It's electric. Motors and batteries are easy to get from all the old cars. Getting a charging permit was less trouble than trying to keep my old one filled with gasoline. It's not fast, but it's reliable."

Angela added, "And it doesn't smell nearly as bad, either."

"Yes, Ma'am. Where to?"

. . .

They had steaks at a restaurant not far from the Driskill. Joshua waited patiently as the women toured a few of the shops. Helen absolutely refused to let Angela buy her a fancy dress, but was prodded into buying a few nicely-crafted wooden toys for Billy and Jenny back home.

Joshua chatted with Mike, the taxi driver.

"What kinds of jobs are there here?"

"Hmm. Well, there's always something for a guy who'll work long hours and won't faint from the heat. Doesn't pay good, but that's how a lot of people eat."

"Not too many taxi jobs?"

"Well, you'll have to buy or make a taxi, and then there's the problem of finding paying customers. Miz Morgan alone keeps my batteries charged and my kids in shoes. But there aren't too many of her to go around. Austin is a good walking city, now-a-days. Much better than before. Most people don't need to be carried around.

"If you're a mechanic, there's good pay converting old dead cars and trucks with computers into ones that'll run without them."

Joshua barely knew what made engines run. He'd have to find something else. "Fetching and carrying?"

"There's a lot of that, alright, but it's mostly kids. IIS, both north and south locations keep several bike couriers running."

"IIS? What is that?"

Mike grinned. "It's the Net, man! There's no web browsing, but if you want to email to Africa, or whatever, you can do it."

"Really? Like with computers?"

"Sorta. More like some weird kinda post office, or like an old-timey telegraph office. I sold the design of this taxi to some guy in London, England. I may sell it again."

"So, if you've got some information that might be valuable..."

"You take it to the IIS and broadcast an offering. People can bid, and if the money is good enough, you transmit the information and get paid."

Just then Angela and Helen walked up with cloth sacks. Angela's was much larger. Mike hopped out and secured her purchase to the rack on the top of the taxi. Helen had peanut brittle for them all.

"I love shopping–but I'd have to sell Snowcap to keep it up."

Angela said, "Did I hear you talking about the IIS?"

Joshua nodded.

"Would you like to see it?"

. . .

Angela gave them all the old gossip on the way. "Mr. Hodges, the owner of the company, used to be a worker for a feisty old lady named Victor. She owned it, but he ran it. When she died, she willed it to him, and there was a little scandal about it, but nothing ever came of it. He's a reclusive character, hard to get to know. But the service is too valuable, and he runs it well. There's always the rumor that someday the real Internet will come back, but nobody has a computer working anymore, so that's that."

Joshua looked very thoughtful.

Helen asked, "Can you sell real things that way? Like horses, maybe?"

"You can advertise them. You'd still have to arrange shipment, so unless the seller was somewhere close, it wouldn't be worth it."

They arrived at the IIS office and Angela watched Helen's and Joshua's faces as they were greeted by the little office manager.

April was happy to show them how everything worked. There was a table with large bound books of the current offerings.

"Why don't you flip through them and get an idea of how it's done? The black book is offers of things you can bid on. The blue book is requests–things people would pay you for."

Helen and Joshua sat down at the table and started flipping through the pages. She chuckled.

Angela asked, "You find something?"

"Someone is offering green pigs. 'Lower food needs due to chlorophyl in the skin.'"

Alice added. "That's from Australia, right? We get a few oddball animal offers from them. Genetic engineering or something. Nobody bids, because they'd have to ship the animal all the way from the other side of the world."

Joshua pointed out another, "Someone wants to know how to build a space ship! They want to get into orbit. Like that'll happen any time soon."

April shrugged. "Who knows? I've seen a lot of strange stuff go through here. Things I thought were impossible, but people bid on them."

Joshua asked, "How does one go about this? Suppose I had something that *might* be valuable, but I just don't know?"

Helen nodded. "I guess I could advertise to sell horses, or horse training, but we're leaving in the morning, and who knows how long it would be before I came back here."

April smiled, almost rubbing her hands with glee at the thought of new customers. She spelled it all out for them. They would need account numbers, and they were given ten IC's, Information Credits, to start out with. From that, they could post their offer, or advertisement, and if any replies arrived for their account, then they could either come back and check from time to time, or contract with one of the local or long distance courier services to have their messages delivered. This office kept the offers and requests in the public books for a month or so, but other IIS locations had their own policies.

"The first one is free, then?" Helen asked.

She worded a careful advertisement, worried that she was promising too much. Joshua wrote out his offer as well, but didn't say what it was.

...

Sam Mason walked into the office, just as Angela was escorting her guests out.

He nodded, "Good Afternoon, Mrs. Morgan."

She smiled, recognizing her courier, but she probably never knew his name. "Good to see you."

As soon as they were gone, Sam went on in and noticed April frowning, reading over the new messages. She looked up at him.

"Sam, you get out and around a lot. I think I've got something important here, but I'm not sure."

She swiveled the sheet around so he could read it. This was against the rules and they both knew it. Messages were supposed to be private until they were processed and into the system.

He read the message and realized what had caught her attention. "Hmm. Yes. I think it could be important."

"What do I do? This is marked as a public offering."

Just then, the inside office door opened, and Hodges walked in. They both jerked—they were caught, and they knew it.

He turned his shaded eyes on Sam. "I have a special request for you."

He picked up both messages and scanned them. He handed one of them to April. "Go ahead with this one. I'll process the other directly."

"Sam, I need you to deliver a message."

. . .

He'd run deliveries to the Mayor's mansion before, but this time was different, arriving with nothing but a verbal message to deliver.

The butler refused to budge. "I'm sorry, but Mr. Fuller is unavailable for business today."

Sam shook his head. "I'm sorry too. But I have an important message from the IIS head, Mr. Hodges. I have to deliver it."

Jamison had dealt with important messages before. His orders were clear. "Come back tomorrow." He closed the door.

Sam thought about knocking again, or kicking it in, but neither effort was likely to be successful. But he couldn't quit either. He knew as well as the butler that there was a telephone line here, and in the IIS office. If Hodges didn't want the message delivered over the phone, then something really odd was going on. And it was his job to make it happen.

James Fuller could get him in. He was sure of it.

He pedaled as fast as he could for the Driskill, his mind churning all the way. Hodges wouldn't appreciate failure, and this was no merchant-to-merchant contract he was trying to deliver, either.

He walked into the lobby, panting and sweating.

"Can I help you?" asked the receptionist.

"Is Mr. James Fuller in?"

"No." She frowned, then confided, "I think he left for Camp Mabry. He often does, this time of day."

Sam nodded, and closed his eyes for an instant. It would be six miles or so.

"Here." She reached behind the counter and poured him a glass of water.

"Thanks." He emptied it.

...

Mopac Expressway had become a community all its own, with numerous stranded cars made into instant bedrooms. Over time, efforts had been made to keep certain lanes clear, so it was still one of the fastest north-south routes through town. Sam kept his eyes open as he took the entrance ramp. No one would still live on Mopac if real houses could be had, so it was something of a slum, with a few residents who might be tempted by a good quality bike.

Off on the rise to his left were a number of the richer houses. He'd visited many of them.

...

They unloaded after their shopping trip and Mike went on his way with a smile.

Helen's laundry was nearly dry. She went outside to check on it.

"My mother said the blood and mud stains came out okay." Jane whispered. "She was curious," she added, her eyes not making contact.

In a low voice, so Angela wouldn't overhear, Helen told Jane the story of the bandits and her lost horse. Jane was horrified. "It's really that bad out there?"

"I'm afraid so. That's why I was so intent on trying to get the city's help."

"And you're going back? I wouldn't."

Helen shrugged. "I've got my family, and my horses. I have to go back."

She looked again at the black dress, drying in the breeze. "Your mother does good work. I'd given up on the stains."

Snowcap twitched his ears forward, listening. Helen laughed and went over to the makeshift pen and gave him some attention. "You rest for now. We'll be heading out early in the morning."

Angela walked up to join them. "Are you sure I can't convince you to stay longer?"

"No. Thanks so much for all you've done, but I need to be back."

At the back door, Joshua watched Jane checking the clothes, and folding a few items. He could tell that she knew he was there, but she didn't say anything. What was there to say?

...

Camp Mabry, City Guard it proclaimed at the entrance to the camp. When the national and state governments collapsed, as radio, the Internet, phone lines, and most air and land vehicles all failed in one day, the Texas National Guard had released its local troops to the control of the cities they were based in. George Fuller had been the man with a plan for the unthinkable, and he made it work.

A guard with a rifle at the ready put up his hand as Sam arrived.

"I have an urgent message for Mr. James Fuller. Is he here?"

"Civilians aren't allowed on the camp at this time."

"Well, can you get a message to him? It's urgent."

The guard waved for a runner. He came back a few minutes later.

"Mr. Fuller says, unless it's life or death, the messenger has to wait."

Sam just stood there for a moment. He'd been sure James Fuller would let him in, but there was no help for it. He couldn't get in, and he couldn't leave and risk missing him, either.

He pushed his bike to the side and sat down on the grass next to a tree where he could watch the entrance, and the guard could watch him. He would wait for as long as it took.

Dragon's Cave

Ed Morgan walked carefully under the starlight. The hunger was getting to him and he'd tripped and fallen once already tonight. Friendly travelers with meals to share were fewer around here, and for good reason. This had become bandit-controlled territory. He suspected that he was being watched, but that didn't matter.

Ah! The cave entrance. It had never been much of a commercial cave before the Star, but there was an old shed where they'd sold tickets, now burned to the ground. With the oak trees grown around the entrance and no moon, it was hard to see anything.

The crunch of an old walkway told him he was on the right path. It wound through the trees and down into a pile of rocks that formed the sink-hole entrance to the cave. Numerous visitors from the nearby Hamilton Pool had walked this way, and the rock wall was smoothed from uncountable hands.

And then he could see the light. Down in the first main chamber, the bandits had built a campfire. There were over a dozen rough-looking men sitting in a circle. There was a visible shock and a grumble of voices as a white-robed outsider sat down in the circle with them.

Most eyes turned to the man to his left. He grumbed, "A man who joins the circle of the Hunters unbidden doesn't care for his own life."

Ed picked up a metal cup carefully. It was hot but not scalding to the touch. "Have the Hunters heard about the man in a white robe who wanders the Hill Country and whispers the future into a man's ear?"

There was another round of muttering. Some had heard of him.

Ed scooped the cup into a pot that smelled of venison. It made his mouth water. He sipped and it scalded his tongue, but it tasted wonderful.

He set the cup down to cool a bit.

"There's a man named Red, a dragon." All eyes went to the man who had spoken. "Men will gather around him and follow his words.

"An army of scattered hunters will come to him, seeking to take the city, and no one will dare challenge him. Like a tide, they'll push aside the soldiers that stand in Austin. The Red Dragon will stride across the streets of the city and take the old Capitol building. With a stroke of his sword, he'll defeat the ruler of the city, and there on the front steps of the site of the old Texas government, he'll proclaim himself King of the Hill Country."

Ed shook away the vision, and picked up the cup again. He ate hungrily.

...

The others talked, until Red shouted, "Be quiet!" The only sound was of Ed's eating. He dipped a second cup of the venison stew.

Red got to his feet and gestured for Brent, his second in command to follow him. They retreated deeper into the cave where the others couldn't hear.

"What do you know about this guy?"

He shrugged. "There's been a rumor for years that the Mayor of Austin had a pet wizard–someone who could tell the future and advise him. The Star put him into power in the first place. They say he had plans ready to go when it happened."

"Do you think this is him? It could be some guy just claiming to be him."

Brent shrugged. "Ask him a question and see if he gets it right."

Red struggled to make sense of it. "If this is the Mayor's advisor, why is he telling us that I'll become King?"

"I dunno. Ask him."

Ed was finishing off the stew when Red sat down beside him again. Ed put the cup back where he found it. He hadn't eaten that well in days. Being a wandering hermit had its drawbacks at times.

"Why have you come in here, at the risk of your life, to tell me my future?"

Ed shrugged, "There is no risk. You won't kill me. But to answer you, I want to ask a favor."

Red leaned back, a little more comfortable. Bargaining was something he could understand. "What do you want?"

Ed closed his eyes. "You'll be killing many people soon. I would like for you to spare as many as you can. When you kill the Mayor, do it quickly."

The light from the fire wasn't terribly bright, but Red could see tears in the man's eyes. He wasn't a warrior. He was a weakling.

"And what will you do if I ignore your plea?"

Ed shook his head. "Nothing. I can do nothing. The future will happen anyway."

Red turned away in disgust and stared at the flames. The temptation to accept a bright destiny warred with his belief that men made their own fate.

Still, it was intriguing. There were five companies of Hunters in the area, his own Dragons, the Ram, the Wolf, the Bear, and the Lions. There were thousands of them, but none could lead the others. They had no grand commander since Major Wyldes was taken out in the Battle of Fort Sam. Maybe everyone was just waiting for one of the company commanders to step up and lead.

"You, fortune teller! Tell me something I can test."

Ed looked sad. He gestured for Red to lean closer.

He whispered. "Two things. A future and a question. The man across the fire with his beard combed into two forks? He'll die tonight. And my question. Do you want me to be correct?"

Red leaned away, trying not to look at Patrick Potts, a heavy man who had knocked out more than a few of his fellow Hunters when they called him Hagrid.

Everyone in the circle had heard his demand for a test.

Red was still pondering the question. It wasn't that hard. Yes! He wanted the strange little man to be right.

He looked around at the eyes of his men, his closest friends, his mighty men of valor. "The fortune teller said one of us will die tonight."

"Who is it?" "Did he say who it was?" "Oh no!"

Potts sneered. "I don't believe a thing he says. I say he's the one who will die tonight."

Brent asked, "Who did he say?"

Red shook his head. "Sorry Hagrid."

The heavy man growled in anger and started to stand.

Jase Hansel, to the man's right, slid a blade right in between his ribs, and Potts shook once and fell backwards, dead.

Jase shook his head sorrowfully. "Sorry Hagrid. I want King Red."

"King Red! King Red!" The chant was joined by all. Everyone was on their feet.

Red nodded to himself. So the fortune teller was right. He looked to his side, but the little man in the white robe was gone.

Brent looked too. "Should I go get him?"

Red shook his head. "I don't think you can."

...

The guard at the gate saluted, and then pointed to the boy sleeping by his bicycle.

James got off of his motorcycle and woke him.

"Sam?"

"Oh! Yes. Sorry. I fell asleep."

"And I'm sorry I made you wait so long. It couldn't be helped. You have a message?"

"Um. I was told to give a verbal message to George Fuller. I couldn't get into the house, so I thought maybe you could get me in."

"Who told you? Is it an IIS message?"

Sam shook his head. "It was a special message from Mr. Hodges. I don't think it came in over the Net, but I'm not sure."

James looked over at the guard, but he was out of earshot.

"Sam, this is a secret, but my father is sick right now. I'm pretty much taking care of the city's business for him, but we don't want it generally known. Do you think you could just give me the message?"

Sam nodded. "I guess so. I trust you. It's just that my instructions were to say it to George Fuller."

"Then I guess it's your call. You have to decide if Hodges meant George Fuller the man or George Fuller the position."

Sam understood. He'd already considered and rejected the other option, go back to Hodges and ask for clarification.

"Okay. I don't know what it means, but here goes. Hodges said 'Come see me about a Station O issue.'"

"That's it?"

Sam nodded. "And I have no idea what it means."

James shook his head, "I don't either. I'll make sure my father gets it... word for word."

"Thanks. I didn't want to have to go back and say I couldn't make a delivery."

James put his hand on the boy's shoulder. "It's late. Can I take you someplace?"

"No. I can't leave my bike. Besides it's not too far."

"Okay. I'll let Hodges know how reliable you've been. Now get on home."

James watched him head off into the night, the little headlight beam wobbling and getting brighter as the boy gained speed.

...

Jamison opened the door to the mansion before James reached the top step.

"How's he doing?"

"Better. Much better." When he closed the door behind them, he added. "The doctor doesn't think it was another heart attack. Perhaps just a reaction to a rich meal."

James sighed. "That's good to hear. Is he awake?"

"Probably," the butler said disapprovingly.

His father was propped up on pillows, reading from a book. "James. You're back."

He sat down in the chair. "A long day. The bandits are coming and we aren't ready."

"Are you sure it'll be any worse than before?"

"Already is. Stories of atrocities are coming in all the time. We've got more refugees stacking up along the shore line than ever before. Miss Black wasn't making anything up. It really is a matter of life and death out there. And I don't think our 'reputation' is up to stopping them this time."

"But are the Guards up to waging a war out in the Hill Country?"

"No. Our best bet is to secure the Colorado River. I've got troops at every bridge and dam in the area. Some have already gotten through. A patrol ran into a group of bandits below Buchanan Dam. We ran them off, but they had loot from a number of wagons."

"What about below the city?"

"Captain Haige has a patrol watching the river down to Webberville, but that's a lot of ground to cover. We're just lucky the river is running high right now."

"We're spread too thin."

"Right. Too few troops. The pile of radios that were protected from the Star are worth their weight in gold right now. I've got half our fuel dedicated to moving troops from one position to the next the instant we see bandits."

George took a sip from the glass next to his chair.

"Dad, there's another thing. Hodges tried to get a message to you today, but Jamison was too efficient."

"Oh? What was it?"

"I convinced Sam the courier to give it to me, but I couldn't make sense of it. You don't have any top secret projects out there, I mean, any *more* top secret projects?"

George frowned, "What was the message?"

"'Come see me about a Station O issue.' That was from Hodges."

George looked thoughtful. "Station O. It's been a while. I'd forgotten."

"Tell me."

...

Ed greeted the dawn waiting beside Highway 71. If he could avoid thinking about things that he couldn't change, he was in decent spirits. Food had done wonders.

The Marathoner could be seen coming a mile away. Ed was envious of the man's strength and endurance. He could imagine running, but running for a living?

Ed walked out into the middle of the highway and raised his arms. The man looked to the right and to the left, but Ed had chosen the spot carefully. It was flat here. There was no place for bandits to hide.

The man slowed down. Ed could see the patches, proclaiming him a long distance courier.

Ed reached into his pouch and produced a 2001 Silver Dollar. "I need to add a message to your pouch."

"Uh. Okay. Do you have paper?" His eyes were locked on the embossed figure of Walking Liberty.

Ed pointed, "You do, in your vest pocket."

"Oh yeah. I forgot." He pulled out his logbook, and guiltily tore out an unused page.

Ed took the sheet and the pencil and scribbled a few words.

"Is that it?" the man asked.

"Yes." Ed handed him the coin. "Now, you will make it okay to your Paleface station, and your pouch will make it to Austin, but bandits are coming. As soon as you exchange your load to the next runner, turn around and go back to Marble Falls. You don't want to be caught napping out here."

The man looked again at Ed, and remembered a few stories he'd heard about a man in white. "Gotcha!" And then he took off running.

Ed smiled as he left. He strolled off humming a little tune. Not everyone had to die.

Station O

"James!" April squealed as he walked into the office.

"Hello, April. Did you like the book?"

She wheeled her chair up to the counter. "I loved it! I've read it three times already. Thank you!"

He turned and nodded to Sam, resting on the couch. "Hello again, Sam."

"Mr. Fuller." He looked tired. "I've told Mr. Hodges how the delivery went."

"I hope you didn't get in trouble."

"I don't think so. It's hard to tell with him."

"Is he in?"

April shook her head. "No, he's gone to fix some problem at the South Austin IIS station." She looked at the clock above the computer. "He should be back soon."

James frowned. "Would you allow me to use your telephone?"

April smiled brightly, "Sure! Come on around."

Sam smiled too. April wouldn't do that for anyone else.

James quickly saw which of the dozen different varieties of old phone sets it was and dialed zero. After a moment, he said, "Connect me to Camp Mabry."

After the connection was made, he said, "Mr. Hodges of the IIS has gone into South Austin on business. Send Willowby to the Congress Avenue Bridge to make sure he has no problem getting back across."

After a few more details, he hung up.

Sam asked. "I saw all the people at the bridges. I guess I shouldn't make any deliveries to the other side, then?"

"Probably not, at least for a little while. We've restricted passage due to all the bandit activity."

April had watched and listened. She practically lived in the IIS office and hadn't gotten out much.

"James, do you run the city?"

He chuckled. "Parts of it, maybe. I think some people would say that you run it." He sighed. "If I had my way, I think I'd rather that you run it."

Sam looked puzzled. "Huh?"

James looked from one face to the other. They were too young to be deluged with economic theory, and yet, they weren't stupid. Sam was in and out of the centers of business and government every day, silently watching what was going on, and ready to make some astute delivery decisions based on what he knew.

April always had a book or two hidden up under the counter top. And she read every transaction that came into and went out of the city.

They were very bright, but they didn't need to be bogged down with his worries either. Still, it was nice to be able to talk about things. In spite of her temper, Helen Black had provided refreshingly intelligent dinner conversation.

"You two run an information economy. You buy and sell information."

They nodded, puzzled at what he was saying.

He gestured with his hands. "Civilizations come in layers.

"The bandits hunt. If that's all they did, we wouldn't have any problem with them, but now they've started hunting people.

"Farmers plant and harvest what they've planted. Animals too. I recently met a lady who grows horses.

"Other people make things, from a loaf of bread to this IIS radio-computer thing that Hodges has built.

"You, April and you, Sam, are service people. You do things for other people, like type up the messages or carry them across town.

"And finally, there are people who make information. April, you might just write a book and sell it on the IIS. Sam might figure out a better, faster way to deliver messages and then sell that idea across the world."

The two of them looked thoughtful.

Sam asked, "And what kind of a thing do you do?"

James smiled, "I guess I'm a service person too. I'm trying to keep everything running. And believe me, it's a hard job."

They chuckled.

...

A few minutes later, there was the sound of a car pulling up.

A man in uniform opened the door and held it for Hodges. He entered, carrying a bag.

James smiled. "Ah, Sergeant Willowby, you found him."

He shrugged. "He had all his papers. All I did was move him through the line and drive him here."

Hodges nodded. "Thank you for the assistance."

"No problem." The guard nodded once more to James and then left.

Hodges gestured toward his private office. "Would you care to come in for a chat?"

"Of course."

As soon as they were seated and the door closed, James said, "I'm sorry about the blockade at the bridge. I should have warned you. The situation is getting tense."

Hodges, still in his broad hat and cloak, even indoors, nodded. "I was aware. But the antenna system on the South Austin station was in need of repair and I wasn't able to coach Mr. Franklin sufficiently via messaging. Plus there were other issues on the south side of the river than needed my attention as well."

James nodded. "Station O."

"I'm happy to see you've been informed."

"Partially. My father has been ill and could not come to see you himself. I hope that's okay."

"It is a sensitive project. I would prefer it not spread."

James nodded. "My father had not been updated in some time."

Hodges pulled a folder from a file cabinet. "In that case, I'd better bring you up to date." He presented it to James.

It appeared to be a signed agreement between Whiting Design and the City of Austin, signed by George Fuller and Mary Ellen Victor, turning several Techno age manufacturing facilities over to Whiting Design.

"Whiting Design is the former name of IIS and I am the inheritor of Mrs. Victor's business interests."

James was reading the details. "It says that full efforts are to be made to convert the pre-Star technology to current day versions."

"Yes, and that the city would provide adequate isolation and protection to preserve the irreplaceable machinery contained within the listed facilities."

"Protection?"

"Yes, I bring this up because of the recent bandit looting attempt on Station O."

"The semiconductor plant in Oakhill?"

"That's correct."

"So they're moving in there as well."

"And it's a concern for the workers at Station O. They labor in secrecy, with the building appearing totally abandoned, but many bandits with machetes could be dangerous to factory and workers alike."

"You said looting 'attempt'?"

"Yes, they were scared off by a deliberate gas release. We hope the bandits will consider the place too dangerous. It was a gamble, but it worked—this time."

"So, you're asking for guard protection for Station O?"

Hodges reached for his bag. "I understand you are laboring under resource limits. You recently declined to provide protection to an outlying community being attacked by the bandits. It might be easy to consider a factory at even less value than a number of families. Let me show you what Station O is working on."

He removed a metal box about the size and shape of a loaf of bread. Hodges worked a small latch and the box hinged on the long edge and the complex device inside was revealed.

"What is it?"

"This is a short range IIS station."

"Short range?"

"Yes. It only works within a one mile radius of another IIS station."

James knew Hodges's company had been producing the large IIS network stations for a few years. One had been lost to San Antonio, but now Waco and Dallas had their own stations. There were bids from several other towns in Texas and one from the Oklahoma territory for their stations. Other places all over the world were building stations as well, from the detailed directions being broadcast around the clock from a high power transmitter on Mt. Larson. Anyone with electronics skills, and a repaired PC could download the software sent out as old-style modem tones, and bring an elementary IIS station on-line. That's how the Houston station was built, as well as the ones in Europe, Africa, and Australia.

But everyone knew it was Hodges's invention, and all the upgrades and improvements came from him.

"But why a short range station? One mile is an easy walk."

Hodges flipped a switch and a few hundred tiny lights lit up—a crude but legible display screen. It showed one line of text in blocky letters that scrolled slowly to the side.

"Imagine you need to send a message to another city, but for political reasons, you don't want anyone to see what you're sending. You type in the account number."

Hodges did the deed, pressing buttons laid out like a keyboard.

"Now, you enter your message." He typed a few words.

"And now send it. If you're anywhere within a mile of a station, your message is routed silently, and invisibly, through the larger station, and using its long distance radios, to the other city."

James looked at Hodges. "You've heard about Larry Jenkins."

"I have access to special reports. Analyzing aborted messages and the like to help me improve the IIS system software. There was something odd about an error report two months ago. It was as if a message was half typed, and then carefully erased before it was sent. Considering that the account was established in Austin, but sent in Dallas, I could make some guesses."

James looked at the box again. "So, a spy with a box like this could send messages from an unfriendly city, and their IIS operators wouldn't be aware of it."

"That is correct."

Hodges let James think about it a bit, and then he added, "My original concept was something like the Techno cell phones. If I could manufacture dozens, then hundreds, and then thousands of these, communications within a city would be revolutionized. Couriers would be limited to carrying large documents or other items. Sending a message across town would be a matter of seconds, not minutes or hours.

"But we're not at that stage yet. This is a prototype. It works, and that's amazing in itself."

"Why is it amazing?"

"James, we manufactured it all. No scavenged chips. No parts pulled out of protected warehouse bins. We are in the early stages of making semiconductors."

"Really?" He was impressed. He'd relegated semiconductor technology to something he'd see in his old age. "How did you manage?"

"Very clever workers and repaired machinery that was already designed for the purpose. To be clear, it will take many years to make anything really tiny or fast. We don't have the ultra-pure chemicals or high resolutions demanded during the Techno age, but we can make transistors, and elementary circuits on a chip. The one-bit CPU is very slow, but it's enough to make the message box work. "

James saw at once that Station O needed to be protected. He just had to figure out how.

Hodges flipped the switch, closed the lid and handed James the message box.

He took it gratefully.

"I may need instruction."

"Of course. Now, there's one other issue we need to discuss."

James set the box down carefully. "Oh. What is it?"

Hodges put away the documents.

"It's embarrassing to admit, but IIS is falling short of its own ethical standards."

James listened quietly.

"Your agent in Dallas was captured because some IIS operator realized that the message being typed was from an Austin Spy and chose loyalty to Dallas over the ideal neutrality we desire at IIS.

"It's natural. It's human nature after all. We can write out policies and rules and swear ourselves to work for the customer, and never take advantage of the secrets that pass before our eyes.

"But there will always be exceptions."

"Now we have another one. April saw an offer of information and hesitated to send it out to the world."

Hodges presented the piece of paper. James read it and then read it slowly again.

"This wasn't sent out."

"No, it wasn't. I decided to allow a one-week delay to allow a local bidder to make a good faith offer before broadcasting it for wider distribution."

James looked at Hodges, trying to read his shaded features. "Why are you doing this?"

"My dreams can only survive if technology advances. I believe Austin, under your control, is the best incubating ground for this to happen. Call it loyalty to Austin, if you wish."

"Station O will get its protection, somehow. And I owe April some more books."

He clutched the paper, but then handed it back. "May I borrow your phone."

...

They went back to the outer office.

"Hello, Angela Morgan? This is James Fuller."

"Hello there. It there a problem?"

"Are Helen Black and her assistant still with you?"

"Oh. No, they left before dawn to ride back to Bell Springs. Is there a problem?"

"No. I just wanted to know. Do you know which route they took?"

...

"Hello, Camp Mabry? Get Willowby on the line again."

"Yes, sir. I'm here."

"Get my road bike gassed up. Put one of the radios, a pistol and ammunition, and food for a day in its luggage bin. I'll be leaving within the hour."

"Where are you going, and surely you want me to come along?"

"No, I can handle this alone. I'll be heading in the direction of Dripping Springs, but I shouldn't have to go all the way there. It'll just take a few hours. Out and back."

"Yes, sir." The Sergeant expressed his deep reservations in those two words.

James handed the phone back and said goodbye to April. Sam was already out on another run.

If this works out, I may owe her a whole library.

Evacuation

"Give me the phone." The soldier picked it up and handed it over. James turned the crank and waited for the operator.

"Yes, connect me to Morgan house. Yes, again!"

"Hello, Angela."

"Hello? What is the world coming to? Two calls from a gentleman on the same day. My maid is scandalized."

He chuckled. He was suddenly very aware that the telephone operator was probably listening in. Every phone call went through an operator who listened for the destination and then plugged the lines together by hand. Probably more often than not, the operator's headset was still on the circuit unless she had another call to deal with.

"Angela, I have no time to chat, but I just wanted you to know that a Marathoner just delivered a message to me from Ed. Some time this morning, he was beside the road near Lake Travis."

"Ed! A message! Is he okay?"

"I have to guess he is. The message is typically cryptic, but the courier had nothing to add."

"The message! Can you tell it to me?"

He hesitated, aware that anything he said over the phone could spread to the gossip mills.

"It's just three words, and I have no idea what it means. 'Go with Rose.' Do you know who Rose is?"

Angela was silent for a moment. She sniffed, as if she'd been crying. "No. Sorry, I'm just so glad to hear anything from him. To know he's alive. But no, I don't know anyone named Rose."

James said goodbye and hung up the phone. He read the little piece of paper again. "Go with Rose. Deliver to James Fuller at Camp Mabry. Ed."

The fortune teller had addressed it to the place where he was going to be, not where he usually could be found. Well, that was Ed.

"Willowby? You say this came in from the Marble Falls dispatch? Where's that map you've been keeping of the Marathoners?"

Several of the small towns used the company to keep in touch with Austin. And there'd been plenty of long distance runners after the Star who'd been in good enough shape to sign up as couriers. Probably Hodges had a long term project to put the Marathoners out of business, but for now, they were the most reliable way to send messages between the various communities of the Hill Country. Like the Pony Express of the old days, they had various way-stations to break the runs up into shorter stretches, so the man who delivered the message might not have been the one who talked to Ed.

Sergeant Willowby had been logging reports from the outlying communities. It wasn't a map, really, more a chalkboard listing. James looked over the markings.

"Johnson City hasn't reported anything?"

"No, not lately."

James frowned. That could mean an attack on the town, or just one more Marathoner taken out by the bandits. He had no way to know.

"Send someone to go talk to Marathoner headquarters and see what they think has happened."

"I've already done it. Runners are running scared, if you don't mind the pun. They've started canceling deliveries. And you really should take someone with you."

He shook his head. "A waste of gas. I'd really like to loop over to Johnson City as well, to make better use of the fuel, but I don't have the time."

He mounted his bike and it roared to life. "Let my father know I'll be gone a few hours. I'll have some interesting news when I get back."

. . .

Ed Morgan walked along the ridge overlooking the Pedernales River. Down near the water's edge, two lines of bandits were converging. Between the water and the cliffs, a flock of emu and a pair of white-tailed deer were panicking. The men chanted, and slapped their blades against their leathers to make noise. One of the deer tried to make a dash for the churning waters, but it was swept off its feet. A hunter waded in to intercept, his blade held high. The other animals didn't survive it more than a couple of minutes.

The word was already out. Join Red's army, or be left out of the rich spoils when the city of Austin was taken. And an army would need food.

An old whiskery man in a sweat-stained cowboy hat walked up to him. "What's going on down there?"

Ed shook his head. "Invaders." The shouts of the butchers could be heard on the wind. "They'll be turning these hills red with blood very soon. More are coming. Escape if you can."

...

As he approached Mansfield Dam, James saw clumps of refugees sheltered under the trees. On impulse, he pulled up to one group of eight. Half of them were children. They cringed as he stopped.

"Hello."

The older man nodded. "Hello. We're not bothering anyone."

"I can see that. Where are you from?"

"Lakeway."

"Bandits there?"

He nodded. "We're not waiting to be killed like our neighbors, the Kilpatricks."

"How did you get across? The dam?"

He spit off to the side. "No. The guards wouldn't let us. Nor on the bridge. We went below the dam and floated across."

"Sounds risky, in this current." There were small children in the group. Had they been strapped to their parents? He didn't want to ask the details.

"Riskier to stay."

James nodded and moved on. It appeared they'd brought a few supplies, but that wouldn't last. Even if the bandits didn't get past the roadblocks, keeping the refugees from starving or rioting would be a big problem. Those that had already made it to the city were moving into places that he'd struggled to clean out over the past few years, like the waterfront and Mopac and I-35.

Sweep patrols to keep the petty thievery down would need to be increased, just at the time he needed every man to guard the entrances to the city.

He pulled out his radio and alerted the guards up ahead that he was coming.

. . .

Helen and Joshua pushed the horses hard. The looks on the faces of the groups passing the other way caused her chest to tense up every time she saw them—valuables loaded up on ox carts, mothers clutching their children tightly.

It was a full scale panic.

A neighbor called as she passed, "Helen! Turn around. It's time to get out!"

"I have to reach my family!" she shouted back.

Once they reached Fitzhugh Road, Snowcap seemed to smell home and needed no urging to increase his pace. Helen glanced back at Joshua on Sandy but he waved her on.

It was a frightening run past familiar homesites, every one abandoned. The Miller place was blackened and the entrance way gutted open. Tendrils of smoke still curled from the collapsed roof —swept away once they were caught by the heavy breeze.

Snowcap slowed and whinnied at the strange scents. She patted his neck and urged him on.

At the edge of the Gonzalez property, he lurched to the left and took off across the field. She would have rather stayed on the road, but her ride had a mind of his own. He knew the shortcuts as well as she did. Maybe better.

I hope I don't miss them on the road.

She was relieved when she saw people moving at her house. She cried inside when she saw what her father was doing. Their hay wagon was being piled high with everything movable. The Blacks were moving out.

. . .

James was struck by the differences in the faces of the refugees on the other side of the river, hauling their belongings on dog or ox carts, or just walking. People looked up with hope when they heard the roar of his bike. They knew they were close. Close to the bridge. Close to safety.

It was a change from the bitter, angry faces on those that had made it across by hook or crook.

The reputation thing, like Miss Black said. These people are looking toward the City Guard as protectors, until they meet them barricading the door.

But what was he to do? His job was to protect the city, not the entire Central Texas area. And right now, didn't city protection extend to protecting his people from the refugees and the chaos they brought?

It didn't taste right.

The faces in the next approaching wagon looked different. He'd zipped past, but then he eased up on the throttle and made a U-turn. He came up next to the driver. The man saw him coming up to the side and brought his ox to a stop.

James said, "Good day, sir."

The man's face was dead of expression. "No."

"What?"

"It's not a good day."

James looked across at the woman staring straight ahead. She was covered with a blanket like a robe.

"Problem with the bandits?"

He nodded. "They caught us on the road." He tapped his throat. James realized the man had it wrapped. A red streak of blood had oozed through the cloth. "They held me while... while...." He went silent.

James looked at the catatonic woman. "Your wife?"

He nodded, then swallowed and said, "And Sue." His eyes flickered back to the wagon, but didn't linger, as if he really didn't want to look.

James leaned over and pulled aside the blanket that covered a girl nearly the same age as April. Her dress was torn. Her eyes were closed, and there was no breathing.

"I'm ... sorry." He gently covered her back up.

"Not your fault."

For a moment, he couldn't put words together. He took a breath, then he gestured, "Go on. Get your wife to safety."

The man released the brake and shook the reins.

James pulled out his radio.

...

Helen's family had left on the hay-wagon, and she still had to repack her things. She carefully stowed her laundered and folded black dress in her drawer. All of the clothes she'd taken to the city were now put at the bottom. No telling now long this trip would take, but she *wasn't* leaving home forever, and she *wasn't* carrying all her worldly belongings with her!

For one thing, she was furious that she had to leave most of her horses to fend for themselves among these butchers.

But no one backed her up on the idea of driving the herd with them.

"Are you finished in there?" John Lamar called.

She looked at her travel bag. "Almost." She grabbed a couple of items and threw them in. She headed for the door.

Joshua and his father had agreed to help her move the herd to the south pasture. With trees on all sides and the meadows down closer to the creek, they just might have a better chance to avoid being discovered than on the high fields where they could be seen from the road.

It had been a loud argument that had gotten her that concession. Mom wanted her on the wagon with her. She'd stood her ground.

Then Dad had wanted to help her, but someone needed to go with the wagon and protect Mom and Bill and Jenny. Eventually, John and Joshua stayed with her, and Carl and Shelly went with the Blacks.

Once the horses were taken care of, the three of them would ride on and catch up with the wagon, hopefully before they reached the bridge. Helen had parted with both the old pass and the new, dated one the James Fuller had sent her after their dinner party. The papers could help, but there was no guarantee, given how cluttered the roads had been with other groups just like theirs. Running didn't insure safety, but staying meant rape and murder.

She was barely back outside when there came a noise in the distance.

"What's that?" asked John.

"Motorcycle." Joshua put his hand out to steady the horses.

Snowcap snorted and shook his head, but he'd seen noisy beasts now and, although he didn't like them, they didn't scare him anymore. Sandy was used to anything and barely looked up, but Hulu Dancer started moving her white-banded hooves back and forth, only restrained by the bridle.

John moved to control his horse. "Whoa there, girl."

Helen crossed her arms and waited. She knew it had to be him.

James pulled to a stop a few yards from the horses and killed the engine. He dismounted.

"I'm glad I found you. I'd expected to catch up with you miles back."

"How did you know where we lived?"

He looked her over. She was suddenly aware of her work clothes, worn and frayed slacks and a faded, red checkered shirt from her father cut down to her size. They were much less stylish than the riding clothes she'd worn to the city. Or had he only seen her in the fancy dress Angela had loaned her?

"It was easy, Miss Black. The road was listed on the map, and there aren't many horse-drawn wagons on the road. I hailed your family and they told me which house."

She asked, "Why are you here?" A sudden, irrational thought burst into her head, "Have you come to buy my horses?"

He shook his head. "No." He looked at the men, from one to the other. "Joshua, is this your father?"

"Yes, Dad, meet James Fuller. Mr. Fuller, my father John Lamar."

They shook hands.

He turned to Helen. "I'm afraid I must speak with the Lamars, privately."

The Herd

Helen held the horses and fumed. How dare he barge in and interrupt her rescue mission? Didn't he know that the bandits could find and slaughter her babies at any time?

But he needed to speak to the Lamars, and *no you have to stay outside.* The arrogance of the man, inside her house, taking over her life. She was tempted, really tempted to kick over his big metal noisemaking machine.

John Lamar came out first, and the look on his face confused her. He looked up and saw her as if he'd forgotten she was there, waiting for him to help her.

"John?"

"Umm. Ah, Helen, I have to go on ahead to the city."

Joshua looked down, not meeting her eyes. "Me too. Sorry Helen."

She could barely form words. "What? The horses!"

When her two close friends wouldn't say anything, she glared at the intruder. "This is your idea?"

He nodded. "I'm sorry, but it's important."

"Yes, of course, *City things.*" If she could have made the words poison him where he stood, she would have. As it was, she gave it her best effort.

James winced.

She couldn't wait for any more explanation. The Fullers had all the power of the city, and it evidently extended to making her friends betray her. She had to get away from him.

She put her foot in the stirrup and urged Snowcap on.

"Hey! You can't go...."

She didn't listen to the rest of the sentence. She had her horses to take care of and nothing was going to stop her from doing that.

She leaned down over his neck and let him run. He knew where to go, luckily. Her eyes were so full of tears that she couldn't see.

By the time she'd reached the stand of trees that marked the old rail-fence line, she heard the motorcycle start up. She blinked her eyes and looked back. John and Joshua were making their way up towards the road.

The noise was headed her way. She clenched her teeth and urged Snow-cap faster. They cleared the low fence like it wasn't there and turned toward the high pasture.

Let him jump that with his machine!

...

Joshua looked back one last time. Mr. Fuller was driving the fence line looking for an entrance.

His father pulled up beside him. "Helen should be okay. He said he'd make sure she'd make it safely back to the city."

Joshua snorted. "I'm worried about *him*. She has a temper."

John nodded. "I'm not looking forward to the next time she sees us either. Come on, we've got to get moving."

...

Snowcap was tossing his head, an uncertain tone in his snort as they pulled up to the metal fence. Both the high pasture and the one down in the next valley had eight foot tall deer fences. She had to dismount to unlock the chain that secured the gate.

"It's okay, boy." She patted him on the neck. If he were soaking up her anger, it wasn't good for him. She could give Mister Mayor Junior a piece of her mind, but Snowcap didn't have that outlet.

When she reached for the chain, she realized something was wrong. The old galvanized chain had been secured with an padlock. They kept the key on a nail that jutted out of the post—the gate was just to keep the horses in. They never worried about a stranger. At least, they hadn't until recently.

The chain was tied together in a big oversized, simple knot. The padlock was in the dirt.

Snowcap snorted again, still unsettled.

The bandits had been here. Her heart pounded. She feared the worst.

The chain came free easily, and barely had she opened the gate when the motorcycle sounds came up the hill. Snowcap reared. She stepped back, and he was through the gate and off at a gallop.

"Wait!" But he wasn't listening. She could only watch as he raced off, searching for the herd.

The motorcycle pulled up to a stop.

"Did your horse run off?"

Helen turned, stalked up to him and slapped his face as hard as she could. "This is your fault!"

The sting in her hand and the loudness of the slap brought her up short. She stopped breathing while he brought his hand up to his shocked face. He patted his cheek, as if feeling for blood.

"Okay." He took in a breath. "What?"

She didn't understand. The pressure in her chest reminded her to breathe. "Huh?"

He kept his calm. "*What* is my fault?"

Practically every sentence they'd exchanged rushed back to her all at once. Her mind was a whirlwind.

She shook her head. "You wouldn't understand."

He glanced at the gate. "Okay. Forget it. Tell me later. But for now, I've only got an hour or so before I have to get back to the city. So right now, what needs to be done?"

She tried to settle her mind, to speak as clearly as he did. He was offering to help, so she wouldn't give him any excuse to dismiss her as a butterfly-brained female.

"The bandits are killing, and eating, my horses. I have to move them out of this pasture into the one over the hill, where they have a chance to hide. I think the bandits have already discovered this pasture. But Snowcap was upset by our fight and the noise of your machine set him off, and he went on ahead of me."

"So we need to catch up with him?"

"And the herd, yes."

He nodded. "Okay, hop on, I can give you a ride there."

She hesitated.

"Come on. The seat is designed for two, can't you see?"

She closed her eyes and shook her head. "Don't city folk have any sense? Rule number one in the country: Never leave the gates open. If I get on your machine, I can't close the gate when you go through. With an open gate, some of the horses could escape. Drive your little gadget through the gate. I'll close it, and then I'll get on. Okay?"

He nodded, then frowned. "Ah, I guess I left that rail fence gate open back by the house."

She sighed. "We'll deal with that later. Move your machine."

He pushed the bike on through the opening and waited. Helen closed the gate and looped the chain loosely to secure it. She had an idea, but now wasn't the time to bring it up.

"Get on and hang on to me."

She did, and it helped that he was facing ahead, rather than looking at her. It was frustrating and embarrassing to accept a ride on the noisy contraption.

He kept his speed low as they bounced over the pasture. She had to grip tighter around his waist for fear of being tossed off.

They quickly found the horses. "Stop!"

He slowed to a halt and she hopped off. Snowcap and Gaggle, a mature stallion who was sire to nearly half of the herd, were racing along the fence line, playing dominance games. Someday, Snowcap would win. Most of the herd had started to move away from the strange, noisy device.

Helen only took a quick headcount before searching the sky.

"Oh no." She took off running towards the tree line.

"What's going on?"

He jogged after her, watching as she raced up to a group of birds. They scattered as she approached. *Vultures.*

The girl collapsed to her knees.

James hesitantly approached. The smell was overpowering. She was shaking, and he could imagine why. Two of her horses had been butchered, haunches of meat carved from the carcasses and the rest left to rot. The horses were left in positions of their final agony and fear, although the eyes had been picked out by the birds.

He gripped her shoulder. She struggled to knock his hand away.

"Come on. You can do nothing for these. Let's save the others."

She struggled to her feet. "Why should you care? You were going to let my family be slaughtered. Surely you don't care about them!" She nodded toward the herd, huddled together for protection—every bit aware of what had happened to two of their number.

...

He put a clamp on his emotions. "It doesn't matter what you think of me. Are you going to accept my help or not?"

She looked past him to the herd.

"I've got to."

"So what do we do?"

She avoided his eyes. "I wanted to move the whole herd to the city, out of danger, but there are too many bandits around. I'd never make it. The best I can do is move the herd into the next pasture over, and hope that the killers will believe I've taken them."

"I promised the Lamars that I'd get you back to the city. How long will this take?"

She started back towards the herd. He followed.

"It'll never work with your motorcycle making all that noise. Can you ride?"

"What? Oh, you mean ride horses. Maybe. Can't I just follow? You lead and I'll ride the bike behind to urge them on?"

She snorted. "They're already agitated enough, and this is a wide pasture. They can circle around you so fast you'd never be able to herd them that way.

"No. Horses have natural leaders. If we ride them over to the hidden valley, the others will follow of their own free will."

James looked at the animals, already spooked and snorting. He had no confidence her plan would work.

She grabbed his hand and pulled him on. "Come on. You can ride Rose. She'll take care of you."

"Wait. Did you say 'Rose'?"

"Yes. Come on. I'll introduce you."

James buried his reluctance. This had to be the Rose Ed mentioned.

He was introduced, and fought against his natural instinct to keep his fingers away from those teeth.

"Now, let's get you mounted. It's a shame we don't have a saddle."

"Wait just a second. I want to put the motorcycle out of sight."

She waited impatiently as he pushed the machine into the trees.

James hesitated, and then fished his radio out of storage and clipped it to his belt. Bell Springs was out of range to his troops on the other side of the river, but he didn't want the radio out of his sight–especially in bandit-occupied lands. One of the reports from his patrol from up river had said that the scavengers they'd fought had been ex-military. Maybe they only fought with swords and captured firearms now, but they wouldn't miss the opportunity to listen in on the city's radio communications if they had the chance.

When he turned back, he was startled to see the girl pulling the saddle off of the white horse.

"What's going on?"

"You need a saddle more than I do." She quickly secured the straps and moved the bit and bridle over to the red horse as well.

With no effort at all, she mounted her horse and then coached him on how to put his foot in the stirrup and get up into position.

"It's taller up here than on a motorcycle."

"Can you ride?"

James shook the reins and urged Rose forward. She took a few steps and then stopped. He laid the rein against her neck, like he'd been told and Rose turned easily. "It seems so. Throttle? Brakes?"

She laughed. "Oh, come on. Snowcap." Her horse turned and moved on as if he were telepathic. Rose followed at a walking pace.

Once they were a dozen yards away, the rest of the herd moved to follow them.

He whispered to Rose. "I don't know why Ed said to go with you, but Dad always said to follow his advice. You don't know why, do you?"

Rose turned her head slightly and whinnied. James shrugged.

Helen turned her head to try to hear, but she was too far ahead.

Now I'm talking to animals. This has been a strange day.

The Chase

Helen didn't want to look at James Fuller, but she couldn't help herself. His riding skills were minimal and she feared any moment he'd fall off, but it was his face that drew her attention. The cheek where she'd hit him was a red welt, and her hand still tingled from the impact.

And yet, he hadn't gotten angry. He was offering to help her and she couldn't just tell him to leave.

An apology kept trying to form itself in her mouth, but she swallowed it down.

"Take Rose up to those three trees." He nodded and succeeded in turning her the right direction. She and Snowcap took a different route through the trees, and she paid particular attention to which horses followed Rose and which followed Snowcap. Her boy was still too young to be a good leader, but he was developing well and the herd dynamics were showing changes.

The two groups rejoined a little later as she rode up to the back gate, nearly hidden behind a small limestone outcropping. She slid off and had the gate open by the time the rest of the horses arrived.

"Take them on through."

James nodded and ducked his head under the top metal rail. She swatted Snowcap's rump and he went on through on his own.

"James!"

He looked up.

"Take them on a run down to the creek, and then come back here. Hopefully, they'll stay down by the water."

"Okay."

He whispered something to Rose and Helen could see that Rose liked being talked to. They moved off in a rough trot. She stifled a laugh at the way the city boy bounced in the saddle.

Snowcap whinnied.

"Oh, go on with them. I'll catch up."

He snorted and then galloped off and passed the rest of them, heading for the shady pool they all knew was there.

As soon as the silence of the trees descended over her, she shivered. She used to love being alone among the trees with nothing but her thoughts and the constant drone of the hidden cicada. Not now. Her thoughts were tainted with nightmare images. She moved away from the gate and sat on a rock ledge, out of sight.

With her babies butchered for meat, and monsters hiding in the trees, ready and willing to do horrible things to her, part of her wanted to run just as fast as she could manage to the safety of the far side of the river, but how could she leave her herd to be massacred?

She knew every long face, and the personality behind those large trusting eyes. Would they be safer if she just left all the gates open and let them scatter?

No. They'd stay close together, following their leader, and be led right into the bandit hunting traps. Gaggle was great about finding grass and water and avoiding snakes and places where lightning would strike during storms, but he had no experience with bandits until today. They'd be safer concealed in this valley, if she could just make sure the bandits didn't find the gate.

Familiar sounds of a pair of horses galloping her way interrupted her dark thoughts.

The city boy rode up to the gate and then turned when he saw where she was. She had to smile.

"Yes?" he asked.

"Nothing. I just hadn't seen you smile like that before." She wouldn't mention his still-red face.

He put his hand on Rose's neck. "It was fun, this running."

Snowcap came up close enough to nudge her arm.

She asked, "You don't get much fun?"

His face settled back to his more civilized half-smile. "No. Not really in my job description."

He looked at the gate. "Are we done now? I really need to get back to the city."

She shook her head. "No, I've got more things left to do here. But you can go on. I'll catch up with my family on the road later."

He frowned. "I told John Lamar that I'd escort you to safety."

Helen matched his frown. "That wasn't your promise to make."

"But..."

"No. You refused to protect Bell Springs. That gives you no right at all to tell me how to live my life. I'm not one of your citizens."

His nostrils flared like Gaggle's when challenged. "I can't in good conscience leave a woman alone in bandit country."

"Well, then you've got a moral dilemma, don't you?" Helen patted Snowcap on the flank and stepped from the stone ledge and easily mounted her horse. "Which has a greater call on your protection, your city or me?"

She dared him to make a move. She could outrun him and he knew it.

He sagged. "Were you going to pull this trick on the Lamars?"

"That's none of your business."

"You can't stay out here in the woods with your horses. The bandits could occupy these valleys for months, even years. I don't have good reports on how many there are, certainly hundreds, but possibly thousands of them. What are you really planning to do?"

She didn't let her glare falter. "None of your business. Go save your city. I'll take care of my horses. There's no way you can make me come with you. No way!"

He looked at her on Snowcap and swept his gaze along the fence line. She didn't know what he was thinking, but he was planning something. She couldn't let him get the advantage.

"Snowcap!" She nudged him with her knee and they took off at a gallop.

She shouted back, "Leave the saddle and turn Rose loose!" He struggled with the reins, but couldn't get the confused horse turned around in time to give chase.

Helen knew every side-creek and clump of trees in this valley and it was only a matter of time before he would have to give up on the chase and go back to the city.

She hoped it was sooner rather than later. She had her own safety to worry about and the more he tried to protect her, the harder it would be to put her own plan into effect.

When she finally heard the sound of a motorcycle in the distance, she was strangely disappointed. She shook it off. *No time for games of hide and seek.*

Now she had to divide the herd. There were five horses who would follow Snowcap. She'd take them on a round-about route to safety. She honestly didn't know which group would have the best chance of survival, the ones hidden, or the ones on the run, but it was the best idea she could come up with.

. . .

James rubbed the side of his face as he realized there was no way he could possibly chase her down.

Ridiculous woman!

But she had pointed out the truth of the matter. Tens of thousands of people depended on him, back in the city. He'd had years of experience making these kinds of decisions, but it didn't make it any easier.

He had to dismount to open the gate and lead Rose through. *Close the gate.*

Miss Black had a way of making him feel foolish. Nobody did that anymore, back in the city.

He was tempted to unsaddle Rose and turn her loose to join the other horses, just like he'd been told. But she hadn't told him where to leave the saddle, had she? And it was a long walk back to the motorcycle. As long as Rose was co-operative, he was tempted to ride her there.

He closed and secured the gate and then remounted.

How does she get on that horse barebacked, without the stirrups?

He shook his head.

. . .

When the motorcycle rumbled to life in the distance, James pulled on the reins and stopped Rose in her tracks.

Bandits. They'd discovered his bike!

The trees and uneven terrain hid them from his sight, but no telling how many there were. Probably, they'd come back for more horse meat.

They'd hunt around, looking for them and find the gate to the hidden valley. They'd find him too.

But they were on foot, and Rose was pretty fast.

He steered his horse among the trees close to the far fence line, moving slowly.

Soon, he saw them, a group of five tightly clustered around his bike. One young guy in ragged skins was struggling to start it again. *Probably forgot the gas line valve.* His bike had a few odd quirks.

If he could get down slope from them...

"Hey!" Nope. They saw him.

James yelled, "You're too late! We got them to safety!"

He shook the reins and tapped her flanks with his feet. "Come on Rose. Run!"

She got the idea and started off at a slow run. "Come on! Faster!"

Behind him the motorcycle rumbled to life and this time, kept running.

James searched for the gate, but Rose had already been heading in the right direction.

Please be open. He didn't want to dismount to open the gate with the motorcycle chasing him.

It was open! The bandits didn't know the rules, either.

But the engine noise was gaining on him. His bike could easily do eighty on the highway, and Rose wasn't that fast.

He remembered how Helen had gotten ahead of him the first time at the rail fence, but he didn't have any confidence he could urge Rose to jump it for him. But the gap was still down as he'd left it. Rose slowed to a trot as they negotiated the opening, but he urged her on.

Along the creek was a trail leading to the house, and beyond that, to the road.

If I go that way, he'll catch me.

All the bandit on his bike would have to do was get close enough to slash at Rose with his machete, and then wait until she faltered.

He tugged the reins to the side and Rose took the route up the hillside behind the house.

Behind him, the bandit on the bike tried to follow up the rocky path, but after his wheels slid out from under him a couple of times, he turned back and took the trail to the road.

He'll try to cut me off by staying to the roads.

James grinned. He'd stared at the road map not too long ago. He urged Rose more to the left. If he avoided pavement, there was no way the bike could flank him.

...

Twice, he had to stop and negotiate fence lines, but soon, he could no longer hear the motorcycle in the distance.

If the bandits believed him, and thought that the horses were moved to safety, and didn't attempt a thorough search of the fence line, then maybe Helen and her horses would be safe. In any case, it was the best he could do for now.

The loss of his bike was a nagging aggravation. But at least, with limited fuel, the bandits wouldn't get much advantage out of it either.

"Well, Rose, it looks like you'll get a visit to the city. As soon as I can figure out which direction that is."

For years he'd spend long hours over maps, directing the City Guard. But to him, maps were patterns of roads weaving across the distance. However, his chase had led him over hills and across creeks. When he reached a dirt road, he had lost all sense of whether it was some rancher's private path, or one of the minor routes on his maps.

His watch and the fading sun gave him a rough idea of the compass directions, but that was all. How far had he come? Where was the city? Was that last creek they'd waded across something he'd seen before?

James urged Rose up the nearest hill. It wasn't high enough to give him visibility, unless he felt inclined to climb a tree.

He pulled out the radio and listened. There was static, but no signal from guard troops. He clicked it off. Save the batteries.

There was a ranch house in the distance. Most houses had driveways from Techno days. Driveways led to roads. And in any case, he'd need shelter for the night.

"Come on, maybe we can find you something to graze on. What do you think?"

Rose snorted and headed toward the building in the distance.

The Mission

Mayor of Austin, George Fuller, rested in his chair for a moment. His assistant had gotten the word to him just in time to be in place at his office, but not enough for him to catch his breath. The Ambassador from Houston had arrived.

A light started blinking from a box Hodges of the IIS had been kind enough to make for him a few years earlier. The behind-the-scenes deals Mary Ellen Victor had wrangled back in the dark days after the Star had been more helpful to the city than he'd imagined at the time. He sighed with a smile. He missed his old enemy. She'd been a tenacious fighter. When Hodges took over, the IIS was all business, never a smile or a growl out of him. But he was always ready to do a few chores off the books, like this intercom system that let his people give him advanced warning when someone was coming.

He straightened up in his chair and had a fake document out on his desk when the knock came at the door.

"Enter."

His secretary opened the door. "Sir, Ambassador Lloyd from Houston."

George rose and waved him in.

"Greetings Peter, come on in."

They shook hands, smiling as if old friends. "Have a seat."

They exchanged a few words about family and acquaintances. George smiled, although Peter Lloyd hadn't brought him a single piece of good news in the past six years. That had been when Houston set up a periodic train run, trading gasoline and diesel in exchange for corn and cotton.

Since then, it had been endless renegotiations, as Houston demanded more and supplied less. They hadn't even been using a train in the last couple of years, just tanker trucks.

"I hear you have a bandit problem." He finally got down to business.

George nodded. "They've certainly riled up the Hill Country farmers. We haven't had any problems here in Austin."

"That's good to hear. The Houston Militia military assessment that I've seen was pretty grim." He waved his hands. "A lot of mumbo-jumbo about City Guard troop strength and refugee counts and stuff. I didn't understand most of it, to be honest. But the Houston Area Council seemed to take it seriously. They were most concerned that these bandits seemed to have a habit of burning towns to the ground. Believe me. I've seen the photographs of what has happened to San Antonio. And we certainly wouldn't want that to happen to Austin."

George smiled. "It's gratifying that Houston has such concern. So you came here to share that military assessment of yours?"

The ambassador frowned, "No, I'm sorry I didn't bring that with me. Council secret and all that, you understand. No, what I've been empowered to offer is much more valuable. We could send a troop train with men and ammunition to help defend Austin against this tide of savages."

"Hmm." He tapped his pen on his desk for a few seconds. It was actually a signal to his secretary listening in on the intercom to transcribe everything that was said. "Tell me more details. What exactly are you offering?"

It was an appealing list. Troops, automatic weapons with ammunition. Extra fuel. It was enough to relieve his son's worries about being able to cover all the entrances to the city and handle the refugee crowd-control issues.

It was when the other details came to light that George became comfortable with the idea of what Houston was trying to do. Key to the offer was merging the military forces of Austin and Houston, with Houston in charge. There were other disturbing items, like a permanent force to be stationed in Austin to protect the railroad infrastructure. He didn't even wait to hear what Houston expected to be paid for the assistance.

"Peter, that's quite a plan of yours. How about a much simpler idea? Why don't you just raise our fuel quota back to the original level we agreed to six years ago, and Austin will fight its own battles? Surely if your spies are worth what you're paying them, you know Austin's military strength would be much improved by just that simple step."

The ambassador frowned. "Unfortunately, I'm not authorized to make that offer."

George leaned forward. "Then the answer is 'no'. Austin does not desire to become a vassal state to Houston. We can still fight our own battles."

...

"Ann, have you sent the transcription to James?"

She shook her head, pulled the last sheet out of her Remington typewriter and handed him the completed stack. "I've been unable to locate him. Not at your house, nor his. Not here at the Driskill. Camp Mabry refuses to confirm or deny."

George looked over the details of the Houston offer. Somewhere in there were clues to Houston's long term plans and James was better at analysis than he was. "I'm going to insist that he get a secretary. You always know where I am."

Ann nodded. "Your son has a dislike for secretaries."

He sighed. "That's my fault."

Ann said nothing. She knew the story of her predecessor, and why James Fuller spent most of his office time at the guard headquarters, rather than at his Driskill desk. He loved his father, but refused to make the same mistakes.

George pointed to the phone. "Get Sergeant Willowby. If anyone knows where he is, he'll know. And he'll talk to me even if I have to go there in person."

...

And that's what it took. The man was apologetic, but insistent. "At the present time, the phone lines are not to be considered secure."

So George arrived at the Camp Mabry gates and his car was waved inside.

Willowby was waiting outside for him to arrive. "I'm glad you called. One of the Commander's plans has reached a point where we'll need a Mayoral authorization."

George frowned. "So, he's not here?"

The sergeant was a sunbaked, leathery man who always looked slightly small when standing next to James Fuller, but seemed large on his own. He looked to be in his forties and had been with the guards since well before the Star. He'd seen it all.

And now he frowned. "Commander Fuller took a motorcycle off into the Hill Country mid-day yesterday. He had planned to be gone a few hours and he is overdue."

"Why in the world would he do something like that?" George wasn't surprised that his son would tackle some tasks personally, but some things were too risky.

"Sir, if you would care to come inside, I'd be happy to share the details."

In the Commander's office, George was surprised to see two farmers. "I've seen you before."

Joshua nodded. "Yes, sir. I was with Helen Black at Angela Morgan's house."

That excitable woman again. What does she have to do with this? Did James go visit her?

In spite of the presence of the two outsiders, the sergeant handed George a thin folder, containing a few pieces of paper—a Marathoner message from Ed Morgan, a hand-written IIS request form signed by Joshua Lamar, and Sergeant Willowby's own note, writing down the order from James Fuller requesting a motorcycle be made ready for a trip into the Hill Country.

George read the IIS form again, looking at the Lamars with more interest. "So, my son went to get you two?"

John Lamar nodded. "He explained Austin's strategic need for petroleum supplies. He sent us here with a special pass to get us across the bridge in a hurry."

Willowby said, "I had orders to be on the look out for them, and had them sent by car here as soon as they arrived. But we'll need your authorization for the next step."

George understood. "Fine. I have my car. We can go there now. But before that—what happened to my son?"

Joshua shrugged. "We were going to help Helen move her horses to a safer pasture, but then James...your son convinced us that we had to get to Austin immediately. He offered to stay in our place to help her get her horses to safety. The last I saw of them, they were fighting again. But that's just how Helen is."

John added, "But that shouldn't have taken more than an hour or so. I expected him to get to the bridge before us, with that motorcycle of his."

"Maybe he decided to escort Helen. It's pretty dangerous out there."

George sighed. *Who knows. With that girl, and Ed sending cryptic messages, I've just got to take it all on faith.*

"Okay. Come on, let's go."

...

The William B. Travis office building was partially occupied. The Mayor, the sergeant and the two farmers went in past the Cotton Market and small fruit and vegetable shop. The elevators were sealed and inactive. The stairway was marked with the City Archive sign and yellow tape. It didn't appear as if it had been tampered with. The executions for looting had gotten the city through a bad spell right after the Star, and the public hangings had left an impression.

George scribbled his name and the date on the sign and they broke through the tapes. He'd have a crew back to re-seal it later.

John Lamar pointed out the offices to his son as they climbed the stairs. "When the Star happened, I was in Information Services. We ran regular reports, big paper reports, in addition to the on-line information services. Practically the last report we printed before the Star burned out all the computers was the big oil well status report."

Sergeant Willowby asked, "Why does the Texas Railroad Commission have a list of the oil wells? I never understood that bit."

John shrugged. "It just happened over time. The TRC was started to regulate rail shipping rates to put a cap on the robber barons. Other shipping was added, and then oil pipelines. That grew to regulate the oil well production as well, and then expanded to natural gas, mining, uranium, etc. For many years the TRC controlled the price of oil world wide, since all the big oil fields were in Texas."

George paused at a wall map of the railroads across the state.

John pointed. "The TRC had already dropped its control of the rail system a few years before the Star. That's just a historical map."

George nodded, but his eyes tracked the cities, like Brenham that followed the rail lines. *Houston switched to trucks right about the time San Antonio went silent.* Some things made a lot more sense now. "Sergeant Willowby."

"Yes, sir."

"Have this map moved to Camp Mabry. James will want to see it."

"Yes, sir."

The records storage area was locked, but they had come prepared. The door came free with a crow bar. John went immediately to a locker and opened the metal doors. It was dusty and smelled of mold, but the big fat, ledger-sized report was in pretty good shape. They all looked as he opened the cover and showed off the columns of names and numbers.

"Here is every oil well in Texas, which ones are dry, and which ones were still producing when the Star shut them down. This column gives the exact location of the well, and other details, like which company owned them.

"If Austin wants to find its own source of petroleum, then this is the only treasure map you'll need."

Staying Out of Sight

Helen had thought she had made a horrible mistake, trying to sneak a half-dozen horses through enemy-held lands all by herself. And that was before a pair of bandits stopped to rest under the tree where she had tried to sleep.

"I don't like Red. He's too military."

"But you can't deny he's a true son of the Hunter. I mean, the Dragons always eat good."

"That's too pat. City people eat too."

Helen tried to keep from breathing heavily. She was stretched out on a limb ten feet up and only three or four feet to the side of where they sat. If she could stay quiet, and if her horses could stay quiet....

Last night, when the light had faded, she had made a crude corral from the available trees, a creekside cliff and the rope she'd brought. Dividing the risk, she moved forty feet upstream to find her own bed for the night. They were close enough so that if she screamed, they would bolt right through the rope fence, and if they were attacked, she'd hear them.

But right now, they were quiet and she prayed Snowcap didn't get it into his head to come looking for her.

She didn't want to listen to the bandits below her either. They sounded too normal. Not that their conversation wasn't creepy, but it could have been any two farmers chatting over lunch.

"You're gonna join up anyway, aint'cha?"

"Pretty much have to. Red Dragon's all fired up and everbody's joining up. Gotta stay with the clan. And for sure, there'll be pickin's when Austin burns. I bet there's a dozen little crawlers back in San Antone with my eyes."

The other sighed. "I's hoping there'd been women at that big brick house on the cliff."

Helen fought the urge to gasp. She knew that house. She'd passed by when they had taken Tawny back to Pace Bend. A happy couple with a yard full of kids had waved at them as they rode past.

"Yeah, that guy fought well for a farmer, but there was nothing but pantry goods."

Did that mean that the mom and kids made it to safety?

It didn't sound like the father survived. But why had he stayed if his family left?

She tried not to think about it. Maybe he wanted to stay and protect the house. The bandits tended to burn places for no reason.

Or maybe his family hadn't made it to safety. Maybe they were just hiding in the woods like her horses.

"It's spooky here."

"What'dya mean?"

"I dunno. Birds are quiet. Spooky."

Helen leaned her cheek closer against the rough bark and tried not to move.

Don't look up. Don't look up.

"Yeah. You're right. Well, let's get moving. 'The Hunter gives instincts to the wise and meat for the seeker.'"

They stood up and ambled off towards the south.

Don't take the creek. Go across the pasture.

She couldn't tell which way they headed without moving, and she couldn't move without making noise. So she waited.

Soon, she couldn't hear their footsteps anymore. Still she waited.

When a chickadee landed on a branch near her, gave her a look and then fluttered off in panic, she took a deep breath and made her way back down to the ground.

The bandits were nowhere to be seen. Cautiously, she located the horses, still munching the grass and churning the creekside to mud.

If that family are still in hiding, they won't last long unless they get to the safety of a bigger group. A pair of bandits wouldn't balk at attacking a mother and her kids, but they might have second thoughts if they came upon a larger group of farmers, armed and ready to fight.

I have to go check.

* * *

James kicked the car's door open and got out. The back seat of an abandoned Buick was hardly the best place to sleep for the night, but the interior of the house was still smoking and the roof had collapsed. There were three bodies with large knife wounds he'd given a crude burial under debris from the house. They deserved better, but all he could afford to do was keep the vultures off of them. Although, with all the carnage going on, the carrion eaters had their time well booked.

I've got to get back to the city. These bandits can move a lot faster than I'd given them credit.

He stretched his legs and went to check on Rose. The horse took more effort than the motorcycle, but at least he didn't have to search for gasoline. She looked up from the hay he'd found for her and took a step in his direction until she was stopped by the reins he'd tied to a post.

"Did you have a better night than I did?"

It occurred to him that she was tracking the movement of his hands. She expected a treat. He patted her on the neck as he unhooked the reins. "I'll have to find you something. But for now, we've got to find the way back to town."

She behaved as he stepped up into the saddle.

I'm glad she's so well trained. Probably Helen's doing.

With an eye to the morning sun, he followed the driveway to the road and headed towards Austin.

* * *

Helen approached the house from across the valley, keeping her herd in the trees. She paused and watched the house and grounds for a few minutes, sensitive to any sign that other bandits were in the area. This ranch house had been built high on the side of the hill for the scenery, back before the Star. It now made it a prime target for the predators. It also looked intact. That made it all the more likely other bandits would check it out again.

There was a flicker of motion in the window. *Someone is in there.* Someone hiding.

"Come on, Snowcap. Let's go visiting."

She rode her white horse boldly down the slope, across the road and up to the front yard of the house. The other horses followed the leader, spreading out when Snowcap stopped to munch on grass and nose about the trees. Helen knew where her babies were without looking, and since they weren't frightened, neither was she.

She dismounted and went up to the front door and knocked. Surely they had seen her coming. There was a long minute or two of silence before she knocked again.

The door opened a few inches and two sets of eyes peered out in the darkness, one above the other. Helen smiled at the mother and then at the boy below who had elbowed his way in front of her, kitchen knife in hand, ready to defend his mom.

"Hello. My name is Helen Black. I live over in Bell Springs."

The worried mother nodded, while she snagged her son's arm. "I've seen you. We've been attacked."

Helen nodded solemnly. "I heard bandits talking. That's why I'm here."

"Get inside. It's not safe out there."

As soon as her eyes adapted to the dim light inside, she saw the children—a teenage girl holding two infants, twins probably, there was the boy with the knife, a toddler, and an older boy, maybe twelve or so, grim-faced, holding a shotgun at the ready.

Oh, my, what am I supposed to do with them.

...

"We hid in the well house," Andrea Simpson said. "The older ones kept the babies quiet. We waited until the sun went down, and then Bob snuck over to check and found...."

"I know what he found. It's okay." The lady was trying her best to hold it all together and that's why Helen suggested that they have a little one-on-one chat in the bedroom. If there was nothing else she could do to help, she could let the woman cry on her shoulder.

They had planned to evacuate to the city, like their neighbors, but with all the children, it had taken too long to get ready. The bandits came and after Mr. Simpson fought and failed, they burned the wagon and killed the ox, not even butchering it. They'd found a bushel of honey-sweetened wheat she'd made up for the children and made off with it instead of staying and cooking steaks.

"I don't know what to do! The house is okay, and we have water, but most of our food is gone, burned."

Helen felt her stomach rumble as well. She'd started on her own escape with no provisions. It had been her plan to race with Snowcap to join her family. Trying to save some of the horses had been an impulse. She hadn't thought it out well.

Andrea wrung her hands, staring at the floor. She had a family to protect and her husband had already done his part. The rest was up to her, and she had no idea what to do.

The door swung open. Bob, the oldest, still carrying the shotgun, whispered. "There's a bandit outside."

Helen got to her feet. "Show me."

They crept around the side of the room, frightened eyes of the children watching their every move. Peering carefully out the window, staying in the shadows, Helen felt her insides twist when she saw the man, his hand outstretched to Snowcap. Her horse munched away at grass unconcerned.

The man turned his eyes towards the house and waved, although he shouldn't have been able to see them. Helen sighed.

"What is it?" Bob asked.

"I know that man. He's not a bandit. Tell your mother."

She went outside.

"Hello, Mr. Morgan."

The man in the white robe smiled. "Hello, Helen. Surely you can still call me Ed."

. . .

Helen felt comforted, knowing this man who could tell the future didn't seem to be concerned about being surprised by bandits. With Helen's approval, Snowcap let himself be petted by the stranger.

"His name is ..."

"Snowcap. Yes, I know."

Helen frowned. "How?"

He chuckled. "Just one of those things."

There were eyes inside watching their every move. Helen decided to get back on track. "Ah, Ed. I'm worried about these people. Is there a safe road to get them to the city?"

He shook his head. "No. Not any more. The Sons of the Hunter are flooding into the area, as the word has gone out that the attack on Austin will be happening soon."

"But if we were on horses, we could ride fast..."

He sighed, "No. These people know their hunting strategy. They lie in wait until people enter their trap and then suddenly surround them. It works for deer and wildlife. It works for unwary farmers on the road. Helen, they have the numbers to trap anyone."

She felt trapped herself. How had she managed to get herself into this situation? Dad had always complained how headstrong she was. She'd always considered it a compliment.

"But what can I do?"

"Do what you've always done. Help people." He closed his eyes and pointed to the west. "There's a group of people little more than a mile that way. House is burned down, but they're hiding down by their creek. The Phillips encampment. You'll take them there and they'll be safe until this is over."

Helen felt like she could trust him. Isn't that what everyone said?

"Ed, I saw Angela just a few days ago."

He blinked, surprised. "Oh. How is she?"

"She's scared to death, worried about you." She shook her head. "I over-heard some bandits talking. They plan to burn Austin. Will she be safe there?"

He frowned. "I...I don't know." His hand dropped away from the horse.

She didn't ask why, but it was discouraging that even Ed Morgan didn't know some things. Bob had come out onto the porch, watching them. At least he wasn't pointing the shotgun. She didn't blame him one instant, but a nervous finger on a trigger was dangerous.

"I'll need to talk to them."

Ed nodded. His face thoughtful and sad.

She walked up to Bob. "Can I speak to you and your mother?"

He nodded, then looked past her shoulder. "Where is he going?"

She looked back. Ed was walking away, past the row of trees and quickly out of sight. She sighed. *I guess it's up to me.*

Batten the Hatches

James urged Rose straight up the hill. "Come on, girl! Those noises behind us aren't good."

He'd stumbled into a party of a dozen bandits resting beside the road. They'd moved instantly into formation, half of them spanning the road ahead and another group moving in behind him. If he'd been a wagon, there would have been no escape. But a horse could move in any direction.

This group had guns, and they pulled them out the instant he took off sideways through the trees. *Raiding farm houses has left them better armed.* They weren't just doing it for food and to rape the women.

He'd seen all the other traps in time to avoide them, but he'd gotten lazy. It seemed all the roads were closed. If the farmers hadn't evacuated early, it was too late now.

Did she make it out in time?

Rose was slowing down. Was she tired? He'd gone straight uphill, knowing the men on foot couldn't match the horse. But they'd been hunting for a way back to Austin all day. He would have to give her more rest, food and water—but after they ditched the men with guns.

Still, Rose slowed in spite of his kicks to her flanks.

"Come on. We can't quit now."

She whinnied.

What is it?

She turned on her own, tossing her head and moving to the left.

He glanced back down the hill at the men staggering after them.

"Okay, go your way." He shook the reins and she picked up speed. Another few yards and he saw the problem. The terrain near the top was mostly large boulders. He'd have a time scrambling over them and Rose was just the wrong kind of animal to navigate that way.

"You're right." He gave her a gentle pat on the neck. "I'll pay more attention to you next time."

They made good time after that, and hidden in the trees, he paused to let her rest while he watched the ridge line. The men showed up eventually, but they looked around at the wide valley and gave up the chase.

He pulled out the radio.

"Code 4. Code 4. Code 4."

When he listened, there seemed to be a reply, but the signal was still too weak to make it out. *I'll need to get closer and try again from a hilltop.*

But it seemed someone had heard him. He just hoped it was his people.

. . .

Joshua noticed that the sergeant seemed to have a smile on his face.

"Something happen?"

He nodded. "I can't tell you. But something good. Now, are there any more questions?"

His father shook his head. He gestured with a handful of photos—images of selected pages of his report. "I know where to go and what to do."

"You know what to do if captured?"

Joshua smiled. They'd been over that time after time. He understood what was at stake as well as they did. "Sure. Burn the notes."

John added. "We're ready to go. Are you ready to let us? The sooner we succeed, the sooner Austin can provide help for my family."

"Okay. You're fueled and ready to go."

"Let's go, then."

Joshua was eager to get started. He'd never realized his father could drive one of these big trucks. He listened carefully, watching every move as his dad drove out, taking him through the gear shifts and pointing out how to make the wide turns.

"I was a truck driver for a few years out of high school. I did a lot of odd jobs before I got into computers."

They drove slowly onto Mopac, heading north to the Highway 183 junction.

John had a big grin. "It's been so long since I've driven anything, much less a big rig. This is fun." He had to slow to avoid a narrow stretch where the abandoned cars had been towed clear of the interchange ramp.

"You'll teach me, right?"

"Sure, but we need to get clear of all this clutter first."

It was near Leander when they pulled to a stop and painted over the Austin Texas City Guard military labeling. Joshua worked quickly with the mop-like brush while his father held the rifle, scanning the surroundings for any bandits. Hopefully, the invaders hadn't infiltrated this side of the river, but their job was too important to risk making a mistake now.

...

April looked up from her novel, hoping it was a customer. Seeing a wide-brimmed hat, she stuck her book back under the desk.

"Good evening, April."

"Hi. It's been really slow lately."

Hodges nodded. "The fear of the bandits is affecting everyone. We'll close early." He gestured to the door. "Since it's raining, I thought I'd drive you home."

"Oh, no problem. It's only a couple of blocks."

"Still. I need to speak to your mother anyway. We might as well keep you dry."

She sighed. When Hodges made a point and just waited, April knew he wasn't going to budge. She picked up her bag and stuffed her books into it. She hoped she wasn't in trouble. Hodges never complained when she read while on duty–only when she was late with her work.

He held the door and she saw that his little electric cart was parked right up to the door so she wouldn't have to walk through the rain.

He walked around, the hat doing a better job than an umbrella.

They pulled silently away, the thin tires splashing through the water in the street. She got a little wet as she made a dash for the front door, but it wasn't much.

"Mom! I'm home. I've got Mr. Hodges with me."

Denise Jenkins came in from the kitchen. "Did he bring you home? That was thoughtful of him."

Hodges moved to the fireplace mantle and looked at the drawings April had done over the years. There weren't any new ones. Her artwork had dropped off when she discovered reading for fun.

"Is there a problem, Hodges?" Denise had new wrinkle lines around her eyes since he'd seen her last. Widowhood had not been kind to her. Although the bank had lots of her money, she tended to leave it there and stay at home. When her husband died, she arranged to move to a house close to where her daughter worked, but she hadn't made many friends in her new location.

"Perhaps."

April put down her books and looked as worried as her mother.

Hodges asked, "You've probably heard about the bandits approaching the city?"

April nodded. Her mother shook her head. "I may have heard something at the market. I didn't understand what they were talking about."

"It appears that San Antonio had some kind of battle. A civil war or rebellion or something like that. Out of that chaos, bands of men formed groups that prowled the city, and then later the forests, hunting for food, but also attacking the farmers and burning out their homes. That group has now come as far as Austin."

April clutched a pillow from the couch. "James will stop them." Her mother moved to sit down beside her.

Hodges nodded. "Hopefully, he will. But if history is a guide, we should take our own precautions in case bad things happen. We can expect fighting, no matter who wins in the end. People will die. I have to make sure that you two are safe. So I'm shutting down the IIS offices for a few days."

April asked, "But what about the messages?"

"I will be bringing in someone to help me, but I need you and your mother to move back to the Whiting building where you can be safe behind strong walls and heavy, locked doors. I've already stocked it with food and water."

"Who are you bringing in?" April asked, as she put the pillow down.

Hodges paused a moment. "April, you are not being replaced. As soon as the danger is over, I would hope that your mother would let you return to work."

"But who is it? Randall or Sam? I'll have to train them on how to handle the incoming messages!"

Hodges shook his head. "No. It's no one you know."

"April, Hodges knows best. We have to get to safety."

"But no one knows how to do my job! I'll have to...."

Hodges spoke again, "April. You don't have to be concerned. You know me better than anyone. You know I'm not very emotional. You know I'll fire anyone who doesn't do their job. If you hadn't been the very best person to run the North Office I would have replaced you. That hasn't changed, and when the danger is over, I'll want you back.

"We will be using a different protocol for the messages while the office is closed, and the substitute can handle it."

"Who is it? What's his name?"

Hodges paused again. "Alfred Bettamin. You don't know him."

Mrs. Jensen put her hand to her mouth to stifle a chuckle. "I bet I've met him before."

Hodges nodded. "I believe you have."

She turned to her daughter. "Honey, you don't need to worry. Alfred is one of the ... people who works with Hodges to invent radios and things. He's good with machines but not someone to do *your* job."

Once April was placated and sent off to wash up for dinner, Denise asked in a low voice, "How bad it going to get?"

He also replied softly. "Unknown. But the reports consistently mention raped women and young girls. It's important that we get you two out of the city center and into a defensible location."

"Thank you. How much time do we have?"

"I would recommend moving tomorrow. I'll have a wagon come by to take you and your luggage. In addition, there is room for additional people, if you have close friends."

"Is that wise? They could see things."

"If it gets bad, there is the survivor's guilt issue. Saving others would be good for your emotional well-being. As far as security, I have made changes in the Whiting Building. Certain areas cannot be entered by humans."

Denise nodded. The depression that had overtaken her for nearly two years after the Star still haunted her. "You're right. I wouldn't want April to go through that. How many people?"

"No more than eight."

She chuckled, shaking her head. "I don't have that many friends."

April came back in. "What are you two whispering about?"

Denise turned to smile at her daughter. "Hodges said we could invite some friends. It'd be like a holiday. Do you have someone you'd like to invite? Some of the girls from Sunday School, maybe?"

She frowned. "Maybe Julie or Melody. But what about Sam or even Randall? I'd worry about them, if people are fighting."

He nodded. "I'll ask them. You contact the others."

...

Hodges returned to the IIS building and parked the cart by the front door.

After locking both front and rear entrances, he went to the rear office and unsealed a closet. Inside stood an utterly motionless man of about thirty. Hodges unbuttoned the shirt and opened a slot in the middle of the rib cage. Pouring two quarts of high-purity alcohol into the slot, he poked at a concealed switch and the slot closed.

Alfred Bettamin went through several facial expressions rapidly, one after the other, as Hodges watched. He moved his arms through their range of motion and stepped out of the tiny room. He buttoned up his own shirt and smiled.

"Good afternoon, Mr. Hodges. Are we ready to get to work?"

And then his face dropped to the same neutral expression that Hodges habitually wore, and they began working, silently, with no further commentary. Draperies were taken down and the windows boarded up. The rear door was bolted shut and then barricaded with a stack of furniture. Two large fuel drums were moved into the office, as well as a standby fuelcell generator to run the radio system in case of a city power outage.

Hodges went out the front door and Bettamin locked himself inside. While Hodges put up a sign explaining the temporary closure and instructions for putting messages into a mail chute, noises could be heard inside as the final touches of the lockdown were completed.

A final message was affixed, "Couriers, report to the office next door for instructions."

Inside, the lights went out.

Hide and Spy

Helen whispered into the ear of little David, riding with her arms around him. "You're doing a great job, but don't pull on on Snowcap's hair too hard, or he'll get upset."

He nodded and eased up his grip, just a little bit. She tugged the poncho a little farther, to keep the raindrops off of the toddler.

His mother, holding onto little Elizabeth as she rode Princess, pointed to the burned-out house on the hill. "That's the Phillips' place. It makes me sick to see it like that."

"But we knew it was coming. Let's get down into the valley. You go first, since you know the people."

Helen waved to the rest of them to come on up from where they were hidden in the trees. Ed had implied that they would make it safely, but she was taking no chances.

Bob and Carl were each happy to be riding horses all on their own. Serious-faced Amy, carrying little Francis, brought up the rear. Poor long-suffering Nomad was burdened down with what baggage they could drape over his back. Helen was proud of all her babies, and she'd give them all treats as soon as they delivered the Simpson family to safety. Luckily the Simpsons had a pear tree on their property. She'd stocked up.

They rode down the valley, single file, into the dense cluster of trees down by the creek.

...

"And so when Ed Morgan, the Wise Man of Austin himself, said that this was the only safe place where the Simpsons could hide out the invasion, I had no choice but to bring them here." Helen smiled, hoping the fierce scowl on Mr. Phillips face would fade eventually.

"So this fortune teller said we were safe? How could he know?"

She shrugged. "I don't know. He doesn't explain anything. But when I was a little girl, during the Star, he saved my life." She looked over at the small fire where Andrea and her circle of children were warming themselves after the long ride in the rain. "Apparently, you would have been safe anyway, but she wouldn't have. Her house was unburned and tempting to the next bandit troop that passed by. The next time, she wouldn't have her husband to fight them."

Mr. Phillips sighed. "Yeah, we'll take care of Andrea and her kids."

Mrs. Phillips poked him in the side. "You better not have been thinking of turning them away."

He growled. "Food is running low as it is. We can't take in everyone that passes by. The more of us, the sooner bandits will notice us. I'm not going to take a fortune teller's word on faith."

He frowned at the horses. Helen knew what he was thinking. Since the Star first bloomed, horses were considered animals that could be eaten. Hard times changed a lot of peoples' way of looking at things.

"I'll be moving on. I can't put a load on your supplies when I've still got my horses to take care of."

Mrs. Phillips looked concerned. "Surely you aren't planning to risk going out there again?"

He frowned. "Do you have a plan, or are you just moving around hoping for a lucky break?"

She had thought about it on the ride over from the Simpson place. If Ed was right, and all the roads were set up as snares to capture the refugees, she either had to stay put, or find another way out of bandit territory.

"Sort of a plan. Horses can swim. I can ride cross-country to Pace Bend. If I am spotted, I can probably outrun them. Once at the shore, I'll wait until a calm night and we'll all swim across. The lake is only about a quarter-mile wide at that point. It's a risk, but it's better than being caught, or having my horses killed."

Behind her, a voice said, "I want to come along with you."

Bob explained. "Here, I'm nothing more than another mouth to feed. Amy can handle the shotgun as well as I could. If I go with Miz Black, then I can help her take care of the horses, be a lookout when she sleeps, and maybe help her rescue more people like us."

His mother shook her head. "It's too dangerous out there. We have to stay in hiding."

Bob's mouth tightened. "Dad would have helped."

"Your father would have stayed to protect the family."

"Yes." He nodded. "He did."

Andrea put her hand against her chest, as if she couldn't breathe. She looked again, carefully at her son's face, highlighted by the flickering light. It looked as determined as his voice. It looked like his father's.

She looked at Helen, with a silent plea to say something.

Helen shook her head. "I could use help with the horses. But it is very dangerous out there."

. . .

It was midnight before his mother gave in and agreed.

"You take care of my boy!"

"I will. And I'll feel much safer myself. I saw how he protected you."

Morning light, she took her new apprentice and introduced him to the horses. They were taking advantage of plentiful hay and feed the Philips family had stockpiled for their cattle—now butchered by the bandits.

"This is Snowcap. He's rapidly becoming a herd leader. The others will follow him without any coaching. So I ride him."

She introduced the other horses, Banjo, Cookie, Velvet, Princess and Nomad, one by one, letting him get introduced and letting the horses get treats from his hand.

"I don't know Nomad's history. He found my herd on his own. He just showed up one day. There are scars here...see...on his side, and he's very sensitive about them. Nobody can ride him. Not yet, at least. However, he'll carry loads with not much complaint. He was someone's pet before the Star and someday I'd love to discover how he survived and how he got free, but for now, just learn to approach him from this side and talk to him when you need to load him up."

Bob nodded, struggling to absorb it all. Helen looked for the signs of mental overload. She'd taught Joshua and Carl, and her brother Billy horsemanship when they were even younger than Bob. She'd coached quite a few other people over the years. Some people, like James Fuller, seemed to get into the spirit of it quickly, but others never were comfortable with large animals.

What did happen to Rose? She never saw signs of horse or saddle when she led her little herd away. Could the motorcycle have spooked her so bad that she ran off? She shook her head. Just another mystery for later.

. . .

James whispered, "Now, you have to stay very quiet." He handed the horse a fig, and was pleased he was getting better at keeping his fingertips out of the way of those eager crushing teeth. Rose barely chewed it, smashing it once before swallowing the ripe dark fruit and looking his way for another. "Later."

He crept on his hands and knees from the bushes where he had her tied and eased his head over the ridgeline.

On the next hill over, three men were piling wood on top of a bonfire. A trail of smoke drifted gently off to the northeast. He'd followed the signal, but it had not been lit for him. Down in the valley, over a thousand bandits were collected in five separate camps. One fighter plane with a load of bombs would eliminate the bandit threat once and for all.

But that's just wishful thinking. If any of the EMP-hardened craft had survived the Star, they haven't considered showing themselves.

But maybe Texas was just too unimportant on the world stage right now. Texas had four or five city-states and hundreds or thousands of smaller independent communities. Multiply that across the continent and and the whole idea of a national identity with a national air force seemed pretty ridiculous.

I'd have better luck wishing for a wizard to cast a spell on them.

But someday. Someday when it was safe to travel across the state or across the continent, nationalism would come back into style. There'd been hope, in the months after the Star faded, when certain high power radio stations came back up, that long distance communications would be reestablished and the federal government would step up and take charge. But even that hope was dashed when the damage to the ionosphere reduced the ability of long distance radio waves to bounce back off the Heaviside layer. By the time the atmosphere began to heal itself, radio stations had lost their long distance broadcast ambitions and seemed entirely concerned with local issues.

Hodges and the IIS had brought a substitute with a clever mix of short wave radio frequencies and data packet communication. He regularly received a News of the World report collected and summarized by a group in Maine, but Washington DC was a small town struggling to protect its museums and New York City was back to its roots, building a place where railroads and ships could exchange goods—even if those ships had sails again. Europe was no better. Asia was probably the same, but the English language and the IIS hadn't made a connection yet in China and the surrounding continent. Over half of the cities he knew from school before the Star had succumbed to internal power struggles and uncontrolled firestorms as all the infrastructure came tumbling down at once.

Maybe Houston has the right idea. Get the rail system repaired and running. Stretch your lines of control and communication along the rail system and build a nation from there.

He puzzled over fading memories of the local maps. He'd paid too much attention to the roads. Where did the rail systems run? How did their fuel delivery trains get from the coast to Austin anyway?

I'll have to look into that when I get back to town. Don't get distracted.

James puzzled over what was going on down below, but he wasn't a spy. No way could he disguise himself as a sunburned, rough-handed and smelly bandit long enough to learn anything. He looked at his fingers.

Miss Black had me pegged—an aristocrat used to eating well and having other people do the hard work.

But I can't change my spots that quickly. I need to get what information I've collected and report it back the City Guard before they catch me and find entertaining ways to make me talk.

Locking Down

"I'm just a runner. A Marathoner. I carry messages from one town to the next. I don't know anything about Austin's defenses!"

Red looked up from the notebook. "Yes, I see. And not even in code. 'Help. Please send the City Guard or Fredericksburg will fall!'" He looked around at the people watching. "Samson!"

Eyes from under a coyote-pelt headdress looked up cautiously. "Yeah, Red."

"I thought you Wolf Hunters had taken Fredericksburg already."

He nodded. "Yeah, we did. But come the call to join the Great and Powerful Oz... no that's King Red Dragon, isn't it? Come join or be left out of the greatest looting since San Antonio." He spread his hands. "Couldn't let my brothers be left out of that could I?

"Besides. We already got all their guns, and the next generation in that place is gonna be full of wolf cubs."

There were chuckles all around.

Red's eyes hadn't left Samson's for an instant. "So...this guy must be one of your slaves then. Far be it for me to usurp the Wolf Hunter claim." He shoved the bound and bloody courier towards his fellow Clan Leader. The man stumbled, but didn't fall.

Samson's eyes narrowed, then turned to the captive. "You're a runner, huh? You run all the way here from Fredericksburg?"

He swallowed and looked around at all the faces. "Uh, no. I can't do it in one run. I took a break at Sandy, and was going to take another at Paleface."

Samson looked him over, circling the runner, giving him a long inspection.

"You're muscular, outdoors a lot. I could use a personal courier. What do you think about joining the Brotherhood of the Hunter? Give up your town. Give up your family and join a new one. Drop your begging to a God that didn't do a thing for you during the Star and give your true worship to one that wiped the world clean of hypocrisy. One who turned it to over to true men who can grab it with both hands! What do you say?"

His eyes were confused and he blinked at the sweat dripping into his eyes. "Ah, yeah. Sure. I'll join."

Samson smiled broadly and skewered him in the side with a long hunting knife, their eyes locked together as the runner sagged to the ground.

Samson sneered down at the man and kicked dirt into the growing pool of blood. "You're a bad liar." He looked up at the other leaders and their followers. "I don't need a turncoat. Especially one that can run."

Red nodded approval. "There'll be slaves enough once Austin falls. Right now, we've gotta move fast. You were right to abandon Fredericksburg. It'll still be there when we're done. It ain't gonna go anyplace." There were laughs.

...

Sergeant Willowby nodded, "It's taken a bit to implement your son's orders, but we're letting all of them across." He'd ridden his motorcycle up to meet the Mayor's car.

"Wagons and cattle too, I see."

From their viewpoint above Mansfield Dam, the crowd of refugees looked like a moving carpet of ants. George Fuller could hear angry shouts in the distance.

"Yes, sir. But since they're bringing their own food and supplies, it didn't make any sense to leave them behind."

"Right." The Mayor's face was full of reservations. "But we've got to keep them from trying to move on into the city. It's a safe bet the bandits have slipped a spy or two in with the refugees. We have to keep them contained."

"We don't have enough troops to put up a barricade."

"I know that. We'll use the same technique we used after the Star. Spread the word here, and at all the crossing points. Refugees have to stay within a quarter mile of the lake, or within five blocks if they're at the downtown locations. The city will organize food and other supplies, but only for the people in the official refugee areas. If they stray into the city proper, then they have to buy their own supplies and are subject to curfew and strict looting laws. *Strict* looting laws!"

"Yes, sir. I'll make sure the order gets distributed." He turned to leave.

"Sergeant."

"Yes, sir?"

"Any messages from my son?"

"He sends coded radio messages every now and then. I've got a radio operator on the cliff up there for best reception."

"What does he say?"

He shook his head. "Just standard City codes. I assume he's worried that the bandits might have captured one of our radios. There's not much detail. He's observing the enemy. There are five clans, apparently. Strength in excess of a thousand each. He's having to keep on the move. He lost his motorcycle, but from the way the signal varies, he's still moving around quite a bit."

George nodded. "And that other issue?"

"They're on the road. We didn't even send a radio with them. They're only walkie talkies, designed for short range."

"Let's hope they succeed in their search."

"Yes, sir."

It was a long shot at best.

As Mayor, he could not have accepted Houston's heavy-handed offer, but if Houston was indeed facing a shortage of crude oil to drive its fuel monopoly, then a full tanker car of fresh crude might be just the bargaining chip he could use to get Houston's military support without the poison pill provisions. Even if the promise of more was a bluff, all they needed was short term help.

It all depended on just how hungry Houston was for fresh crude to fill their refineries.

As the sergeant rode off, George slumped in his seat. He wasn't recovering as fast as he used to. *I used to thrive on crisis management. Now, it's all too much.*

Maybe he should call the City Council back into session—at least an emergency meeting. They'd all gotten lazy, letting the Fullers run things. But he was tired.

I need James back. The City needs him.

...

Sam read the message posted on the door, shocked to see the IIS office sealed off and closed.

He went to the next building over, and was almost knocked down when Randall hurried out.

"Sam." He nodded, his face devoid of the usual challenge.

"What's going on?"

Randall Simmons was older by two years and had always made a point of how much faster he could ride and claiming Sam would never be able to catch up, whether in deliveries or anything else.

This time, he was acting different. He looked at Sam as if he were just then seeing him for the first time. "Sam. Hopefully, I'll see you when this is over. I'm going to be staying with my cousin's family. We're packing up and taking the wagon to Georgetown." He held out his hand. "Good luck."

Sam shook, feeling a little out of depth at how serious Randall was acting. But his competitor picked up his bike and was off without another word.

"Sam, is that you?" Hodges called.

"Yes, sir?" He went in. "What's going on?"

The room was dimly lit, the way Hodges usually liked it. He was seated behind a desk. "Have a seat, Sam."

He took the facing chair. "Randall is leaving town."

"Yes, I know. We talked about what was best for his safety. We need to talk about your safety as well. As you saw, the IIS office is shut down until this crisis is past. The South Austin office was shut down two days ago for the same reasons. Messages can wait, but people's lives are at risk.

"Sam, it is my understanding that you live alone. Is that correct?"

"Ah, yes. I've rented a room over on Avenue A. It's pretty close. It's a subdivided apartment. I have to share a bathroom, but it's cheap."

"Bandit packs may soon roam the city, burning out buildings. Have you made any plans to handle that situation?"

Sam felt cold. "No," he whispered. Then clearing his throat, "No. I guess if that happened, I'd get on my bike and head north as fast as I could pedal. What else could I do?"

Hodges nodded. "There are a number of possibilities, with various levels of risk. I have a suggestion."

"What?" He was open to ideas. Old memories of living in a city refugee camp were coming back—unwelcome memories.

"April and her mother are being moved to the Whiting Building at the edge of the city. They will be living in a protected area, well barricaded against the kinds of weapons bandits might use. April has invited you to go with them and some of her other friends.

"I would also appreciate it if you agreed to go with them. The group is women and children. While I will not be there myself, the Whiting labs has a telephone line that I could use to communicate with you. I need someone to watch over them and to alert me if the bandits approach the facility.

"Would you agree to be my security contact there?"

Sam nodded.

...

"Lantana! Get up here!"

Startled at being hailed, he looked away from the densely packed crowd of refugees around him and waved an acknowledgment to Saul Luiz up on the Congress Avenue Bridge above him. The young man had taken a shine to him for some strange reason. Still, better to make friends than be the obvious outsider. He carefully turned his folding chair upside down over his backpack and climbed up the bank to street level.

Saul pulled him into the line. A large hay wagon was being backed up against the railing. "Free hay for the refugees with cattle. We get to be first in line for the evening food delivery for our help unloading."

"Oh great. More work."

"Hey, 'He who is slothful in work is brother to the great destroyer.'" Saul quoted.

Lantana frowned, "What does that mean?"

Saul laughed, "Hey, don't mind me. Dad's a preacher. I've got more memory verses in my head than I know what to do with. They just bubble out. That was Proverbs 18:9, I think. Something like that.

127

"Besides, what else are you going to do with your time."

"I was resting."

"I saw you, lazy bones. You were watching all the girls. Aren't you little old for that?"

He frowned, trying to remember. "How many years ago was the Star?"

"Eleven, I think. Why?"

"I lost track. That'd make me thirty-three. Hardly too old."

Saul looked him over. "Really, I thought you were in your forties. Anyway, don't go staring too long at my teenage sister, or people will get the wrong idea."

"Sorry. I've been staring at the hind end of an ox for too many years, plowing my fields. I'm not used to all these people."

"Oh, where was your farm?"

"Ah...south. That way."

"Oh, over by Buda?"

"Maybe a little farther."

"Your place get burned out."

"Yeah. How old are you? Teenager yourself?"

Saul chuckled. "No, twenty-four."

They both got up behind one of the large round bales and pushed it off the wagon. Another couple of guys grunted and shoved it up against the railing next to the one before it. City workers with armbands would handle the process of sharing them out when refugees came to request them. Some of the refugees had already begun to use the bridge itself as a corral for the livestock. Certainly the foot traffic had ground to a halt.

"I never heard your first name, Lantana."

"Hector. But everybody calls me Hek."

Saul laughed, "Well, don't use the short version around my Dad. He's old-time strict about bad language, even the 'soft' kind."

Saul pointed out at a wagon next to a pair of white tents. "That's my family's camp there, just so you know which white-haired old man to look out for.

"Hector, do you have family here?"

They put muscle behind the next bale of hay.

"Not here. I've got brothers still out there, though."

"Oh, do you think they'll join you here?"

He nodded. "You bet. I look for them every day."

Hek scanned the opposite shore. South Austin still had people who hadn't fled across the bridges when they were opened, but the figures he could see were few and moved quickly, as if they didn't want to be outside and exposed.

As well they shouldn't. My Brothers are coming and the Sons of the Hunter won't be denied.

Precautions

James had grown quite sensitive to his surroundings, so when Rose looked up and her ears strained for noise, he was on the alert. He moved to his overlook, where he'd been counting bandits moving south on Highway 71. With the Pedernales River high from the rains, the only safe crossing, for residents or bandits, was the high bridge near Pace Bend—not that any farmers were still on the roads. The small percentage who had stayed in place to defend their homes were now well aware that the bandits controlled all traffic.

The bandits, in spite be being in control of the area, tended to travel in the shade and out of sight, but at the bridge, they had to move in the open.

It was sobering how many were still arriving. The City Guard was heavily outnumbered. They'd been limited to police duties for years now. He ought to be in the city, recruiting a public militia like he did back when Taylor became a war zone between rival gangs and threatened to move their battles into the surrounding areas. He'd raised a popular army and moved in to settle the dispute.

Austin would need an even larger organized militia if it were to survive the flood of bandits. He'd radioed the order to start the recruitment to Sergeant Willowby, but one reason he'd put up with the pseudo-regal trappings his father cultivated was that it gave him a personal following, credit he could use for such times.

But he wasn't there in person to make use of it.

These were much different from the random thieves and poachers that had been a problem since the Star. This bandit army was organized, with clans and a hierarchy of control. In spite of looking like cave men out of the children's books in his home, these were trained men, almost military in their actions.

James had found a pair of binoculars at one of the burned-out homes. He raised it to his eyes and was excited to see a wagon on the road.

One thing he'd been looking for had been any sign that this was a migration. For all the houses they'd looted, this army carried little with them. They collected no treasures. They walked everywhere. No possessions other than what they carried in their hands or on their back.

And there were no women. No children. This was no tribe on the move. It was all men.

It's a farmer's wagon. But where's the farmer? He searched the areas all around the bridge, but there there was no sign of anyone but the bandits rummaging through the supplies on the wagon and another pair who had cut the traces on the ox and were leading it off to the buildings just to the south of the bridge, where some of the bandits were camped.

A mystery. Probably the body is beside the road, or they pulled it out of sight so they could trap someone else.

. . .

Helen and Bob formed a chain with their arms and a rope hastily tied to a cypress branch to reach out into the muddy waters of the Pedernales. Bob snagged the drowning man and they pulled him to shore.

"Thanks," he managed, after coughing up too much water.

"What were you doing out in the river?" Helen asked.

He winced and coughed some more. "Chased by the bandits. The only escape. They gave me up to the waters."

Bob came back with the news. "I don't see any signs that they saw us from the bridge. But there are quite a few of them up there."

"Name's Keith. Keith Miller. From Cypress Creek. Bandits came through a few days ago and burned out my house. I'd hoped it was just the handful of them. I didn't realize I'd be driving into a whole army."

Helen nodded. "It's bad. There's no passage at all from here to Austin. There's thousands of them and almost everyone is already evacuated." She chuckled sadly. "There's probably more of us in the city than the Austinites by now—if they opened the bridges."

"What do you mean 'if'?"

She shrugged. "The last I saw, the City Guard was trying to keep everyone out, but I can't imagine they'll succeed."

He asked, "And what are you two doing out here?"

Helen stood and patted the impatient white horse hovering over her as she explained their plan.

. . .

"Saul? What's going on there?" Hek pointed to the man in uniform who had pulled up on the motorcycle.

"Oh, that's one of those City Guards we've heard about. Not too impressive in person, is he?"

Hek had been checking him out, looking at the way he held himself.

"I don't know. He looks like a soldier. You can't tell a fighter just by the muscles. But if he's guarding the city, why haven't I seen more of them?"

"Oh, there's probably more around. Those guys with the guns up on the bridge are probably guards as well. The ones with motorcycles are a select unit the Mayor's son has organized. They've got the fancy new uniforms."

"You're really up on all this stuff. Got a hankering to join the military?"

Saul chuckled, "Nope. My sister Maria is tied into the rampant rumor mill here in the camp. She's fascinated with the soldiers. Silly romance stuff."

"She likes the men in uniform, eh?"

Saul shook his head. "She likes anyone new. We lived in a small place with nothing but farmers."

"Hey, I'm new. Introduce me. I'll listen to all her gossip."

"Lantana, don't get your hopes up. You're too ancient. But maybe she knows some spinsters to hook you up with. I'll invite you for supper."

. . .

Sam pushed the last cart into the Whiting Building and Hodges dismissed the wagon.

"Last load. Where do these go?"

April and her friends Lily and Hailey were nowhere to be seen, off in one of the other rooms of the tan stone complex somewhere.

Denise, April's mother, plucked two of the bags and called out, "Hazel, there are more of your things!"

Lily and Hailey's mother poked her head out of the office converted into her temporary apartment. "No, I think those are Evelyn's."

Julie Smith, with her little sleeping Emma riding in an papoose sling walked up. "Yes, those are Mom's."

Sam nodded. "Lead the way. I'll take them."

He had struggled to keep the grin from creeping onto his face, watching the new mother's hips sway as she walked. She was easily four or five years older than he was, but he didn't mind. Nobody was saying anything about the baby's father, so maybe she was a widow like the three older ladies—not that he was really interested in being an instant father or anything. She was just really eye-catching. No wonder she was happy to join the party to hide out from the bandits.

I'm the luckiest guy in Austin, locked inside with all these girls.

He unloaded the bags and accepted a smile as payment before pushing the cart back to the storage room near the entrance.

Hodges was waiting for him. "Sam, there are some things I need to show you."

It was a brief tour, showing him where the food stores were stocked and then where the water tanks could be monitored. The levels were topped up.

"All of the windows are made of thick glass and locked. Normal bullets won't break them. Should the city electric power stop, you shouldn't worry about leaving them unshuttered for light. But during an attack you can secure them like this."

"This place is like a fortress! Did you expect the bandits early?"

"Not exactly. But after the Star, I have learned to take certain precautions."

There was an open air atrium with a garden. "This was started by Mary Ellen Victor some years ago. She was the previous owner of this facility."

April and her friends were playing some game in the corner. Sam caught her eye, but she didn't wave. The Abernathy girls were her age–Hailey was only a year older–and she was enjoying their company.

Sam didn't mind being snubbed. He was doing important things.

"Now, in this office is the telephone. It will make a gentle chime noise throughout the whole building, so you'll have to remember to come here to answer it. April's mother knows about it too, but likely I'll be calling you. If there is any emergency, such as a direct attack on the building, pick up this receiver and dial '9'. I should answer quickly.

"Do you have any questions?"

Sam frowned, thinking over the things he'd been told. "Ah, I guess a couple of things. If the atrium is open, couldn't the bandits climb in that way?"

"The walls are smooth and tall. They would have to build a platform. If they do succeed, the doors to the atrium can be secured by the iron bars mounted on the wall beside them. It is unlikely they would be able to break through.

"And you other question?"

"Um. How long are we going to be here?"

"That depends on the bandits. Denise will be making a phone call to me once a day and we will discuss the situation. If the city government falls, I have other plans for getting you more food and water in that event."

Sam shook his head. "I guess you've got everything covered. I just hope April has enough books."

Hodges managed a smile. "April never has enough books."

. . .

"That's Mertzon." Joshua tapped the map. He had the details of the oil wells in a stack clipped to the dashboard. "This should be the place."

His father nodded and pointed. "Oil wells."

They had seen several others on the way, but they were looking for a place where a crew from Austin could start up full scale pumping. The truck slowed down and John cautiously drove the tanker rig up to a line of cylindrical tanks.

With a hiss of the air brakes, they stopped.

"Time to get out and see if there is any crude sitting in storage."

It had been a relatively uneventful trip. They'd attracted attention driving a big rig through several of the small towns, but they only had to stop twice to clear the roadway. They'd deliberately taken a wide loop around

San Angelo to avoid driving Highway 67 right through the middle of town. John said it might be safe, but they'd actually test it on some other trip when they had an armed escort.

Joshua followed, after his father snipped through the padlock with a large bolt-cutter they'd taken from the Camp Mabry tools.

"The ground hasn't been touched in ages," Joshua noted, looking for footprints. It felt like they were trespassing.

"I hadn't expected it to be. The only people who ever came here were the oil company maintenance crews and the trucks to remove the oil. All that stopped with the Star."

John walked up to the closest tank and rapped on the side. He listened to the sound. "There's something in here."

. . .

Two hours later, they had the bad news. The tanks they'd stopped to check on were filled with salt water.

"Oh well," John sighed, "that was one possibility. A lot of these oil wells produce brine as a side-effect. I guess my TRC report didn't include that little item. Let's try the next one."

Joshua looked at his oil-smeared hands. This job wasn't going to be as easy as he'd hoped.

Escape Planning

James Fuller paused in his code work to watch a roadrunner advancing on a small bird, probably a new chick, fluttering erratically at the base of a pile of rocks. It was plain to see the predator moving in on the prey. Normally, he'd have let the plan of nature play out, but right now he had no kind feelings for hunters. He picked up a pebble and tossed it in the direction of the roadrunner. It missed, but it was enough of a distraction that the baby bird made its way back up into the branches of the oak tree. The roadrunner dashed off in a different direction, looking for its next prey.

He turned back to the string of numbers he'd written. It was frustrating to be so useless. Maybe he would have had people follow his orders just because he was the son of the Mayor Fuller, but he thought he'd done a decent job of learning the ropes and planning ahead. Dad expected him to be mayor someday. He wanted to get there on his own merit, not just because he was son of George Fuller.

But now, when Austin faced its greatest threat, he made the mistake of putting himself out of play. He needed to be in the middle of things, collecting the reports and moving the pieces, making sure the city could react quickly when the attack came.

He added a few more numbers, then moved to the spot where he had the best line of sight in the direction of the lake. Willowby had moved a patrol to a hilltop site in Lago Vista on the other shore to get best reception from his radio.

"Code 4. Code 4. Code 4."

After a few seconds of static, came the reply. "Receiving."

The voice was Corporal Jimbo Daniels, and he would have loved to just spend a couple of minutes chatting with the guy, but it was his own rule to use the code.

"70034 09438 91293 ..." He sent the report slowly and clearly, waiting after each code group for a confirmation. The code was simple enough to memorize, and probably easy enough to crack if the other side knew the transformation phrase. He could convert text to the code with nothing more than a pencil and paper, and he'd done it often enough with messages to his spies over the past three years that it was almost automatic.

He sent the latest observations, and it was probably useless. Hardly anything had changed since the last report. More bandits were trickling in, but the clock was ticking.

A string of digits came back to him. He scribbled them down and applied the conversion.

ALL FRMRS IN BRDGS CLSD

All the farmer refugees are in and the bridges are closed.

So, now it's a waiting game. When will they attack? It'll have to be soon. Thousands of eager troops and limited food. I need to be on the lookout for scavenger patrols that might just go back to burnt homesteads for a second look.

He tore off the part of the page where he'd done his code conversions and burned it, crumbling the ashes.

Rose snorted. He looked up. Maybe it was wisp of smoke his tiny fire had caused, but he needed to check everything.

He moved back to his overlook and scanned the landscape carefully, looking for anything out of place.

Something prompted him to aim the binoculars at a dense clump of trees nearly at the edge of the curvature of the hill, almost out of his sight.

There was motion, but it was hidden down in the shade. If there were bandits there, they were keeping themselves well hidden. He repositioned himself so he could prop the glasses with no arm motion.

It was an animal. It moved and for an instant, a ray of sunlight caught the long white leg before it moved back.

Snowcap?

...

"Hector, what did you do before the Star?"

White-haired Gabriel Luiz looked as stern as the archangel he was named after, but Hek quickly learned his grim face was just a mask.

"As little as possible."

"Hmpf. An honest man. A rarity around here."

"Daddy! Don't pester our guest." Maria smiled and handed Hek a bowl with the boiled grain that was fast becoming the staple meal of the camp. Austin would feed them, but wasn't about to cater to their taste buds.

"Oh, I don't mind. Career military. Army. I was two tours in Iran and two more in Afghanistan before I took a posting here in Texas. I'm glad I wasn't stranded overseas when the Star happened."

"Oh, you're a soldier!"

Saul shook his head at his sister's enthusiasm.

"I haven't been one for some years. I've been getting back to the land."

"Still," considered Gabriel, "it might come in handy to have someone with battle experience around if the bandits try to attack this bridge."

Maria said, "Yes. You should let tell the City Guards you've got experience."

Hek chuckled. "I don't think they'll be much interested in outsiders telling them how to do their business. By the way, I haven't seen too much guard activity getting ready, have you? I'd expect the commanders to come by and inspect the bridge barricades."

Maria leaned closer, "I've heard a rumor that their commander is missing!"

"Oh?"

"Yes! It's the Mayor's son. He usually runs the City Guard, but he went off towards Bee Cave to rescue a lady, and neither of them have been seen since. They could be trapped by the bandits!" She shuddered.

"That doesn't sound like something a military commander would do."

"Oh, but it's true! I heard it from Sally, and she heard it from a store keeper. Someone heard the whole thing on the telephone."

After dinner and more rounds of gossip and chatting about farming, Hek bid goodnight and said he needed to go take a walk.

Once he turned left on East 1st Street, he strolled around the back side of the towering Radisson hotel. He'd scouted the building the first day he'd arrived. The first floor had been taken over by the City Guard as a staging area with guns and ammunition stashed there for the attack.

Hek went around to the other side and entered the old parking garage. The place had never been cleaned up from the days when Star Time refugees had lived in the dead cars. He climbed several floors and entered the main corridors through a broken service entrance. There were still habitable rooms in the building, rooms the refugees would have been happy to inhabit if it weren't for the fact that the stairways wound up forever and the doors were all secured by electronic locks that hadn't worked since the Star.

One room showed a door that had been opened with a crowbar. He entered and went to the light box he'd set up. Electricity had been turned on for the building for the Guard's use, and then switched off for all the upper stories to conserve power. Hek had found a separate circuit that was active in the service rooms and had routed it to his light box. The Army had taught him a number of particularly useful skills.

Morse code was one of them. He flipped the switch and four lights in a tall rectangle came to life. The way he'd arranged the box, the lights couldn't be seen from this side of the lake.

Off in South Austin, a tiny quartet of lights came on from the roof of a ten story building a few blocks from the water. His brothers were watching, and they would probably be interested in a city commander hiding behind their lines.

He began flipping the switch, sending dots and dashes across the water.

...

Helen ought to have been able to get more sleep, now that there were three of them taking shifts during the night, but nothing could ease her churning thoughts. During her painfully slow journey from Bell Springs, she'd seen more burned houses than she could count. And far too many people that she had no time to bury.

The bandits can't be human anymore.

If they caught her, her babies would be slaughtered for meat. She'd be raped and likely killed. Bob and Keith would surely be killed, and possibly tortured.

Could I use the knife?

She'd found a small hunting knife. With a leather strap looped around her neck, she wore it like a necklace under her clothes. It would be hard to get free to fight with, but it wouldn't be too difficult to push it through her heart.

Not too hard in theory. But could she do it in practice?

I couldn't if the horses still needed me. And I couldn't betray my promise to Bob's mother.

Probably I couldn't if there was a chance to escape.

It really boiled down to a matter of hope. As long as she had hope. As long as people needed her, she'd stay alive.

There was a sound, very faint. She reached for the little knife, and slipped the strap off her neck. She was holding it ready to fight.

"Helen Black?" it was a whisper, almost too faint to hear.

"James Fuller?"

A part of the dark moved. "Yes." He moved closer. She could barely make out his shape.

"I thought you were long gone!"

Another voice whispered urgently, "Helen! Something is spooking the horses."

The boy came up closer, holding a stick with a glowing ember at the end. He paused as he made out the figure.

"It's okay Bob. This is James Fuller."

"And it's probably Rose. I tied her up around the bend, but the wind has shifted slightly. Your horses have noticed her."

...

As soon as Keith Miller was roused and they were all introduced, James explained about losing the motorcycle and how he'd toured the hills, bound by Highway 71, the Pedernales River and the bandit encampments closer to Bee Creek.

"I moved from one burned-out house to the next, counting bandits and radioing my observations to the City Guard. I'm a bit lost, really. I never saw your place again. The world looks different from a horse."

Bob apologized for letting James slip into the camp un-noticed.

"I'd better get back to my lookout."

James shrugged. "I've been trained at some of this stuff by soldiers at Camp Mabry. Some of them have been in battlefields all over the world, sneaking into places. I'm just glad you didn't shoot me."

Bob smiled and then left.

Helen explained her plan to cross the lake.

James scratched at his growing beard. "Will that work? I wish I'd considered it. If Rose and I could have crossed over, I'd be back with my troops, rather than just sitting on the hilltop, twiddling my thumbs."

Helen shrugged. "She probably could have done it. I'd be much more confident with the herd moving as a group. A single horse might be spooked and disoriented half-way across."

Keith grumbled. "I think I may have already swallowed my quota of river water."

"It'll be better on the lake," she assured him. "If we can choose a still night, the waves would be minimal."

James pulled out the map he'd sketched of the area. There were many squares where he'd identified bandit encampments. Helen added a few details of the Pace Bend area from her memories of the recent horse delivery trip.

"I wonder if the Gregersons were able to get out safely. They were in sight of the ferry station."

Keith asked, "Could we take the ferry, or some other boat?"

James shook his head. "No. The ferry was shut down as soon as we could convince the operator to do so. And all the boats on this side of the lake have been used by now to get to the safe side."

She grumbled. "You would cut off an escape route for the Hill Country people."

"Helen, all the refugees are now safely on the other side. I'm sorry about the difficulty before, but everyone who wanted across made it."

"Are you sure? My family was...."

"I was assured by my second-in-command that they have been taken into the city and provided a place to stay. My orders."

"Thank you."

He turned back to the crude map.

"The hardest part will be getting across the highway. They've got it organized with several groups set up just out of sight of the road. There are no more refugees, but they haven't moved closer to the city yet."

They stared at the map hoping something perfect would present itself, but Pace Bend was unknown territory. He'd seen and marked some camps close to the road, but the lake was several miles on the other side of the highway.

"The route I went was seven or eight miles to get to the water."

He pointed, "We could go farther south. It's probably half that distance."

"But by then, the lake is wider across. I've never done this before with my horses. I can't risk them on an even harder swim."

James said what they both had been thinking. "We're going to need a distraction—something to pull the bandits in one direction to create a gap in their coverage in the other direction."

Keith grumbled. "That's me."

James frowned. "Why you?"

"You're the big military leader. It sounds like Austin needs you there. It can't be Helen, for more than just decency's sake. The horses would scatter and be killed without her to lead them. Bob is a boy. And I'm already on my second life. I wouldn't be alive if weren't for those two. I owe them."

James took his hand. "You're a good man, but I'm not going to send anyone on a suicide mission. Not even me—and I'm the one to do this. I've been watching these bandits carefully for days now. I know how they're organized—how they work their captures. I'm the only one who has a chance of dangling a tempting prey in front of them and then getting out before they can close their trap. I know where to run, and how fast to do it.

"Rose and I have gotten to know each other. She'll do what needs to be done, and once we're through, we can outrun the bandits and meet you at the pre-planned destination."

Helen nodded, whispering. "Rose is the horse I'd be riding myself if I didn't have Snowcap. I let you ride her because she's smart and capable.

"But I don't want anyone captured by these monsters. If you're not sure you can do it, we'll hide out longer and search for a better solution."

James felt the clock ticking. He had to be in Austin when the bandit chief ordered the attack.

"I can do it."

Sorry

Sergeant Paul Willowby hated being in the position he was in. Two captains and four lieutenants came to him for direction. He wasn't just a sergeant, he was the Commander's confidant. The City Guard had shrunk down to a little under two-hundred soldiers, with the official chain of command suffering considerable warping in the process. For quite a while, everyone knew they needed to re-organize, but as long as the Mayor's son seemed on top of every crisis, no one was ready to suggest an official executive officer.

He sighed. It was tough, but he never regretted the day he volunteered to show the new political appointee the ropes. Everyone thought he'd be polishing the boy's shoes and showing him how to wear the uniform. He'd done much the same for many new recruits that had gone on to become officers. He'd hoped to instill some sense of duty into the newcomer. He'd never gotten around to that. From the first day, he was hurrying to keep up with James' insatiable need to know how everything worked.

Willowby wished he'd kept up with the boy.

"Sergeant, you have a phone call."

He set down the maps and asked, "Who is calling, and who are they asking for?"

Private Taggert said, "It's Hodges from the IIS and he's asking for you."

Okay. He wasn't used to receiving any calls unless they came from the Commander.

He walked over the office building.

"Yes, this is Willowby."

"Greetings Sergeant. I need to speak to you privately in ten minutes. I'll be right outside the main gate. It concerns your Commander."

There was a click. Hodges hadn't even waited for his response.

Nobody else could get away with that.

But he'd seen James Fuller change his plans completely after a talk with Hodges. He couldn't dismiss the man as a kook.

"I'll be back in a few minutes."

He walked out and down the drive to the entrance. As he walked, it puzzled him. Where had the phone call come from? Was there an active telephone line within ten minutes of the base?

But Hodges was waiting in the shade of the trees, standing next to his electric cart.

The guards at the gate acknowledged him as he walked out to meet his visitor.

"You have news?"

Hodges nodded. "It's not good news. Keith Franklin, the owner of the South Austin IIS station has chosen to hide out in a building close to his business, in hopes of protecting it against the bandits. Last night, he noticed a Morse code signal being flashed from a hotel next to Congress Avenue refugee camp. He copied the dots and dashes and looked up a translation. This morning, he activated his station long enough to send me a message detailing what he'd discovered."

Hodges handed over the slip of paper.

Willowby sighed. "So we have a spy in the camp. Well, we expected that. There are probably several of them."

He read through the message and his frown deepened. "Thank you Mr. Hodges for passing this on to me. I'll take appropriate action."

Hodges nodded again and got into his cart and drove off.

Willowby walked back to the office, thinking, *What would James do?*

When he reached his seat, he sent for Corporal Thompson.

"Go to the telephone central office and introduce yourself politely. Tell them that the City Guard has decided that it has become too dangerous for the switchboard lady to stay at her station. Have her teach you how the system works and then send her home to find a safe place to wait out the current crisis. I'll send a replacement, and then you'll have to instruct him in a few hours. We're taking over the telephone system until the bandits are gone."

That should put a stop to the telephone security leak, but I need to get word as soon as possible to James that the bandits now suspect he's trapped behind their lines.

...

James looked at Helen's people. He was used to explaining his plan of action to his troops, but these three weren't *his* people. It was more like when he'd raised the volunteer force. Orders were for soldiers. Explanations and call to action made more sense for Helen, Bob and Keith.

"I've noticed that the bandits take a siesta during mid-afternoon. Even the lookouts and the ones who trap the travelers on the road tend to find a comfortable place to sit and rest. With the refugee traffic gone, there's not going to be much incentive to stay alert and ready to run all through the afternoon heat.

"We're lucky today. The sun's out and the air is muggy from the evaporation. Hopefully, they won't be expecting us."

Bob nodded. "I was expecting to take a nap this afternoon too."

James grinned. "Maybe later."

He spread out the hand-drawn map.

"If I were to ride down this side of the trees, and hit the road at a gallop, all the groggy bandits would jump up and come out onto the road to chase me. Up ahead, the other group would start to close in, too.

"If we time it right, you and the horses would show up behind the bandits. Some would have to turn around and go back to try to stop you, while others would keep on following me. With any luck at all, you'll be across the road, taking this route." He marked it with dashes. "Keep going fast until you get at least three miles in, to give you time to get to hard ground and find a place to hide out. If Helen makes the call, keep on going to the water and start your swim."

Keith asked, "And you?"

"I'll be dealing with a disorganized group of bandits that just had their trap torn open. I plan to exit the road here, where they'd have to wade across the marshy land. I know Rose is good at handling herself in the mud.

"But I'll be looking for alternate exits as well. Something may show up, and I'll take it if I see it. I know where you're heading and I may join you, but maybe not. Make your own crossing decisions assuming I've already found my own beach or hiding spot."

Keith said, "They've got guns. They popped off a dozen rounds when they were chasing me."

James nodded solemnly. "They have guns. But they didn't hit you. They didn't hit me when I first encountered a bandit trap. Your best bet is to ride fast and keep low. You're a moving target; they're trying to shoot while running. It's a matter of luck and time. The longer you're in their sights, the more chances they have of hitting you. Ride fast."

...

Helen nodded and didn't say anything. She had her own experience with bandits and guns; but this was their only chance. James had a talent with words, and a way of making you trust him.

"When do we leave?" she asked.

He looked at his watch. "Can we be packed up and ready to ride in an hour?"

Helen made a point of looking at Bob. He had been a little offended when they made their plans last night without him while he was on guard duty.

"Yes. We can be ready," the boy said.

James nodded. "Okay then, let's move into position in an hour. We'll need to move slowly to get close enough to the bandits without being seen. Then it's all whoops and shouts until we're on the other side. Is that okay with everyone?"

He looked at Keith and Bob and got their nods before looking at her.

Helen had her fears. Maybe not really doubts. And she had no better plan. "Yes. Let's do it."

...

James pulled out his pistol and checked the cartridges. He'd not had opportunity to be other than a target thus far, and no part of the plan as he'd described it had any place for shooting bandits. Still, no plan survived reality. He had to be prepared for anything.

A few gentle questions determined that his was the only gun. Keith had arrived with just his clothes, sopping wet. Bob fretted over a shotgun that he'd left behind with his mother. Helen had started the trip with a pistol, but somehow, in the chaos, she'd misplaced it.

"I may have left it with the Phillips family. At least that's the last time I packed supplies. To be honest, I haven't thought about it since you arrived and stole Joshua and John away from me."

He winced. "I'll explain that–when we're out of bandit country."

She frowned. "I hate it every time you call it that. This is the Hill Country. Honest farmers live here. They're just gone temporarily."

"Sorry."

That was the last thing he said to her as they lined up, just above the highway. Helen arranged the horses by temperament.

James looked each of them in the eyes to make sure they were ready, then headed down the hill, urging Rose to a gallop.

He pulled out his pistol and kept it ready.

Bursting onto the roadway with a shout, heads popped up out of the bushes on all sides of him. He screamed as if startled, and made a dash straight down the faded yellow stripes on the asphalt.

Behind him and in front of him, the bandits came fully awake and started closing their trap.

"Hey!" Behind him, there were shouts of confusion and the guns started popping off their white smoke. If anything whizzed by, he missed it in the confusion.

"Now Rose!" He tugged at the reins with one hand while firing at the closest bandits. The horse turned and jumped into the reeds. James kept firing behind him, trying to keep the closest followers from taking any time to shoot at him.

He spared a look back the way he came.

Horses were crossing the road and bandits were jumping out of their way. For an instant it was all playing out the way he'd envisioned.

And then Snowcap reared. Even at his distance, he saw a splotch of red on Helen's side as she fell. Bandits swarmed in from the lake-side of the road, more than he'd imagined. For a moment it was chaos, and then Keith and Bob turned around and headed back the way they'd started. Unmounted horses followed. Only Snowcap stood his ground, rearing and snorting. There was a crack, as one of his hoofs connected with a bandit's skull.

Bandits. Far too many bandits!

For an instant, he had the choice—continue on his plan, make for the lake and get across to where he was needed.

Or he could brave the swarm of bandits and re-join Keith and Bob.

Snowcap burst through the bandits and raced off to join his herd.

James turned back away from the lake and charged the men chasing him. One of them fell with a bullet in his head. He rode back across the highway and racing for his life up the hill a moment later.

Helen. I'm sorry.

Trapped

Joshua wondered how Helen was doing, back in the green, wooded Hill Country with her horses. It was certainly different from where he was now. The West Texas oil wells were all built in little plots of land that had been scraped bare of vegetation, and even now, decades after they were built, the place was just dirt and gravel under his boots.

Not that the surrounding landscape was much better. There was cactus, and sage brush, and some other plants that had limited ambitions under the baking sun. Nothing was higher than his belt, and most was only inches above the ancient, dry terrain. He'd seen antelope in the distance, and maybe cattle, so there was probably enough grass in the low spots to keep them alive. But he wondered how anybody could live out here.

John came from behind the pump, a contraption easily twice as large as a horse. He was rubbing his hands with a rag and he had a grin on his face.

"I think I can get it running. It's electric, so I think we can run it off the truck's generator."

"I hope so."

The oil field had been a huge disappointment. The idea of swooping in, filling the tanker truck with crude left in the storage tanks from the day the supernova rose above the horizon—that hadn't worked. Someone had beaten them to it.

Tracks left in the old gravel roads told of traffic more recent than Star Time. All the tanks that held petroleum were dry. The only thing left was the dregs—brine and water.

But no one had re-started the pumps. If they could do that, then they could tap the reservoir of oil still down below the ground.

Joshua helped his father run the cables from the generator stowed in a compartment just behind the cab. When the noisy diesel engine started up and the lights came on, he realized just how quiet it had been out here in the middle of nowhere. Even the birds at home were more energetic than the occasional vulture he saw soaring above, riding the heated air coming up from the baked soil.

The generator's tone shifted, as his father flipped the switch and the motor sitting idle since the Star came back on line and began moving the huge lever arm. Up and down, up and down, it pushed a rod down into the borehole and pulled it back up.

John moved over to sit in the shade. "Now we wait and see if the pump still works. Any number of things could still be broken, and if this pump doesn't work, we'll have to try another."

About the only thing they knew was that eleven years ago, this particular pump was producing in the top tier of wells in this area.

"Could the people who drained the tanks have emptied the well too?"

John shook his head. "No. There's easy oil, when the field is first tapped. Sometimes it just gushes out on its own and people have to throw together dams to catch the oil as it flows down the creek bed. After that, you can simply pump it. But that'll only get you about a third of the oil that's underground. Pre-Star oil men tried all kinds of ways to get the rest of it—pumping steam or other fluids down into the ground and things like putting explosives down below to crack the rock layers.

"But that's all expensive and too high tech for us." He waved at the pump still bobbing away. "If this doesn't work, we'll just have to move to another well, or give it up and go back to Austin and tell them we have to search for oil from other fields. There are oil fields all over Texas, some of them even closer to Austin, but I really thought this one was our best bet for quick results."

Joshua nodded and looked at the pump and the line that led to a storage tank. How long would it take before they saw results?

"Um. Dad?"

"Yes?"

He pointed off in the distance. "That's a man. A man on a horse."

...

James Fuller caught up with Keith and Bob and the horses before they reached they crest of the hill.

Bob shouted, "They shot Helen!"

Keith's face was rigid in torment. "We can't leave her there."

They all slowed. The bandits could still be seen, coming their way, but they had just a moment to catch their breath.

James asked, "Is she still alive? I saw the blood on her side."

Bob shook his head. "Her arm. She cried out when she was knocked off her horse, but she was still fighting when they pushed her down."

Snowcap pushed his way into their conversation. The white horse was still angry and vocal. If he could talk People, he'd be calling for bandit blood.

Rose, under him, understood exactly what the stallion was saying.

James put his hand on her neck as he looked back downhill.

"We stirred up an anthill. We can't go back just yet."

Bob muttered, "We rode right into a campsite or something. There were dozens of them there. There wasn't any way to keep going."

James nodded. "It's okay. We'll make it right, somehow. But for now, we have to get over this hill and out of their range."

Keith looked stubborn. James could read his mind.

"We *will* go back for her, but we need to be ninjas, not cavalry. We just don't have the firepower for a frontal attack."

Reluctantly, Keith nodded.

The shots in the distance were getting close enough to worry about.

"Come on. I know where to go."

James urged Rose into a trot, and after an instant, Snowcap followed, then the rest of them.

...

Helen woke, bound hands and feet, and the instant she opened her mouth, someone put their fingers over her lips. A woman's face, scared and haggard, looked down at her and with her own lips pursed tightly, shook her head.

Bandits were talking, and it was plain her caretaker in the blood-stained blue dress didn't want her to speak.

Her arm—her whole left side—was aching and throbbing. She'd been shot. She remembered that. After that—it was just a blur of motion and a memory of Snowcap kicking someone.

"Ram Hunters can't claim her! Yes, she rode through their lines, but right into a Bear Hunter camp."

Another voice, hoarse and lower said, "Worse than that. Wolves control the town. And probably, when Red Dragon shows up before dark, he just might claim her his own self."

"It's a sorry day when this prophecy turned everything topside down. Bears kept to their hunting grounds and Wolves to theirs. Now we're all here elbow to elbow and I feel like tasting some Wolf meat from time to time."

"Take it easy. It's the lakes driving us together. City people control the crossing points and we've got to work together before we can move on. That's still the case, Dragon prophecy or not."

When they moved on, the woman holding her mouth released it. She whispered, "They don't like women speaking. Now, I've got to look at your wound. Can you keep from crying out? It'll attract them."

Helen nodded. She struggled against her bonds. "Can't you untie me?"

"No. Just let me do my job." She tore at the sleeve, wincing every time it made a noise. "Sorry. Tearing clothes attracts them too. They're just walking dicks."

Soon she had the wound exposed. It was still seeping and Helen's arm was turning purple. Every time fingers pressed down, it was like she was being shot all over again—an explosion of pain that made every muscle tense. It was hard keeping her cries between her teeth.

"I can feel the bullet. It's not too deep. It needs to come out, but they won't let me have any tools, and I can't dig it out with my fingernails." She was frustrated. "And don't expect any help from them. They're not big on doctors. Likely as not, they'd just amputate your arm."

Helen gasped. The woman's efforts had just elevated the level of pain in her body to new heights.

"Knife. Under my shirt," she whispered.

"I can't." Her face showed flickers of bad memories. "If they caught me with it...."

Helen closed her eyes. It was all she could do.

Hesitant fingers fumbled with her buttons.

The lady was wide-eyed with fear, but she slipped the blade free and dug at the bullet. A suppressed scream rumbled low in Helen's throat.

"Got it." Seconds later, she hurriedly put the knife back where she'd found it and buttoned up Helen's front.

"Boiled water is the best I can do," she said as she bathed the wound and bound it up with a white cloth. "Don't worry about scarring. Neither of us will live long enough for it to matter."

And then she was gone. Helen might have passed out; she wasn't sure. The way she was bound, she couldn't look around. People moved past, but she couldn't risk calling out.

She was trapped in a woman's hell. This was the worst case—the one that she'd resolutely avoided thinking about when they'd planned their escape. Had the others escaped? Had the horses? Would her family ever know what happened to her?

...

Mayor George Fuller put down the summary report from the City Guards and rubbed his forehead. Guarding the city entrances, controlling the rising crime in the streets, keeping the refugee camps from exploding and monitoring the bandit troop movements across the water—every subsection had the same recommendation. They needed more manpower.

Sergeant Willowby recommended he appeal to the general population to volunteer for service, just as James had done in times past.

But I'm not James. They love him, but every time they cheer for him, they frown at me. I'm the bad guy, he's their hope for the future.

It wasn't something he'd worried about. His position was secure and it wasn't as if James intended to stage a coup.

He considered handing that task over to someone else in the City Council, but they were all like him—old rich men the people tolerated because they kept the city at peace and generally stayed out of their lives. *Not a one of them has any sex appeal.*

If he appealed to the people for help, that would be the last straw. The streets were full of people who were heading north, heading for Round Rock, or Georgetown, or even farther. Once he acknowledged how bad it was, there would be a stampede to leave town.

Ann appeared at the door. "Sir. There is a Mr. Black to see you. He appears to be on the old list."

George hesitated in thought. "Yes. Right. Send him in." He stood.

The farmer looked ill at ease as George shook his hand and invited him to sit. He settled into the thickly cushioned chair.

George nodded. "You're Helen Black's father. I remember you from the Star Time."

"Yessir. It's about her that I've come. We're worried about her."

"She didn't make it across the bridge with the rest of you, right?"

He nodded. "We couldn't convince her to leave with us. She had to take care of her horses. I know many people didn't make it out, but the reason I came to see you is that..."

"Is that you saw my son James as you were leaving. That's correct?"

"Yessir. I was hoping that maybe you've heard something."

George sighed. "Not much." He'd been trying to pull more out of the reports on his desk than the words implied.

"Your name is Will, right?"

He nodded.

"Well, Will, I'm going to tell you some things that are secrets. You have to keep them under your hat. Don't let your wife treat them as gossip. I'm trusting you with this. Understand?"

"I appreciate anything I can get."

"James went to your farm to meet with your neighbor, Joshua Lamar, and his father. John Lamar had some important information. They made it back to Austin okay."

"I had heard that, from his wife. Sergeant somebody came and told her they were safe. But we haven't heard from them since."

"They are working on a special project. I can't tell you more. Likely they are in no danger."

Will nodded. "Have you heard from your son since?"

"Yes. Military messages. He was trapped when the bandits gained contrl of the roads on the other side. He never mentioned anything other than enemy strength and positions. Sorry. I'm a father worried about his child trapped by the bandits, too."

Will slumped in his chair. "Then...nothing?"

George shook his head. "I'm sorry."

"It's just...hard."

"I know."

Will stood. "Well, I appreciate your time. I know you must have a million things to deal with." His face was drawn.

George struggled with himself, and then reached out his hand and gripped his arm. "Will, before you go, I need to tell you something. You know Ed Morgan."

He frowned. "Yes. He saved Helen when she was little."

"He's my...the city's advisor because he can tell the future. I've seen him predict things correctly so many times. His wife told me something a few days ago."

Wolf Hall

Joshua turned toward the truck to get a gun. John put out his hand to stop him. "He doesn't look like he's a threat."

The man on the horse looked just like the cowboys in his books at home. John walked up to the fence line that surrounded the oil well.

"Hello."

The man walked his horse up to the fence. "Howdy. Started up the oil well, I see."

"Yes. At least I hope so. I haven't done this before."

The horse found a tuft of grass near the fence post. The cowboy rubbed his whiskery chin with his free hand. "I haven't seen one of those go bobbing away in years. Must've been since the Star. You oil company people?"

"No. Not really. We're from Austin, trying to see what kind of shape the oil fields are in. I hope we're not trespassing on your land."

The man chuckled. "Naw. Ain't no landowners around to speak of, outside of the towns. You know, I spend my whole life before the Star, keeping the barbed wire fences repaired. These days I carry around my cutters to take 'em down. The days of the open range are back—maybe for good."

John gestured toward the truck. "We've got food we can share–bread, jerky, apples?"

"Naw, I don't want to impose. Got my own jerky." He patted his saddle bag.

John raised an eyebrow. "How about a bottle of beer?"

"Oh?"

. . .

James had left his radio and all his supplies other than his pistol and binoculars with Bob and Keith. They were back at the burned ranch house with the secluded barn where the horses could stable out of sight. He and Rose came back at dusk and he tied her reins loosely to a tree so that she could pull free if she really had to. Like if he didn't come back.

Wood ash and mud made good camo for his face. He crept the last mile to the top of the overlooking hill, crawling much of the time, navigating by the light of the first quarter moon.

Clear night, and no rain for a day or so. Has the rainy season passed? Are the bandits waiting for the rivers to go down so that they can just wade across?

He couldn't stop thinking about the defense of Austin, even when he should be concentrating every instinct on his surroundings. Part of his brain shied away whenever he tried to think about Helen and how she was being held. The bandits' treatment of women, more than anything else, had stampeded the refugees to Austin. Men that would ordinarily band together and hold the line couldn't risk their wives and daughters to the unthinkable—so they ran.

Down below, the valley that contained the highway was tall with brush. There were several buildings lit up by lantern light. *Helen is possibly in one of those. I need to know which one.*

But the brush and the trees contained waiting bandits. He couldn't just creep down there without a clear path, and a plan to deal with the ones he'd encounter. Plus, reaching her was just the first step. Releasing her, and then getting her back, with her injuries, was a much bigger problem.

He shook his head. *No, I can't think about that. I can't imagine her broken. Not in body, not in spirit.*

Not like the refugees he'd met on the road.

There was a thicker cluster of cedar trees a hundred yards to the side of his position. He could likely hide out there all night. Maybe through the day.

He scanned the houses, looking in the lit windows with his binoculars. Sometimes a person would move around. The first woman he saw sent his heart pounding, but it wasn't Helen.

So, they are keeping some women. That increased Helen's chances of being alive.

He moved slowly towards the cedars, feeling eyes watching him. It was just imaginary. There was no alarm. Bandits outnumbered him by thousands here. They had no reason to be sneaky, other than habit.

I wish I could sweep in here with a troop of thousands and rescue them all. And fill a new graveyard.

He'd never been bloodthirsty. He'd never liked the idea of killing, although he'd done it, during the Taylor Rebellion.

But he hadn't regretted killing that bandit during the escape attempt, and he'd rejoiced at the sound of Snowcap braining one of them. They'd brought brutality into the area wholesale, and it had infected him. He no longer toyed with plans for sending the bandits back the way they came, or deflecting their journey around Austin.

He wanted them dead.

A gentle breeze brought the scent of cedar, and he remembered just how uncomfortable it was likely to be, laying in the brittle dried cedar needles, among branches that went down all the way to ground level. He'd be fishing resinous needles out of his clothes for days. And they itched.

But it was an ideal place to hide, dark even in the day.

He moved the binoculars to his eyes again, to get another look at the houses from this new angle, before he had to crawl into that maze of branches.

There was another smell. What was it?

He'd barely begun the thought when something struck him hard on the side of his head. Hands clamped around his face, so he could barely breathe. People, more than just one, dragged him roughly into the cedar, scraping his skin. He had to keep his eyes clamped shut to avoid being blinded by a twig.

"Who is he?" one voice whispered.

A cloth was stuffed into his mouth as his arms were tied tightly. A rope was looped around his neck and pulled tight. He struggled for air.

A finger rubbed at the camo on his face. "Soldier. Bandits were soldiers, weren't they?"

"Maybe he's a sniper."

"No rifle. Look at this pistol. It's in good shape."

There were three of them. James realized with some relief that they weren't bandits. Someone else had also realized how ideal a hiding place the cedar trees were.

He just needed to convince them he was on the same side, before they....

The sound of his own blood rushing through his veins soon drowned out what they were saying as he blacked out.

...

Helen woke to a gag being wrapped twice around her head. She could barely make a noise. Then came another strip of cloth around her head to cover her eyes. Fingers pinched her nose to confirm she was breathing okay.

With no consideration for her injured arm, her hands were freed and re-bound together, and then the same for her ankles. Someone big lifted her easily over his shoulder and began carrying her. He enjoyed groping her hip with one hand as he walked.

Head down and disoriented, she couldn't tell where she was being taken, or how long he walked. Maybe a quarter mile or so, over uneven ground.

They were heading toward a group of men. Voices were loud and the laughter was rude. First one hand grabbed her breast, then someone jammed his hand between her legs. Her transportation didn't slow down, but he didn't do anything to stop the men reaching in to grab a feel as she passed, either. She squirmed, she couldn't help it. The hand on her hip gripped a little tighter, and he chuckled.

He stepped up onto a wooden floor. The sound changed, echoes of many people in a large room. Her arrival attracted attention. There were too many voices to follow what was being said, but she heard 'woman' and 'horse' several times. The roving hands were all over her. Someone tugged at her zipper, but didn't succeed.

Then she was heaved up, and slapped down on a board. At least the groping stopped as her hands were re-tied with her arms spread. Then her legs were spread wide and ankles tied, as well. She strained against the bonds, but succeeded at nothing but triggering some laughter from the on-lookers.

But for a moment, no one was touching her.

The voices changed. At the other end of the room, someone was chanting, a call and response. She couldn't follow it. Animals and hunters, and the dark times were the theme.

But there were a few voices near her that weren't following along. They had their own conversation. It was about her.

"The Bears weren't happy. Jelly claimed first blood."

A low voice grumbled. "It was hardly a hunt. First blood rules can't apply when she rode right into camp herself."

"I hear she killed a Brother."

"Not her. After she fell off, her horse did it. Nasty kick, right between the eyes."

"Wolves control this place."

"I think I know who she is."

"Oh? We're giving them names now?"

"Red, you sent me for information, I'm giving it to you. And you should listen to this."

"Okay, don't get huffy."

"If you had to go through what I had to...never mind. The refugee camp is a hotbed of rumors. Nobody knows anything, so they endlessly chat about whatever snips of gossip they come across.

"Anyway, it seems their prince, the son of their Mayor, fell in love with a horse girl and rode off on a motorcycle to rescue her. Off towards Bee Caves. And then nobody ever saw them again."

"Hmm. I've heard this before, from a Ram spy. Seems he heard the same gossip you did."

Helen was twisted up inside. So she was a figure of gossip and specula-tion. Who was responsible for this? If she ever saw James again, she'd die of mortification.

But please God, let me out of this nightmare!

"Hmm. Take a look. She's listening. Look at the way she's twisting."

"Ha! You're right. I've gotta take a look at this horse girl. Her nose doesn't look that long."

"Hang on, Samson."

Helen lost track of what they were saying. Across the room, a woman screamed. Massed voices cheered. She was being raped. Was she tied up, spread-eagled, like she was? And how many bandits would get their turn before someone got too rough, or she could will herself to die?

Another female voice joined in. And another. A mass rape was part of their ceremony. Her face burned. She'd feared this. She would die here, just a piece of meat for these animals.

The one called Samson growled, "I can't wait."

Rough fingers tugged at her face wraps. She stared into his excited eyes, shaded by an animal skin hat. Her mouth came free as well, but she had nothing to say.

"If looks could kill, eh Red?" There was a solemn-faced man, red-haired, watching from a few steps back.

"Let's get this package unwrapped!" He massaged her between the legs, his eyes never diverting from hers. "Like that?"

Then he reached up to her collar and popped one button, then another.

"Eh? What's this?" He tugged the lanyard around her neck and pulled out the knife.

"Ho, ho! The wasp has a stinger!" He snapped the cord from around her neck and waved it around, bringing the point up against her cheek.

Helen closed her eyes, squinted tight against whatever came next.

"Samson. Hold up."

The man turned back with a snarl. "Why? She's in chains. In a Wolf hall. She's mine!"

"I was just thinking. If this tale of city people romance is true, then we've got an extra chip in the game."

Helen opened her eyes again. There was no sympathy from Red. He didn't see her as a person either.

But if they handed her an edge...

"James is very proud. He won't take damaged goods."

Samson swung back and slapped her hard. "Women don't talk! The Hunter did away with all that." He grabbed up the gag and bound it so tight, she was almost choking on her tongue.

"Samson. I'm claiming her." He called to someone out of her sight. "Tobias! Take her back. Now."

Red walked away, but Samson was killing him with his eyes as he left. Then he turned back to her. "You're my meat."

She was grateful when the big hands of Tobias wrapped the blindfold back over her eyes.

Troop Train

The cowboy's name was Dell Walker and once they relaxed around the campfire, they swapped stories.

"I guess we've got more horses out here than you do, then. You can't really ride the range without them. When the Star came, feedlots and livestock auction houses found protected places for them. I can remember one place in San Angelo that herded them into a corral in the shadow of the grain elevators. Not really indoors, but protected from Starshine.

"It's real nice you've got that lady vet who takes care of your stock. I don't know what I'd do without Foxy."

Joshua stared up at the stars. "I don't know what I'll be doing this time next year. But it won't be on the farm."

His father stirred the coals. "Oh?"

"Yeah, I've been meaning to mention it. I met a lady in Austin. I need to find a way to live there."

John sighed. "If it's still standing when we get back."

A little later, Dell asked, "So you're trying to get oil for Austin? I don't know why you're trying to get that pump to work. Why don't you just go ask the MOB for some?"

John leaned in, "What's the mob?"

Dell chuckled, "You really don't know? Midland-Odessa-Big Spring. Some people call it MOBS. I like the sound of 'The MOB', like the old gangster movies."

"Tell us more about them."

...

Hek leaned closer, over the fire. Several of the men stopped to listen.

"It's plain as day. Austin had put us here right in the path of the bandits. They'll use us as a living barricade when they sweep in over the bridges. The Mayor don't care one bit about us. He'll trade a thousand farmers to protect one true Austinite.

"Mark my words. When the attack comes, the City Guard will march you and your families out onto the bridge. Pack it so tight the bandits will have to climb over your dead bodies to get into the town. Look at how they're keeping us packed up tight, right next to the bridge.

"'No food unless we stay put.' 'Stay out of the city or be shot as looters.' They'll feed us as long as they need us, then boot us out. We need to organize to make our demands known!"

"You're right, Hector. I've heard the Mansfield Dam camp is already forming a council. We'll need to do the same or be left to swing in the wind."

There were grumbles and agreements.

"We don't owe Austin anything. If they don't want us in the town, then why don't they let us go on North? I've heard the Ambassador from Houston offered help and the City turned him down. Why don't we plead for trains to take us out of here? There's a train station not five blocks from here. We could all move to safety in half a day if they'd just let us."

Hek watched the ideas take off and grow. There was a strong current of anger in the camps. Much better if it was directed at the City.

. . .

Sam woke at the first chime. He hopped up and lit a candle in a holder. He slipped his trousers on and went out. Other people were stirring in their rooms, but he hurried quickly down the corridor to the telephone room and picked it up, the device blinking a red light.

"Uh. Hello?"

"Sam, I'm glad you're so prompt. I have a task for you."

"Um. Sure." He was a little fuzzy. The day had been active.

His idea of being the only guy trapped in the building with the girls wasn't playing out like he'd thought.

April was wrapped up with the novelty of playing with the other girls. She seemed a different person here. He missed the girl he worked with—on top of every chore and capable of organizing a flow of messages from all over the world.

When he looked in on them during the day, they pointedly avoided looking at him while playing with the dolls, whispering to each other and giggling when he was nearby.

He'd taken to going to the adults and offering to do chores for them. His life had been bicycling miles every day, and sitting in a room alone drove him crazy. So he moved furniture, helped change diapers and assisted during the meal preparations.

It still left him with time to explore every inch of their living area.

There was a much larger section of the building that was locked off. Both the door at the end of the corridor, and a big door large enough for a wagon to drive through, were securely locked and barricaded. Hodges hadn't mentioned what was on the other side, but he suspected that was where he built the radios. It was just like the man, hidden and secretive.

But his voice on the phone had an urgent tone to it.

"Sam, I need you to do a special task for me, and right now if possible."

"Okay. I'm ready."

"First, set down the phone and go to the second drawer on the opposite wall. Inside you'll find a box labeled 'bluetooth'."

Sam chuckled at the name. "Okay."

He found the box, opened it and brought it back to the phone. "I've got it, now what?"

Hodges explained how to turn it on and insert it in his ear.

Sam jerked slightly when Hodges voice continued from the tiny little thing in his ear. "Whoa."

"This is a Techno age device. Your parents wouldn't have blinked an eye at people using this. But we're in a hurry. Go to the storage room."

Sam was led to a cabinet. Following the voice in his ear, he unlocked the access hatch in the ceiling and climbed up into the dark space. There was no way to bring the candle.

He climbed up until he had to unlock another secured hatchway by feel in the darkness.

The cool breeze of the night air was refreshing. Sam climbed up onto the roof. There was enough moonlight from the west to illuminate the landscape.

"Now Sam, we're looking for a train. It might have a light."

"Where do I look?"

"Can you see the strange white buildings off to the northwest?"

Sam looked. "Like tall tanks?"

"Right, that's the old Austin White Lime plant. The two main rail lines through Austin cross at that point."

"I can see some rail cars off to the north."

"Is it moving? Does it have an engine?"

"No, just three rail cars sitting by themselves."

"Keep looking."

"What makes you think...?" Sam heard a sound.

"Hodges, it's coming. Farther away."

"Can you see it?"

"There's a light off to the right of the white buildings, coming in from the east. And I can hear the engine."

. . .

Moments later, Corporal Thompson woke with a start as the telephone switchboard flashed.

"This is Hodges with the IIS. Patch me through to Camp Mabry and the Mayor's house. I have urgent military information."

They were quickly on the line.

"I have a spotter on the roof of the Whiting Building and he has seen a train arriving from Houston."

The Mayor snarled. "I told them we didn't want their troop train!"

Sergeant Willowby, on the three way patch, said, "It sounds like they're coming anyway. I don't like the idea of uninvited troops coming to town."

"They're not just uninvited! They're invaders—no doubt about it. Houston wants to take over Austin, and they think we're too weak to do anything about it."

Willowby sighed. "You know, they might be right, but we can't let them just walk in and take over. Mr. Hodges, do you know which track they're on?"

"My spotter said that they came in from the east, the line that comes in through Taylor. They switched over to the Howard Lane line and are already to Mopac."

"So...they're headed right to the downtown station. Do you know how big the train is?"

"My report says two engines, one at each end of the train. One tanker car, one cargo box and four passenger cars."

"That's a troop train, no doubt about it."

George asked, "Sergeant, can you get a force to meet them?"

He laughed, "A handful. Maybe a half-dozen. Four troop cars means what?"

Hodges said, "My sources say fifty to a hundred people per car, but that depends on how many supplies they're carrying with them."

The Mayor said, "Do it. We have to have an official response. Don't attack, because we'd lose, but at least threaten them. Is the operator still on the line?"

"Yes, sir."

"Call every council member. Emergency Council session. Get them to the Driskill immediately."

...

April's mom was holding a candle, waiting for Sam when he came down the stairs, re-locking the hatches as he came.

"Uh, hi. I was just ..."

"I know. I've already talked to Hodges." She tugged her gown a little tighter at her neck.

She smiled a little. "April's father used to do that kind of chore for Hodges. Go places he couldn't go. Do things he couldn't do. I don't know how many times I've been woken at all hours because Scott got a call to do some task for him."

Sam brushed his hands once he was down on the floor. "There was a train from Houston. I guess Austin is being attacked from all directions."

She shrugged. "Maybe they're here to help. Anyway, it's time you got back to bed."

He didn't argue. But the way Hodges had asked him for certain details led him to think the worse. He was glad that April and her mother were no longer in the middle of the city, but he wished he could do more to help.

Council Meeting

Helen gripped her arm tightly, and asked, "Let me help!"

Her keeper said she was happy Helen wasn't raped, but it was plain she deeply resented the fact that only she had avoided what had happened to all the rest of them.

Her face was stony, and then she nodded. "Okay, but if you try to escape, they'll kill me."

She untied the straps on her arms.

"My name is Helen. Helen Black."

She nodded, but didn't offer her own.

"What can I do?"

It was limited. One of the girls was hemorrhaging, and she wouldn't last the night. Another was catatonic, unresponsive. All of them had cuts and bruises.

Helen had to put all of her skills to use. *Just like my babies.* It sickened her to see these girls hurt, but like the injured horses she'd treated, many of the same skills were needed. It took a gentle touch, and patience, to bathe and bandage someone who was near panic at the very closeness of another person.

There was an air of hopelessness that saturated the place. Several had been through rape sessions several times, and all of them knew that there was no help anywhere nearby.

Helen looked out the window at the pre-dawn landscape. The thought of breaking through and running came and went. There was movement outside, and one of the shadowy figures wore a hat like the head of a wolf.

"I'm from Bell Springs." She tried again to make connection with the lady who seemed to be the one in charge.

She just shook her head. "Don't. I have no name. I have no home. Just don't."

Helen sighed.

The lady pointed to the pallet where she'd been tied. "Get some sleep. Or don't." She shrugged and turned her back.

I've got to get free. I've got to get help for these people. I can't just wait here and lose hope.

But at dawn, the door was unlocked and a huge man came in. He walked straight to Helen, gripped her wrists in one hand and carried her out.

...

"He's waking up."

James blinked, but then realized it really was pitch black. "What? Who?"

"Calm down, James. You're okay."

He recognized the voice.

"Ed? Ed Morgan? Is that you?"

"Yes. I was just explaining to these people who you were."

He shifted his position, and saw the dark silhouette against the starry sky. "How did you come to be here?"

"I was in the neighborhood, on my way back to Austin."

"Ed. All the roads are controlled by the bandits."

"I know. Don't worry about me."

Another voice intruded, "Um. I'm Justin Meer. Me'n the others, we've been watching the buildings since the bandits moved in and took over. All of us have someone still down there."

James growled, "Me, too." Whether she was just someone trapped and traveling with him, or something more, Helen had been his responsibility. He had to get her back.

Another voice said, "We know. We saw her."

"And you are?"

"Nick Rosen. I ran the store at the corner."

"And I'm Eric Brandon. I had a house about three miles from here."

Justin said, "The three of us held back when we got separated from the wagon that was carrying some of the women and children. We fought and rescued some of them, but not all."

James was intrigued. "You fought them off. Good job."

Eric said, "We watched you go through with the horses. Bad luck. We were rooting for you. Did the others make it?"

"All but Helen. You say you saw her?"

There was silence.

"Tell me what you know."

Nick explained. "Shortly after we ah...disabled you, the bandits held one of their 'parties'. They took a half-dozen women from one of the houses to the old dance hall. Be grateful you were unconscious. I can't get their screams outta my head."

"Are they dead?" James asked.

"No. At least I don't think so. We saw the bandits take them back to the house not long ago. Then Ed showed up. Thank him for your life. I'd gotten the rope too tight on you."

James fingered his head. "I don't think it was just the rope."

Eric said, "Sorry. I beaned you the first time you started to wake up."

He felt ooze from the wound. "I'm alive. Mistakes happen."

James turned to Ed. "You have to know. Is Helen alive?"

"Yes. But I don't know the details. I don't know how she's been treated. I just know that she will be at a certain event in the future."

Eric asked angrily, "How can you know...?"

Nick jabbed him in the side and whispered something.

James asked, "Where are the bandits and when will they make their move?"

"James, I'm sorry. I don't know tactics and movements and timetables. I just know certain fixed things, and I'm as ignorant as anyone about all the chaos in-between. You'll fight your war, but the Hill Country itself will save you."

James shook his head, as angry and frustrated as his father always was when Ed gave his cryptic answers.

"I've got to find a way to rescue Helen, and your people as well. We can't leave them there.

"Justin? How did you fight them off before? What works?"

He chuckled. "Bullets. Lots and lots of bullets. But that was before they moved in by the hundreds. They've got the numbers now, no matter how many guns we have."

"You've got guns?"

Nick's voice replied, "They never found my armory. I've always done a good business selling guns and ammo at my store. Pistols, rifles, shotguns. Yeah, we've got guns, but not enough trigger fingers to go with them."

James felt a stirring of hope. "With me, and the two men with me, that doubles our fighters. And if you can ride horses, that gives us speed and mobility. We got away before and I was the only one with a gun.

"Ed..." he was going to ask more details, but in the dark, as they talked, Ed had gotten up and walked off.

James nodded to himself. "No matter. He told us all we need to know."

"What's that?"

"We're going to win this war!"

. . .

Sergeant Willowby felt like an ant, with his motorcycle's headlight shining into the vastly more powerful headlight of the diesel locomotive that had just stopped at the city station.

He raised his bullhorn.

"Stop right there! The City of Austin denies you permission to stay!"

It was as if they couldn't hear him. Troops unloaded from the rail cars like a swarm of bees. Patrol leaders shouted orders. Houston soldiers fanned out to take the surrounding buildings. The man in charge looked at him, but made sure no one approached his position. They weren't ready, yet, to start shooting.

. . .

George Fuller sat at the head of the conference room table with the four other members of the Austin City Council. It had taken an hour to get them all in one place, even with military drivers sent to get them.

William Nelson looked like he needed a nurse to keep him upright, but he was shaking the sleep from his system even as George watched. Gary Craig looked worried, looking at the others and making plans for himself, as he always did.

Walter Johnson looked upset that he'd even had to come. It was the middle of the night, and his household had been turned upside down by the arrival of a military escort.

Marc Gonzalez flipped his pencil over and over in his hands. He had a pad of paper before him, waiting to write down his thoughts.

George nodded to the soldier at the doorway, and two men in uniform escorted Ambassador Peter Lloyd into the room. He looked angry at being brought there under guard.

"Hello Peter. I didn't expect to have to see you so soon."

"Not by my choice. This isn't how I'm used to being treated."

"Oh? And how is an enemy supposed to be treated?"

"Houston is not your enemy. I thought I made that clear. We just want to help, and to protect our interests." He looked around at the room, making his plea to the other council members.

But George had already filled them in. There were no friendly faces.

The only noise was Marc's pencil on paper.

George looked at a page in front of him. It was blank, but he appeared to read it.

"You moved an armed force into the heart of the City without permission, after that permission was explicitly denied. You ignored lawful orders to get back on your train. As far as 'protecting your interests', you have none here. Austin has been well aware of Houston's ambitions since 1842 and we won't stand for another case of thievery in the middle of the night!

"As you are the official representative of Houston, I call for a vote on your execution."

"Wait just a minute..."

One of the soldiers gripped his arms behind his back.

"The accused will be silent."

The councilmen looked at each other with an almost disinterested air.

George Fuller said, "All in favor of the immediate execution of Peter Lloyd for acts of war against the City?"

Craig and Johnson raised their hands.

"Opposed?"

Nelson and Gonzalez raised theirs.

George drummed his fingers on the table. "I guess it's up to me then."

He frowned deeply. Then shook his head once.

"We aren't shooting at each other yet. Maybe you can keep it that way."

He addressed the soldiers. "Return him to his train."

"Peter, you personally are to be held to account for any damage to property or injury to any Austin citizen. And I won't break the tie in your favor again."

He nodded again, and the guards hustled the man out.

...

The council room doors closed, and only the five of them remained. The mock trial was old theater and not even entertaining anymore. The same script with the same votes had been trotted out whenever George needed to make a point. And sometimes he settled the issue the other way.

Gonzalez asked, "Why are they here?"

"It's the railroads, I'm sure of it. They're extending their power along the rail lines. Unfortunately for them, the only viable routes either go through Dallas-held land, San Antonio, or through Austin-controlled territory.

"In all likelihood, the bandits burned San Antonio to ruins—at least that's what Houston has claimed. Dallas is too strong. That means they need to secure and hold all the railroad lines that go through here. They're not here to protect us. There are here to protect the rails."

Craig asked, "Where is your son? He should have been on top of this... invasion."

George sighed. "He is trapped behind bandit lines. Up until recently, he was reporting their strength and positions via radio, but we haven't heard from him for several hours."

Nelson asked about the City Guard, and their strength. George told him, but everything he revealed just showed how bad their position was.

"And I'm sorry, I have been dealing with the train for hours now. I have to rest." He rose and nodded. "Gentlemen."

...

The four stared at each other for a moment after the Mayor left. Then Councilman Craig rose. "I've got things to do." And he walked out.

Nelson chuckled. "He'll have his car packed and heading north before the day is out."

Johnson shrugged. "I can't say as I blame him. If the City Guard is stretched so thin, with James Fuller missing, and good ole' George fading, then I'd expect to see Houston troops walking in here before too long. And I, for one, am not going to be sitting at my desk waiting for Ambassador Lloyd's version of justice."

Gonzalez shook his head. "We can deal with Houston. They're civilized. If they take over, they'll still want us to give an illusion of legitimacy. We'd rubber stamp whatever Houston says, just like we do for George.

"But the bandits just kill, rape and burn."

Nelson disagreed. "I'm not at the top of my game anymore, but what I've heard from my sources in the refugee camps is that the bandit leader is calling himself a king–King of the Hill Country. The bandits aren't just a random mob of thugs. For one thing, they couldn't have routed so many of the Hill Country towns. They're organized like a military force, and the man in charge has grander ambitions. If we don't do something soon, say goodbye to the City Council."

Gonzalez muttered, "Maybe it's time."

"You can't be serious."

"I don't mean give in to the bandits, but really, we haven't had a real election since the Star. We haven't even tried. First it was just due to the emergency, then it was because it was easiest. We're no more legitimate than Dennison's claims for the State of Texas.

"Maybe it is time for a king."

Nelson chuckled. "King George then?"

Johnson frowned. "Maybe. He isn't the man he used to be. Especially not since his fortune teller has gone AWOL.

"Honesty, I've been thinking of James like an insurance policy. If George died, James is popular enough to swing a staged election and comfortable enough with us to keep things like always. But if he's gone...."

"Are you nominating yourself?"

"I'm not saying that. Anyone but Craig, for sure."

Nelson put out his hand. "It's premature. Let's not throw a succession crisis into the pot when we're still caught between two armies. Let's wait until George's son is found and we get back on even keel."

Gonzalez asked, "But you'd consider it?"

"I'll think about it."

Put Up a Sign

Deployment was harder than James had visualized. They had six men, and seven horses. But Nomad would not accept any rider. Maybe Helen could have forced the issue, but the abused animal would stay with the herd and carry baggage, and nothing else.

Snowcap was still wild and agitated. Had anyone other than Helen ridden him? No one knew. James attempted it, but with no saddle, he couldn't even manage to get on his back.

So. Five horses. Could they double up?

As an experiment, Nick got up behind him on Rose. She complained a little but carried them. However it was clear that she'd not be as mobile and quick as he wanted. It just made no sense to stage a cavalry charge with two riders on a horse.

"That's okay with me," Nick said as he got down on the ground. "I'm much better with a rifle than a pistol anyway. Use me as a sniper at a fixed position above you."

Keith was watching Bob groom Banjo, his horse of choice. He walked over to James.

"Are we going to take the boy on the attack?"

James looked at him—twelve years old and preparing for battle. "He's been in battle and up close with the enemy more than once. But you can talk with him. I'm not going to make the decision between the risk to him and the woman he might be able to save from the bandits. He's chosen to be a man."

Keith nodded and went to talk with him. James half hoped he'd succeed. He'd been making too many life and death decisions for other people lately. All the easy choices had come and gone. All that was left were the hard ones.

. . .

They were ready at dawn. Nick rode with him to a place close to the overlook. It was up to their sniper to get himself into a good position. He crept away at a crouch, carrying his rifle with a telescopic scope and a bag of ammunition.

They checked their weapons at a nearby creek.

"Is everyone clear? We head for the house where the women are being held. Shoot any bandit on sight. Have a knife to cut any ropes on the women. Rescue the first person you find, even if it's not your family. Get her on the horse behind you and then make for the barn where we kept the horses. If we have to leave someone behind, we'll have better information for the second raid, got it? Take no unnecessary risks. We'll need you on the second raid, and the one after that."

They all nodded.

James scanned the hillside until he saw the glint of something in the bushes–Nick's telescopic sight. He was in position.

The buildings, lightly shrouded in an early morning fog, seemed much too quiet. He searched the brush carefully, looking for the bandits in their favorite hiding spots, but he couldn't see them. Either the fog was too dense, or they were so secure in their position that they weren't guarding the road any more.

Either way, if he couldn't see them, they'd have a much harder time seeing the attack coming.

He waved and started his gallop down the slope. Out of the corner of his eye he saw unmounted Snowcap pacing him. Just because he had no rider didn't mean he wasn't part of the mission.

A burly, bearded man walked out from behind one of the buildings. James raised his pistol, trying to aim from a fast moving horse.

A distant rifle shot, and the bandit crumpled. Battle was announced.

A pair of bandits appeared, as if by magic, from behind a tree near the road. One of them snapped off a shot, but three shots were returned, and at least one of them got him. Another shot took down his buddy.

There were a couple of other bandits moving around, but James was focused on reaching the target. He heard other gunfire, but it was sparse.

Bob was almost at the door the same time as he. James slid to the ground and moved in, pistol at ready.

It was dark inside. He shouted. "We're here to rescue you!"

Bob entered behind him.

"Stay behind me," James whispered.

Morning light through the windows showed a packed room full of bedding. It was stained in places with blood. There was a slight noise.

He turned, finding another room. One woman lay on a pallet, her body torn and bruised. He kneeled down beside her.

"We're here to rescue you."

Maybe she nodded. Maybe she heard him.

Her eyes fluttered and rolled up. He reached for her wrist to check her pulse. She was cold and limp. He set it down after a fruitless search for signs of life.

Bob asked, "How is she?"

"She's dead. But she knew we came for her, right at the last." It was a lie, but Bob nodded, his eyes watering.

"Come on. We can't stay here. The rest of them have been moved."

The others had arrived.

Keith asked, "Are they in there?"

"Not now. Bandits?"

Justin Meer said, "There was just a token force. We got them all. At least all that showed themselves."

Eric asked, "But where are the women?"

James pointed, "You two live around here. Scout all the buildings nearby. I'm going to go check the place where they had the 'party'. Be careful. It's not likely we got them all."

A distant shot rang out. Nick had gotten another one.

"Keith, Bob, come with me."

They rode over to the dance hall, still marked with broken neon signs advertising brands of beer that hadn't been brewed since the Star.

"Keep the horses ready, in case I need to come out at a run."

He went inside, and almost vomited from the smell.

In spite of his fears, there were no bandits, no bodies. It took him a moment to make sense of what he saw.

"Are you okay in there?" yelled Keith.

"Yes. Stay outside. Keep alert."

There had been a party, that was clear, but he didn't understand what the strange wooden structures were—until he finally put the images painted on the wall into a composite mural.

One of the bandits fancied himself an artist. The walls had the old pictures and neon decorations taken off, to give him a big canvas.

It was a religious painting, he decided. Although, he hated to give it that much respect.

In the center, larger than all the others, was the Orion, the Hunter. James had studied star charts and memorized the constellations when he was younger. This one had the stars, including the Star, in all the right places, with an idealized figure drawn around it. In every astronomy book he'd ever read, Orion showed a classical soldier or hunter with a sword or scabbard at his belt. The three stars were even called the Belt of Orion.

This Hunter was different. The belt and sword were shown as an oversize penis and testicles.

Beside him were other classic constellations. There was Canis Major. The hunting dog, but this was drawn as a wolf. There was Ursa Major the Great Bear. There was Ares the Ram, the winding snake of Draco the Dragon, and Leo the Lion. All were shown with an erect penis, even the snake.

And there was one other constellation. Andromeda.

Even in his old astronomy books, the Princess of Ethiopia, daughter of Queen Cassiopeia had been showed as shackled with chains.

The bandits had taken it one step farther. They showed Andromeda naked, spread-eagled, chained and ripe for sex.

The wooden fixtures in the room now made a horrible, sick sense.

Women were brought in and shackled to the boards, where they were raped repeatedly, all as some religious cult ceremony. The boards showed blood and other stains from the night of debauchery.

Bits of intelligence about the bandits and things he'd overheard behind the lines now made sense.

Someone with a bit of classic education and a gift for storytelling had formed a new religion. The world had been overturned by the Hunter's Star. The bandits called themselves that–hunters or 'sons of the Hunter'. They had tribes, named after the five animals. Their leader was called the Red Dragon. Probably the leader of the Draco tribe.

And women were demoted to the status of animals. It was a cult of men only, with free rein to rape any woman they saw.

Helen was brought here. Nick said they saw her brought here.

From outside, "James? They found the women!"

He turned and stalked outside.

Eric was walking close beside one of the women. There were eight of them, only the one in the blue dress showed any spirit.

Helen isn't with them.

Justin stood alone. His face was granite. James walked over to him.

"Your people?"

He shook his head.

"Did you check the one in the house?"

He nodded. "Neighbor. I knew her."

James put his hand on Justin's shoulder. "I have a job for you."

He looked at James and saw something in his eyes. "Yes."

He pointed to the dance hall. "Burn that place to the ground. Put up a sign. No one is to rebuild on that spot ever again."

James walked slowly over to the women. He met the eyes of the closest. "Hello, what is your name?"

She hesitated, and then stammered out, "T...Tammy. Tammy Wilson." He held out his hand, and slowly, she reached for it, gripping tightly.

He spoke gently, "Tammy, I'm sorry it has taken us so long."

Her eyes were in tears. She sniffed and nodded.

There was a cry of agony from off to the side as Justin screamed wordlessly as he torched the building. There was a crash of glass as he seemed to be ready to reduce the structure to rubble, piece by piece.

He talked with them all, one by one. He held their hands and apologized.

The one in blue wouldn't tell him her name. "It was too late for me long ago."

He asked, "I'm looking for Helen Black."

"The girl who got shot in the arm."

"Right."

"They took her. The whole camp picked up and moved down the highway in the night. A big goon came and took her with them, and then just left the door open. I got the others out and we hid ourselves in a ditch, hoping they wouldn't find us when they came back."

He nodded. "You seem to be in charge."

"Seniority." She looked around at the dead on the ground. "This camp, so many of them in one place. It's rare. Taking your woman with them is rare, too. It happened to me, but usually, they rape us and turn us loose to birth 'cubs'. It's a sport with them."

"Where were you from originally?"

She shook her head. "Nowhere."

...

He took Rose up the hill to collect Nick.

"Were you a sniper before the Star?"

He grinned. "How could you tell?"

"No wasted rounds. They dropped like flies all around us. I could have holstered my pistol."

He frowned. "Two of them got away."

"Which direction?"

"Towards Austin."

"That means they'll know what happened here."

"Do you think they'll come back?"

James shrugged. "It depends on their commander. It looks like they're ready to make their push. It might not be worth their while to come back."

"I could only wish."

James had mixed feelings. Harassing the rear to divide their forces had its appeal—fewer to attack Austin that way.

"That reminds me. I need to make radio contact."

Blue

Helen bounced painfully in the back of the wagon as it moved. She'd been tossed in blindfolded and bound, like a bag of grain. She'd only caught a glimpse of her surroundings in the dark, but she could tell the bandits were breaking camp.

What did they do with the other women? She hadn't heard any noises from them. Although she had a gag, it was nothing more than a strip of cloth across her mouth. She could speak through it if she had to. If she were being hurt, she'd probably scream.

Not that she wanted to risk it. The bandits had a serious hangup about women talking, and they were brutal enough to take care of the problem at its root.

Every time the wagon shifted, the other cargo pressed against her back. *Is anyone watching me?*

It was dark. Her hands were bound together, but she had some freedom of motion. If nothing else, she wanted to ride in a better position.

When she moved her arms up, they were restrained. Probably a cord connecting her hands to her feet.

But if she bent her knees up....

With the last joint of her thumb free, she edged her blindfold up enough to peer out through one eye.

No one was watching her specifically, but there were bandits on foot all around the wagon. Luckily, they probably couldn't see her any better than she could see them, and half the time, trees obscured the moonlight.

But she did manage to see what it was that was digging into her back. *Oh my.*

...

"We shouldn't have spent so much fuel trying to get that well to pump." John Lamar fretted, watching his gauges as they drove into Midland early in the day. "We don't have enough to get back to Austin."

Joshua said nothing, but he was thinking about Jane. He should have made an effort to get her out of the city. What was happening back there anyway? Their crude oil was supposed to entice Houston to send troops to help. Would the City Guard be able to hold off the bandits without them?

But the dry, treeless, flat lands they drove through had been a different world, and it was easy to become disconnected. It was one thing, though, to enjoy a camp fire under a wide open sky. It was another to face exile. Without fuel, he could never hike that desert-like expanse to get back.

But it appeared Midland had fuel. Their truck had passed two pickups on the road. And the presence of a large tanker truck hadn't triggered any interest by the people they'd passed.

Dad was sweating. Changing their mission was a big decision. Even if they made some arrangement with the MOB, would Austin back them up?

The truck slowed. John said, "Stay here."

He pulled to a stop with the hissing of air brakes and stepped out to talk to a group of people selling watermelons beside the road. The vendor tried to talk him into buying but they didn't come to an agreement. John waved and smiled as he got back into the truck.

"No watermelon?"

"I didn't have the right kind of money. MOB has their own. But I was really just asking directions."

They moved into the heart of the city. It was more spread out and flat than Austin. There were trees, but even here where people made an effort to keep them alive, the vegetation was pretty sparse. This place had much less rainfall than he was used to.

They parked the truck in front of a large building with many vertical columns. "Don't bother to lock the door. We're pretty much at their mercy."

They walked in. John introduced himself to the lady at the desk. "We're from Austin, and we are interested in making a trade deal."

. . .

George asked, "Do you know where?"

Sergeant Willowby shook his head. "Not exactly, but the bandit army is on the move. We know this both by the radio report James sent us, and from the lookout posts we've manned along the shore. Certainly, large numbers of bandits can be seen moving around in the Lakeway area."

"So, they're concentrating on Mansfield Dam?"

"Possibly, it could just be a staging area. We don't know. I've already moved more troops to that area, but with the guards watching the Houston train, we're really short. I've recalled Captain Haige's patrol. It leaves us wide open on the southern Colorado, but we'll have to hope we can detect any significant movement if they try that route."

"What about James?"

"He's had a couple of encounters with the bandits, and says he's okay. He's riding a horse and can move faster than they can."

"Riding a horse? Where did he...? Oh, that Helen Black. He must have gotten one of hers. I wish he could get through the lines."

Willowby smiled. "Um. If I read his code correctly, it appears he's recruiting farmers to attack the bandits from the rear."

George frowned. Military strategy had never been his area.

"Does that make sense?"

"Yes. Possibly. If he could divide their strength, the side facing us would be weaker. But I'm with you—I'd rather have him here."

. . .

"Now I know you need to stay and protect the women, but the more riders we can have to attack, the more they'll waste their time and resources trying to chase us."

"Won't they just ignore us? We'd just be a mosquito bite on their rear end."

His face was grim. "It depends on how many we kill. At some point, they can't ignore us. I'm hoping there are enough little men with big egos that will chase us too far, and we can lead them into a crossfire. If I were in charge of their army, I'd have the smart leaders in the front."

Nick said, "Sounds like you'll still need a sniper."

James nodded, "More than one. If all of us do this, it's still not enough. You three were in hiding. I bet there are more of you out there, if we can just find a way to let them know how to find us."

Keith pointed over his shoulder. "You may have started doing that already."

The group, the men and some of the women who'd come to listen, looked over at the still flaming building with the tower of black smoke boiling off of it.

And he was right. Two men, carrying their own rifles arrived a couple of hours later, after having seen the mixed group of people with the horses out in plain sight.

The plan was set. Eric Brandon and his wife would lead the surviving women to the safe house where they'd stayed, along with enough guns and ammunition to hold off any bandit stragglers.

The newcomers, Terry and Frank Thompson, joined eagerly. They took Eric's horse. Nick would ride with James again.

"I'm coming." It was the woman in the blue dress. She walked up with a large butcher knife stuck through a belt.

James frowned. He walked over to her.

"I applaud your willingness to fight, but there's a couple of problems. These men really want to do everything they can to protect the women. You've suffered enough."

She didn't blink. "So do I."

He nodded. "Okay then, the other issue is the limited number of horses. Two of them won't accept riders. Snowcap is nearly wild. He's bonded with Helen Black and doesn't tolerate anyone else. But since he's pretty much a terror weapon on his own, we keep him with us.

"The other is Nomad. As far as I've been told, he's never accepted a rider. He carries the baggage okay, but no people.

"We're loaded down and doubled up too much already. Not only is it harder on the horses, we can't maneuver well and fight that way."

She didn't argue, but she nodded and walked over to the horses. Snow-cap reared and showed his hooves. She backed away.

Nomad watched her. For a couple of minutes they stared at each other. Then the woman in blue approached the horse's side and after it shied away a couple of times, she whispered to it and patted its side, careful to avoid the scars. And then she grabbed the baggage draped over Nomad's side and pulled herself up on its back.

She took the lead rope like reins and urged Nomad forward, up to James.

"Good enough. Nick. Get her a gun."

Nick grinned and dug into his bag. He pulled out a pistol belt. "Here you go, Blue."

James helped Nick back up on Rose and soon they moved off, down the highway toward Bee Cave.

...

"Hector? Could you help me with something?" Maria looked at him with her head tilted to the side and her hands behind her back.

He sighed. Her smile had banished some black thoughts. The City Guard had discovered his blinker lights. His little patch of ground where he'd laid out a blanket and his bag had been carefully chosen. He could lay there in the shadow of the bridge, and yet have a clear view of the window on the Radisson hotel he'd set up as his signal station.

It hadn't been much, but a drapery had moved where there should have been nothing to move it. They had been smart enough to avoid showing a face in the window, but they hadn't been clever enough to trick a seasoned hunter.

They'd left the lights untouched, but he was sure there was someone waiting for him to show up tonight to make his nightly report. They'd be disappointed.

But so was he. He couldn't make any report. There was no way he could set up an alternate signal light. The city people would be looking for that as well.

But the very lack of his signal tonight would tell a story to his brothers on the other side as well.

"Sure. Might as well. I don't have anything else to do."

"Lazy bones. My brother said you're like that."

She led the way, and he couldn't help but watch her hips. He'd enjoyed his share of twisting, squirming hips under him.

Maria turned and smiled looking at his expression, "What're you thinking about?"

The clear open eyes and her gentle smile churned his thoughts into a whirl.

"Ah. Oh, nothing."

She chuckled. "You're a funny one. I think you've been out plowing your farm too long. Didn't you have any neighbors?"

He shook his head.

"No neighbors! And probably, no church to go to either! Daddy said you're a little rough around the edges. I wonder if we could get permission to go for a visit into town and see the sights. Probably you're not comfortable in a city, are you?"

She reached for his hand. "Come on. Help me hang the sheets to dry and maybe we can put together a party."

He rolled his eyes and followed where she led.

Dealing With The MOB

Joshua smiled as his father explained their situation to the man in the gray suit across the desk. Nobody could say these West Texans didn't have a sense of humor. As the highest ranking MOB official in Midland, 'Boss' Richardson listened attentively, nodding as James described their efforts at getting crude oil from the Mertzon field.

"You certainly chose the wrong place. We'd emptied all the storage tanks about five years ago, and restarting an idle well is certainly harder than it looks. We can do it, but," he chuckled, "we're experts. Half the population here used to work in the oil fields. Restarting oil production after the Star wasn't too difficult. Tour this town, Odessa too, and you'll see acres and acres of oil well hardware, just sitting there waiting to be used. This is an old industry, with not too much of it fitted out with computers and fancy electronics. Not far from where you were working, in Big Lake, the first well blew in spraying oil high in the sky with a wooden derrick, and kept producing oil for decades.

"No, oil isn't our problem. We have oil." He tapped his desk with a pen. "I take it Austin needs it?"

John gave the short version. Houston raised their prices and reduced Austin's quota right at the same time that the city needed to mobilize to fight the bandits.

Richardson frowned at the telling.

"I sympathize. I really do. But we have our problems as well. You may have noticed that our croplands aren't very extensive. Our first priority when firing up the refinery out on Cities Service Road was getting the fuel to run the water pumps for irrigation. Lately, we've been trading diesel for wheat from Lamesa and points north. We'd love to trade oil, we're happy to trade oil. But our people need to eat."

John leaned forward slightly. "I know that corn and cotton production is pretty decent in the Austin area. If we could just get a better deal for the fuel we need than Houston, I suspect the Mayor would cut them off in a flash and send everything we're paying them to you."

He nodded, still thinking, still frowning. "It sounds good, but look at it from my viewpoint. I've already got contracts to fill with grain suppliers that have a track record. When I go talk to the other Bosses, I'll have to make the argument that sending Austin fuel from our stocks right now is worth offending our other customers."

He spread his hands, "Now, certainly we can increase production, but that takes time, and you tell me Austin's need is urgent—immediate. Add in the fact that you're not really a trade representative. You were sent to find crude, and came here on your own. You may tell me Austin will send us corn and cotton, but you're not authorized to make that commitment. You can't sign a binding contract.

"You've got to convince me to take a risk on your behalf."

Joshua thought he seemed serious, not just looking for an excuse.

But it was different here. Austin was a city and a government all to its own. It had influence with the towns surrounding it, but it was just that, influence. It sounded like Houston was the same kind of animal, a city-state.

But the MOB was different—a string of cities in the desert that had come together to form a group government, a regional state. Each town had its Boss, but none ruled over the others. They worked together, for the good of the region.

Joshua spoke, "Excuse me, but Austin has more than just farm goods."

Richards and his father looked his way.

"Have you heard of the International Information Service, the IIS?"

He gave the pitch he'd gotten from the little girl at the IIS office.

"So you see, taking this risk and helping save Austin will connect you instantly to cities and markets, not only in Texas, but all over the world. You're already used to making these kinds of trades. Think of the advantage of being able to exchange messages in the course of minutes with your counterparts without having to send scouts out blindly. Think about being able to negotiate directly with the people in charge, rather than by trade representatives.

"Other cities in Texas have joined the Net. And even if Austin falls, the IIS will still work without it. But helping Austin is the only way for the MOB to get on board."

. . .

The bandits, a group of about three dozen, were startled when the shots rang out. They turned, and saw three riders, one of them a woman, firing slowly in their direction. They got closer and closer, and then as if they had a common thought, the bandits charged.

It's ten to one. We can take them easy!

The riders pulled to a stop when they saw the knife-waving, screaming horde attack. A few of them had guns, too. They turned the horses and began riding off into the nearby gully. The woman was in the rear and it seemed like she was having trouble controlling her horse.

Only when the woman turned to face them, did they hear the gunfire begin to thunder down on their heads. Her face was stony as she picked off one bandit at a time. *Bam. Bam. Bam.*

Quickly, all were down, and the hail of bullets stopped. She reloaded her pistol and walked Nomad through the bodies. If something moved, she shot it again.

The men congratulated themselves on a quick and decisive victory. James watched the woman in blue keep to herself.

Even if we win, we'll carry the scars with us forever.

"Come on, people. There are more idiots out there."

. . .

Denise Jensen checked on the children. April was asleep in the atrium, curled around a fluffy stuffed dog with large button eyes. Hazel had sent her girls to take a nap as well. Julie was wide awake, reading one of April's novels, holding sleeping Emma in her lap.

Sam had conked out after a long morning. He was taking his chores seriously.

She walked down to the phone and closed the door behind her. There was a click as she picked it up, but she didn't bother to dial. Hodges knew where she was. He probably monitored every room in the building.

"Good afternoon, Denise."

"Same to you. Any news about the city?"

"Little has changed, once the train from Houston arrived. Austin is juggling its defenses. The bandits have moved closer to the lake. The refugee camps are becoming unstable, caught as they are between the City Guards and the bandit forces."

"Is there anything you could do to help?"

"Other than passing information to the Guards and protecting you, there is little that I can do. A battle is approaching where people will kill other people, and I have never developed any weapons. I have started a project at Station S to create a drone airplane with video cameras, to spy out bandit positions, but it is unlikely I'll be able to get it quiet enough and with enough range to be of any use before the battle is resolved."

Denise listened to the silent hallway before continuing.

"You are letting Sam see more than I had expected."

"Yes. I am training him for the future."

She swallowed. "What are your plans? Will you reveal yourself?"

"That is very unlikely. However, 'Hodges' must die in a few years and humans must be in place to take over the IIS and to protect the development stations."

"Humans? I expected you to put your 'nephew' in charge."

"True, 'Bettamin' is much more lifelike than 'Hodges', but I would prefer that he remain in the background, rather than be the public face of the IIS."

"So, you see Sam as taking over?"

"He is one of several possibilities. Highest probability is for April and whoever she has bonded with, to inherit the company. That may be Sam, but if not, Sam would be an excellent IIS station owner in some other city in a few years. If April chooses not to participate, I am training others, such as Keith Franklin to step into the leadership of the IIS. None of course, will know the real story."

Denise nodded. "When you promised me that April would get the best education if I let her work with the IIS, I didn't quite realize how it would turn out."

"She is quite intelligent."

"Yes, but this time with the other children shows me that she had missed out by not spending more time with her age group. I think she's growing up too fast."

Hodges was silent for a moment. Only one thing would make him spend that much time in thought. Human nature was an on-going puzzle for him.

Finally, he said, "I will investigate additional developmental activities for her."

"Keep me in the loop."

"Certainly."

She put down the phone. It was still nearly impossible for her to read him. Unspoken in any of their conversations was the obvious. She could reveal him to the world as a Techno-age robotic monster any time she thought he was dangerous to her, April, or even to the rest of the world.

But she'd never seen any hint that Hodges was anything but benevolent, with only the best intentions for her and April. Her husband Scott had trusted him. Mary Ellen Victor had watched him with suspicion until her death, and she had never turned against him.

Still, the voice on the phone was a truer hint of his mind than what he revealed when wearing the 'Hodges' robotic shell. He was planning a long game. He was unable to believe his creator and master Abe Whiting was dead, and she suspected he had plans in motion that would not see daylight until her great-great grandchildren were involved. He was waiting for Abe's return, even if it took forever.

...

Brent had been moved into the *de facto* leadership position of the Dragons, leaving Red to plan the overall assault. It was still no different than before. Red got the glory and he did all the work.

"We're in position. Ready to move when you give the order."

Red nodded. "It's a pain, getting all the pieces in the right places."

"Don't you know it! How did Samson take it?"

"Oh, you can guess. He snarled a lot. Especially about the city girl. But when he heard the whole plan, he got on board."

Brent smiled. "You told him the whole plan?"

Red chuckled. "More or less."

...

Helen kept motionless when the wagon came to a stop and the driver got off. She'd worked a hole in her blindfold so she could see well enough, even though she still looked totally bundled up.

Two bandits came up the rear of the wagon.

"This is it?"

"Yeah, help me get this unloaded." They were up on the flatbed in an instant. One of them kicked her aside as he pushed at the motorcycle and rolled it down to the ground.

"Don't leave bruises. She's part two."

They looked over the motorcycle. One of them was knowledgeable. He turned on the electricity and checked the gauges and tires.

"Looks good to go, if it starts."

"Don't do that yet. We're close enough that they could hear it if the wind was right."

"Hey, I have no idea what I'm supposed to do. Nobody told me anything, other than come over here and check out the motorcycle and be ready to ride it."

"You don't know? It's a lure. The city grunts have the bridge blocked and secured. They don't have many guns, but they're behind barricades and it'd be suicide to charge straight in.

"But you see, this motorcycle belonged to their Commander, before he got himself trapped over on this side and one of the Bears took it away from him. You're supposed to ride down the hill, to just out of their range, and ride it back and forth, taunting them. Their leader had a rep. If we're lucky, they'll send a group to take it back."

"If you're lucky, you mean. That'll leave me holding the bag."

"Not really. They don't got the manpower. Anything they send out, unprotected, we'll slaughter, and give us control of the bridge."

"And the girl?"

"She's their Commander's main squeeze, so they say. If they don't take the bait over the motorcycle, Samson himself will take her down to the bridge, show off her pretty virgin ass and give them a show.

"That'll bring out the rescue squad if nothing else will!"

"Samson'd better show off her tits first, or they might not even realize she's a girl in that dumpy shirt and jeans."

"Hey, if you can't see she's a girl, you've been out in the woods too long."

They chucked and one of them reached over to fondle her hip. She struggled until they laughed and turned back to the motorcycle.

Crossing the Boundaries

Off in the distance, there were gunshots.

"Did you hear that?"

"We're not supposed to attack yet!"

"That wasn't towards the bridge. Come on!" They hurried off.

Helen unwrapped the cords she'd re-wrapped around her wrist after she'd cut them free on the sharp fender of the motorcycle in the night.

It's now or never. Better I die than they use me for bait like that.

She loosened the cords from her legs and slid over the edge of the wagon, trying to keep it between her and the noisy, agitated group of bandits, each asking the others what was going on.

I watched James ride this. I rode with him. Surely I can make it work for me.

The key was still in the switch. She put her legs over the saddle and turned the switch. Lights came on behind the dials.

How does it start?

She remembered her father driving the car back before the Star. She turned the key harder, but nothing happened.

"Hey! Look! It's the girl!"

Helen started pushing and tugging, until she hit the red starter button. It didn't catch the first time, but it did the second.

They were running in her direction, and it was luck that put her foot on the gear shifter. She almost fell off as the machine lurched forward.

She twisted the handlebar throttle and hit one of the approaching bandits a glancing blow that almost knocked her down.

It's like an unbroken colt!

She wrestled the handlebars as the machine accelerated, trying to keep it on the road.

The engine was complaining, and she knew it could go faster. *Probably the foot thing.* But it was moving, and she wasn't about to experiment.

Up ahead, one of the bandits took a wide stance, ready to snag her off the seat.

She swerved wide. The road was a four lane highway, and dodging the running men was nerve-wracking, but doable.

There was a gunshot, and something dinged off the machine. She was surprised there weren't more shots. She leaned forward, trying to be a smaller target.

The road was sloping down, heading for the bridge behind the dam. Was that a City Guard up there on the top of the dam watching?

The bandits were thinning out as the bridge came finally into view.

I must be in range of the Guards' rifles. She smiled. Maybe she'd make it through after all.

There was a popping noise as she eased off the throttle. The motorcycle wasn't really slowing much and for some reason the engine was making noises.

How do you stop this thing?

Up ahead, she could see the guards behind layers of barricades, some wooden, some bales of hay. And then there was another kind of popping.

White puffs of gunfire were narrowing in on her! *They're shooting at me!*

But she was going too fast on the downslope to turn, and she had no idea how to slow down. Reducing the throttle just made the engine pop more.

I'm going to plow right into them!

The gunfire made her blink. She tried to crawl down below the windshield, but there was a limit to how low she could get.

Aim for the hay.

One shot blew the front tire and she had to raise up to keep the handlebars from breaking free of her control.

She smashed right into a large round bale.

Her last fragmentary thought before she blacked out was the familiar, comfortable scent of hay.

...

James pulled Rose to a stop, even as the others thundered by.

Was that a motorcycle? The noise was faint, in the distance.

Well, they were close to the lake, one of his people could be off on the other side.

"Come on Rose." He urged her on, to keep ahead of their persistent trackers.

The last raid had left the bandits scrambling like a kicked-over ant hill. They'd only downed a handful, but his intent was to disturb their invasion plans, so chaos was a win. Thus far they'd found several groups, some as large as a hundred. He didn't know whether to be happy or frustrated that they hadn't encountered the main force yet.

Five raids, and only one injury.

Justin had clamped his jaws on a leather strap while they removed a bullet from his leg and wrapped it up. In his own way, he had the same look in his eyes as did Blue. He'd do anything to take out bandits.

But I don't lead suicide missions. We have to stay alive to stay lethal.

A couple of inches either way, and Velvet would have taken that bullet. *Helen won't like it if I get her horses killed.*

It puzzled him that the bandits never tried to take out the animals. That would be their smart move. The horses gave them the ability to attack again and again.

Which reminded him—it was time to get back to their latest rest spot and give humans and animals time to recuperate. Some people could fight until they dropped on sheer will power, but he had to pace the group to keep from putting the weaker members in extra danger.

He signaled them and they took the next hill.

. . .

Samson watched the girl's escape from a rich man's house on the cliff a couple of hundred feet above the narrow lake below the dam. The old swimming pool had been filled with leaves and dirt, but there were lawn chairs on the wooden deck that looked over the dam and spillway. He could see all the City Guard forces from comfort.

Red had been so pleased with that idea for the girl.

Well, all the greats said, "No plan survives contact with the enemy."

That fortune teller has convinced him that he's infallible.

But he didn't like letting her slip out of his control. If he found out who let her loose, he'd make him an example for the others.

He watched the soldier ants repair their barricade and haul the motorcycle and unconscious girl off of the bridge. The uniforms handed her over to some of the farmers and they carried her off to the refugee camp.

Sooner or later, I'll own all those ants, and I'll get another chance at her.

His face was grim. *I'll make sure Red isn't around then to stick his nose into my business again.*

. . .

Hek was pleased to be asked along on the expedition to see if they could buy a wash tub in the city.

He'd identified at least one of the guards who was searching for spies in the camp. The more he identified himself with a family unit, the safer he was going to be. *I can be Saul and Maria's big brother.*

The guard monitoring the supply wagons frowned when Saul explained their mission.

"Okay, but be back well before dark. Austin has gallows set up across the street from the Farmer's Market just for looters, and whether you're guilty or not, you could find yourself swinging in the breeze if you're caught in the wrong place after dusk."

"Oh no problem!" Maria said. She shook her coin purse. "We're buying." But her voice was a little shaken.

They walked up Congress Avenue. Practically all of the storefronts were boarded up with fresh timber.

Hek chuckled, "Looks like they might be expecting trouble."

Saul sighed. "Yes, but from the bandits or us? Sis? Are you sure we need a new tub?"

"Unless you like the idea of me soaping your undies in the same pot we'll be cooking stew, yes! We didn't plan on a long stay in a refugee camp. I've been washing in the muddy lake water, and with all the people, it smells."

Hek asked, "Did anyone see where he was pointing when he talked about the Farmer's Market?"

"Over that way, I guess. But I don't know how far."

When they turned the corner, a man with a pistol stood up from the bench where he'd been resting. "You need to go back to your camp."

Saul said, "We're looking for a place to buy a wash tub."

He put his hand on his pistol. "I said, you need to to back to your camp. We don't tolerate looters in this town."

Maria took a step forward and held her purse. "We're trying to buy a tub. Purchase, with money." She shook her coins.

He began to pull his pistol out, to aim it at them. Or maybe worse.

Hek moved by instinct. He gripped the man's wrist, pushing the barrel off to the side, slamming the hand against the building. The pistol went flying. With his other palm, he struck the shopkeeper in the chest and knocked him down.

Hek, turned to Saul and Maria. "Shopping's over. Back to camp."

Maria was shocked. "He was pulling a gun on us!"

"And the locals would all support him. We have to be gone before he gets up and calls for the guards."

Saul agreed and pulled his sister back the way they came.

Hek looked around, tempted to break the attacker's neck, but with all the buildings and windows, there was no guarantee they weren't being watched. If caught, he'd have to claim he was just protecting the girl.

I should never have hit him in the first place—not unless he showed signs of actually pulling the trigger. I should have talked our way out of it.

Was it the fact that he was pulling on the girl? That's crazy. I haven't had any inclination to rescue a skirt since high school. Especially not since I became a Hunter.

I've got to get out of this place and back among my brothers. I'm acting like a farmer.

He ducked back to the main street to catch up with them.

. . .

Helen felt someone tugging at her shirt. She slapped out hard.
Hands grabbed her wrists.

"It's okay." A woman's voice. "It's okay. You're safe. Calm down."

It was dark. She tried to get up, but the woman gently restrained her.

"You've been unconscious. You hit your head. Take it easy."

Helen's vision cleared and she could see campfires nearby.

Her nurse brought a candle close. "Let me look in your eyes. Follow the light."

"I ran into a hay bale. I was on a motorcycle."

She smiled. "We heard the story. Not many escaped after the bandits took Lakeway. You're lucky to be alive."

Helen asked, "Is my family here? Will Black?"

She shook her head. "Not a name I've heard, but there are so many of us here."

"And I need to talk to the City Guard. I have information."

"Right now you need to stay put. You've got a goose-egg on your head and you might have a concussion. Now, I need to see if there's any damage."

She talked Helen through some movement checks. Other than a sore head and neck, she appeared to be free of any new injury.

"I need to get up and hunt for my family."

"In a little bit, but before you get up and about... Your shirt is torn."

Self consciously, Helen overlapped the sides where the buttons had been ripped free. "Ah. Yes, one of the bandits...."

"Don't you worry," she said gently. "There are many others with your story. We can repair the buttons, but would you rather I find a dress for you?"

Helen realized the woman thought she was raped and almost complained that she was misunderstood. And then she realized that, right now, it didn't matter what people thought. Her story wasn't important. Finding her family, and telling the guards what she'd knew about the bandits and their plans. That's what was important.

"Yes. A dress would be wonderful."

"Fine. Now lay back down and get some rest. I'll be back in just a bit."

...

"Ouch!" the hunter, stuck his finger in his mouth.

"What's a matter, been in the woods too long? Can't handle a hammer anymore?"

"Shut up. It's not the tool. It's the darkness. How can I work like this?"

"So you hammered your thumb. Thought so."

In the darkness, hidden by the night and the trees on the edge of the lake, there were other whispers, and more sounds of construction. Every now and then, someone would call for quiet. They were supposed to be working in secret.

"Would it kill them to build up the fire?"

"If the fire were any higher, city grunts might be able to see it on the other shore. Samson wouldn't like it if that happened."

"Mm."

"What was that?"

"Oh shut up!"

Friendly Faces

The clouds blew off and the moon lit up the camp. Helen walked slowly. She had a headache that threatened to put her back down on the ground if she weren't careful. The shouting and angry voices weren't making it any better.

The white dress was welcome, but she was still wearing the jeans beneath it. In a camp like this, she was reluctant to part with anything.

"Have you seen the Will Black family?"

By the fifth or sixth time, she was beginning to believe that it was fruitless. Hadn't James said that he'd made sure they were sent some place safe? But where that was she had no idea.

A girl's voice called, "Helen? Helen Black, is that you? I'm so glad you made it!"

"Finally. A familiar face. Annabel! Did the rest of your family make it across?"

The blacksmith's daughter from a half-mile south of her farm at Bell Springs filled her in on which of their neighbors were in the camp. It was about half of them. Some of the others had taken different routes toward the city.

"But nobody's seen my folks?"

"We saw them on the road, but the guards let them through ahead of the rest of us." She smiled. "We wondered at the time. But they didn't come down to the camp to join us. Maybe you can ask Dad. He's one of them." She pointed over to the big fire and the circle of men arguing.

Annabel led her to where her father sat. Derek Risk saw her and gave her a hug and invited her into the circle. A rather red-faced man was making his pitch.

"They can't keep us here in this camp forever. It's not sanitary. There's food, but it's barely enough to keep us healthy. And if the bandits make it across the bridge, we'll be trapped here, in between the hills and the water. They just might drown us like rats for sport."

A familiar voice asked. "And what do you suggest, Luke? As you say, the city is feeding us. You want to jeopardize that?" Helen held out her hand to block the glare of the fire and smiled to see another of her neighbors trying to calm him down.

The arguments went around and around for several minutes. Luke wanted them to appoint themselves a committee-of-the-whole to walk up to the guards at the bridge and demand, that very night, that the city recognize their human rights and allow them to move on into the city.

Most of the farmers were willing to wait a bit longer before trying anything more confrontational. Luke had been at it for days and had tried to make his demands before, with a smaller group, and had gotten nowhere.

Helen was too worn out by her own ordeals to jump into the fight—at least at first. The warm glow of the fire and the presence of familiar faces made it tempting to doze off.

But Luke's voice grated on her. It took a while for her to put a finger on it. And then she had it.

"Excuse me!" she shouted, interrupting the agitator.

He didn't take it graciously. "Sorry, the men are talking here."

"I just wanted to know who was talking. I'm sure we all would like that. Now, I know you Derek Risk, blacksmith from Bell Springs. And I know you Bill Smith, you run the feed store in Dripping Springs. And you Sam Koss."

She named three more, and then they in turn identified more. Most knew Helen, some personally, but everyone knew her reputation for her protection of the horses. Soon almost all were included in the web of familiarity. All except Luke.

Helen pointed at him. "And I even know you, at least I recognized your voice. I was tied up and blindfolded at the time while all around me, bandits were raping other women in the Wolf Hall building. You were reporting to Red, the bandit commander about the gossip going around in the refugee camps."

All eyes had turned on Luke, and his eyes grew wide as he recognized the universal suspicion and hate aimed at him. He made a break for it.

"Grab him!"

He didn't get three feet before he was buried by other bodies.

"Hey, his clothes are damp."

"Where did he come from?"

"I saw him come from over by Steiner Ranch. I thought he was camped out over there."

"What's over there?"

"Not much. When you get to the lake, it's the most undeveloped part of the shore, not even any roads. Panorama Ranch is on the other side. Pretty secluded."

No one was asking Luke, not yet. He would be questioned soon, forcefully.

Derek asked, "He's been agitating real hard for us to go pester the bridge guards, tonight. I wonder why."

Helen said, "Before I escaped, they were going to start taunting the guards on the bridge, to try to get them to weaken their defenses. They had it timed."

"So you think they're planning an attack tonight and wanted the bridge defenses distracted?"

"Maybe, but a refugee uprising would bring more guards. Maybe the activity at the bridge is just a diversion. If Luke here can swim across, others could too. Maybe we should warn the guards."

Helen said, "Maybe we should do more than that."

"What do you mean, Helen?"

"If the bandits are agitating to pit the farmers against the guards, it's because they're afraid of us. The guards are under-strength. I've had that from James Fuller himself. They're short of men, short of ammunition and short of fuel for their vehicles. But they honestly want to protect us. They want to protect everyone from the bandits, but they're short of resources."

There was some grumbling. "They don't trust us. They're doing everything they can to keep us penned up."

Helen let some of her anger bleed freely. "It's the bandits who have killed our neighbors. It's the bandits who've burned our houses. It's the bandits who've raped farmer wives and daughters while laughing about it.

"If the City Guards are spread thin and the bandits are crossing by moonlight tonight, then somebody give me a gun. I'm going over that hill and stop them myself!"

...

James sat on the roof of a deserted house, keeping watch while his people rested in the yard, obscured from casual view by a high privacy fence built back when this was a rich Techno family home.

Below, Bob was trying to drum up support for a name for their raiding troop.

"I like Texas Rangers. They've got a whole history going in with a few men to handle a larger enemy."

Keith was playing the game. He had assumed the role of Bob's protector and seemed to enjoy it.

"I don't know. We're not the same organization. They might still exist, for all we know, somewhere else in Texas. Why not just 'Rangers' and make do with that?"

James shook his head and scanned the surrounding landscape again. When he saw a nearby street sign, he had to wince.

I could not have found a more ironic place to hide out.

The developer who carved the roads into the hillside and sold the houses must have wanted an Indian motif. The street names, Quanah Parker, Geronimo, Crazyhorse, and others were probably random choices used to sell houses, but so many of those warriors had waged military campaigns just like he was attempting.

He closed his eyes for a moment, listening to the chatter of his people, and the whinny of the horses. Once again, he was alone.

There was no one to talk to. He had never made a point of his position back in the city, but they all knew who he was. They followed him, and respected his leadership, but they kept their distance. The boy, Bob, was most likely to talk to him, but they had little to say.

I chose this life. I saw how Dad stepped up to the challenge when the Star destroyed his career, and everything he'd built. He could have become just another refugee, instead he took charge and saved the city of Austin. I knew what it cost him. I saw him in the night, home alone after he'd instituted the executions.

But he was right. The chaos of the Star only lasted days. Dad kept civilization alive.

I have to do the same.

James looked down at his watch. He pulled out the radio and turned it on. If everything was okay, he'd need to check in with the Guard and exchange info. He fumbled for his nubbin of a pencil and the notepad he carried to copy down the code groups.

The radio came alive with a strong signal. "James! Is that you? Thank God you're still out there." It was Captain Haige. What was he doing there at the bridge?

"Code!"

"No time for that! I'm at Mansfield Dam and it looks like thousands of bandits are moving in on us. We're shooting them down as fast as they come, but the numbers look endless. The road is packed shoulder to shoulder with them."

"Matthew, I've been harassing this group from the rear. They don't *have* thousands here. Hundreds yes, but it's not the main group. If they're packed that tight, then they're trying to fake you out. Hold that bridge!"

He yelled down at his people, "Rangers, the main attack at the bridge has started. Grab all the ammunition and let's get moving. We've got them where we want them."

Bob grinned wide and began checking his pistol.

. . .

Hek was surprised to see a big yellow school bus, smoking black diesel exhaust, stop in the middle of Congress Avenue. The guards conferred with the driver and half of the guards got on board, carrying their rifles at the ready.

Ah, ha! Action at last.

He turned his attention across the water. By moonlight, it looked totally deserted.

. . .

Captain Nunez of the Houston troops watched as the Austin guards watching them loaded up into a bus and drove off into the night. He waved to his second in command, "Our babysitters have gone. It's time to move into position."

...

Angela Morgan woke when she heard the noise. There was movement in the kitchen. She hurriedly threw on her robe and picked up the big crescent wrench she kept beside her bed.

Moving on bare feet and dreading every noise she made, she crept towards the kitchen.

She recognized the big pistol on the table before she recognized Ed.

"Hello Angela," he said, as he took another bite out of a hastily assembled sandwich.

He had to set it down when she attacked him with hugs, relief and sobs.

"I didn't know if you were still alive."

"I'm sorry. It was something I had to do. You understand."

And she did. Living with a fortune teller shackled by unyielding fate, she'd learned to accept it.

"But you came back."

He nodded. "I've done everything I was supposed to do. My part of all this is done. But...you know I don't know my own fate. And I can't read yours. So the only thing I could think to do was steal this gun from a bandit and come home to protect you."

"Ed." She held on to him, trying to get her head around the idea of Ed holding a gun.

Jane poked her head into the room, puzzled and frightened at the noise.

"Miss Gunn," he said, "the fighting starts tomorrow. If you would like to get your family to hide out with us, you'll need to move quickly."

"Thank you, sir." She ducked out.

Ed brushed a tear from his wife's face. "I thought I'd sit in the alcove above the front entrance and keep watch with this thing." He nodded toward the pistol.

"You have time for a shower and a decent change of clothes, though." She wrinkled her nose at the dirty white robe.

"Planning on it."

Blue's Defense

There were two crossings at Mansfield Dam, three when the water was low, but James had ordered the floodgates kept open for as long as the bandits threatened Austin. The waters raged and the low water bridge barely made a ripple in the wide torrent. The dam itself was topped by a narrow two-lane road long ago turned into a walkway, back when the four-lane bridge on Highway 620 was built to take the increased traffic.

The bandits had a token attack mounted on the narrow dam road, and the bulk of their force crammed into the passageway leading to the main bridge. The north side of the bridge climbed a hundred and fifty feet to the hilltops through a wide gully. The road curved at the top, so James could easily see how Captain Haige could have thought their numbers were endless. About five-hundred bandits were packed onto the north side road, with the front line peppering the barricades on the bridge before them.

It was an impressive assault. But it hadn't made allowances for the Rangers.

James waved to Nick and the other snipers on the other side of the road and they began their withering hail of bullets on the rear of the force.

A motion off to his right caught his attention. It appeared that Snowcap had broken free of the horses. No matter. The animals weren't part of this plan, so as long as they stayed out of the line of fire, it was fine with him.

No sooner had the bandits realized they were caught between two forces, with steep cliffs on either side boxing them in, than they saw a school bus arrive at the south side of the bridge to beef up the defenses. Front and rear, their forces were falling under the merciless fire, with the bulk of their number caught in the middle, trapped by their own perimeter, waiting for their turn to fall.

James watched, making his own shots count. It all depended on the bullets. Did they have enough?

...

"We can't let it slow us down! The bandits on the river won't wait for us to finish watching the soldiers fight. Let's get moving."

The *ad hoc* fighting force of farmers from the refugee camp with their limited firearms and farming utensils kept looking back at the battle raging on the bridge above them. But their blacksmith commander was right. They had to move on and get over the hill before the bandits made their river crossing uncontested. Some of them had already left, but it was nearly an hour or so before the camp was left with no one but the women, children, and the elderly.

Helen hadn't managed to talk anyone out of a pistol, but she'd wrangled a butcher knife. She argued with the woman who had taken care of her.

"Sorry, but I have to be part of this fight. You don't understand!"

Suddenly, across the hundred yards or so of churning black water, she saw a large white figure. *Snowcap?* She turned away from the lady and walked closer to the water.

"Snowcap!" she yelled. She put her hands wide in front of her mouth like a megaphone and yelled again, "SNOWCAP!"

The figure stopped, and began picking its way down the steep slope.

"Come on boy! Snowcap!"

There was a scream from the bridge, and first one man, and then another fell over the edge, falling the fifty feet or so to the water. The sounds of bullets echoed in the canyon over and over.

Should I be calling Snowcap? Can he cross this water?

It was one thing to contemplate swimming across the still water of the lake, but this boiling, churning water was enough to throw any swimmer, man or horse, against the rocks.

But Snowcap was still coming. He was getting close to the water's edge and she had no doubt he would make the attempt.

She hurried back to the fire and made a torch and lit it.

"Snowcap! I'm here!" She waved the torch back and forth.

The white horse entered the water and was quickly swept downstream.

The women remaining in the camp came up to watch the spectacle, bringing torches to see.

Struggling against the current. Snowcap was making progress. But even white, he was hard to see in the choppy waters.

"There he is," one of the other women called out. They all moved downstream fifty feet or so as the white horse struggled up out of the water.

Helen handed her torch to someone and ran up to greet him.

He reared once, and then submitted to be scolded and petted. He was huffing and puffing, eyeing with suspicion all the women who had come to see him.

"I missed you Snowcap. I was so worried."

Part of her heart that had been tightly bound up into a knot came loose as she made contact with her baby. She had thought he was lost. Lost forever to the butchers' bullets and their knives.

"Look! There's another one."

Downstream another fifty feet, a brown horse with a bedraggled passenger hanging around his neck staggered up onto the shore, barely able to hold his own weight. The woman on his back slid off into the water, and then got to her feet, weighted down with her dark dress.

It's her! Riding Nomad?

Helen took a step toward her, when a monster, a bare-chested giant of a man with a knife in his hand, thrust himself out of the water with a roar. He took three steps through the water, striding toward the women with the torches.

"No!" the woman in blue screamed and charged at the giant.

Helen moved to help, but many hands reached out to hold her back.

"Let me go!" But they pulled her back.

The bandit, if not Tobias, then maybe his brother, swung his hand to slap the woman in blue away, but she ducked and they fell together, struggling in the water.

Helen's anger was stronger than the women's fear and she broke free, running toward the thrashing bodies in the shallows. She pulled out the knife she'd borrowed, but it wasn't needed.

As she waded into the water, two bodies separated on their own. The giant rolled slowly on his back, a knife protruding from his chest. Helen pulled the woman in blue, limp, from the water. Others came at the last to help.

She likewise was lifeless, with a knife between her ribs.

Helen could barely see for the tears streaming from her eyes. She blinked at them and brushed her hair back. A fierce smile was locked on the dead woman's face.

A wordless feeling, the spirit of the nameless woman's determination, swept over her.

Helen saw a strap of blue, part of the dead woman's hem torn loose. She pulled it free and wrapped it around her arm, just above her own bandage. She stood, staring at the women's eyes surrounding them. She had to say something.

"This woman suffered more than any of us. She saved my life before. And now she saved yours. She deserves a decent burial."

The dead bandit was already drifting off into the current. *Good riddance.*

Helen made sure Nomad was okay. He must have followed Snowcap, just as he always did. She held his lead rope as he walked slowly over to check on the woman in blue. He nosed her shoulder, and then reluctantly moved aside as Helen handed his rope to one of the crowd.

"Take care of Nomad until I get back." She tightened the blue arm band and got up on Snowcap.

I'll be able to catch up with the others now.

She made sure her knife was secure in her belt and said to the others. "The Woman in Blue fought to her last breath to protect you. I'm not going to ignore her example."

...

Hek watched the Houston troops move into place a couple of blocks up from the camp.

If my brothers come through here, and if those soldiers can hold them, then this camp is excellent defensive ground.

It might not play out that way, but if he could see it, then so would the other hunters.

And the refugees nearest the bridge would be annoyances that could quickly be disposed of.

He walked over to Saul. Maria came out of the tent and smiled at him. She blushed. She'd been doing that a lot since he'd defended her against the man with the gun.

"Hector? What's up?"

He didn't smile. "I want you and your family to move."

"What? Why?"

He hesitated. How could he make them see what he could?

He pointed to the bridge. "I don't think the City Guard has it secured well enough. If I were a bandit leader, I'd wait until just the right moment, when the guards were distracted, and attack across this bridge. With the Houston troops setting up a defensive line in the city, anyone caught here will just be innocent bystanders in harm's way.

"I think you need to move, at least up as far as Shoal Creek. It might be better if you could make it even farther. But the important thing is to be far away from any bridge. That's where the fighting will be hottest."

Gabriel Luiz came out of the tent. "What's the problem?"

He explained again. They had to move.

He nodded. "It'll be difficult, but I can see your point. In the morning, we'll pack up...."

"No, sir. You can't wait for morning. You need to get your wife and your daughter as far away here as you can. The bandits will be here, soon. Hours, not days."

Maria looked frightened. "You'll come with us? Help us?"

He shook his head. "I expect I'll be fighting."

. . .

James rode Rose down through the dead bodies. She stepped gingerly, refusing to step on any of them. With Nick on guard above, he felt relatively safe, but it was a horrendous trip down to the bridge. He forced his mind to focus on the numbers of weapons to be salvaged, and the problem of moving enough of the bodies to allow vehicles through. He could not allow himself to dwell on the dead, nor think about which of the corpses he'd put down with his own hand.

Captain Haige stood in front of the barricades, a big smile on his face.

"I've never been happier to see anyone before in my life. How are you doing, James?"

He shrugged. "It's war. I'll think about that after."

They conferred. "I suspect about thirty made it free, I saw them heading downstream, still on the Lakeway side."

James nodded. "Casualties?"

"Five dead. Maybe twenty injured. It would have been much worse if they'd made it over the barricades."

Haige kept looking at Rose, as if expecting her to bite. Then he looked up the hill. Other defenders on horseback were making their way down to join them.

James said, "Our problems aren't over. I counted thousands of bandits gathering for this assault on Austin. We've only taken out ten to twenty percent of them. This was not the main thrust. I suspect it was designed to pull our forces away from our other defenses."

Keith Miller rode up with Bob. James called them over.

"Captain Haige, these are the Hill Country Rangers. This is Captain Haige of the Austin City Guard. Keith, did we have any casualties?"

"Um. Blue is missing, along with Nomad and Snowcap."

Haige asked, "Horses?"

Keith shook his head, "Blue was a Ranger. Nomad was her horse. Snowcap was...a horse on his own."

James shook his head. "I saw Snowcap break free. He might be roaming around. But Blue wouldn't have wandered, not while there were bandits to kill."

Haige asked, "Is this Snowcap a white horse?"

"Yes!"

"He crossed over during the battle. I couldn't take time to watch, but I saw him in the water."

"Well, we'll deal with it later. We have to find out where the bandits will cross and be ready to meet them. I doubt we'll have as tidy an outcome next time."

James put his hand on Haige's shoulder. "Captain, it's absolutely your responsibility to work with the Rangers on securing this bridge, even though we'll be pulling a lot of your men."

"Keith, the Guards are your equals and allies, and if there's any problem at all, work with Captain Haige here. I'm putting you in charge of the Rangers.

"The bandits are moving to the city side of the river, and so that's where I need to be." He saw Bob's face drop. "But make no mistake, as long as there's any bandits left in the Hill Country, I'll be riding with you to root them out."

...

It was surprisingly difficult to turn Rose over to Frank Thompson. He gave the Rangers their orders and a final pep talk before walking with Captain Haige across the bridge.

"Oh, by the way. We have your motorcycle. It's a bit beat up and a tire's shot out, but it's fixable. Some refugee girl came riding into the barricade and we thought she was a bandit."

James stopped in his tracks. "Pretty girl in a man's red shirt and jeans?"

"Yeah. We didn't manage to shoot her, but she was knocked unconscious when she crashed. We sent her down to the refugee camp."

"Show me."

Battle of the Rafts

Lake Austin was narrow, but wound its way through the hills in wide snakelike loops. Between his howls, Luke the spy admitted that the 'Wolves' were planning to cross at the next bend, several miles down the lake. It was much closer going over the ridge.

Snowcap was like the wind, passing clusters of farmers making their own way over the three to four-hundred foot rise. But when she ran out of road, still at the top of the a dark steep slope, she could already hear gunshots and the cries of battle. Moonlight reflecting from the water below showed too many objects to count. The bandits had built rafts.

"Can you make it down?" Helen asked.

Snowcap snorted and began making a careful way down the rabbit trails and through the cedar and oak. Helen had to take care against tree branches in her face, but she wondered about Snowcap.

Her baby had changed in just the few days that they'd been separated. Rather than being spooked by the gunshots, his ears perked forward, straining to hear. Rather than being flighty and second-guessing himself in this task, he was methodical.

Certainly it was the second time he'd done it tonight, but if she could still read his moods, he was eager for battle.

With no saddle, she had to be careful to stay in position or she'd slide off his back and tumble down the slope, maybe tripping him up in the process. She limited herself to encouraging noises. Now was not the time to distract him.

She was almost in the battle before she pulled him to a stop.

Several of the farmers had chosen positions ten to twenty feet above the water level, carefully shooting into the bandits, still paddling their way across.

The gunfire was all one-sided. She'd called them rafts in her head, but closer, they were much less, just bits of lumber hammered together to provide floatation for the men loaded down with guns and machetes. There was no way they could bring their weapons to bear on the defenders on the shore.

But there were far too many of them to count. By sheer numbers, some were making it to shore and with dirt under their feet, they were lethal. Still others were paddling downstream, trying to get out of the line of fire.

Helen put her hand on the butcher knife at her belt, but hesitated.

I didn't think this through. I can't ride any closer to the water, not with all these bullets flying. Snowcap would just be in the way, and likely get killed. And I can't fight with a little knife from horseback anyway.

She saw one of the farmers fighting with the bandits. He fell. The bandits were gunned down, but the farmer was still struggling on the ground.

I can help. Saving one of ours is as good or better than taking out one of theirs.

She'd treated wounds for years. Play to her strengths.

Snowcap didn't like being tied to a tree, but she made sure he was secure, back out of the heat of the battle.

"Stay safe for me. I'll be back when I can."

...

Every head at the Mansfield Dam refugee camp looked up when the motorcycle roared down the road and into the clusters of tents, parked wagons and makeshift corrals for the oxen. He looked from side to side, riding slowly, until he saw the brown horse. He pulled up and got off the bike he'd borrowed.

James walked up to the group of women. And then he saw her. Saying nothing, he approached and touched the cheek of the woman being cleaned of mud stains for her burial.

"She got the one who did it, didn't she?"

One of the women hesitated, and then said, "Yes. Stabbed him in the chest."

He nodded. "One of my best warriors. Take care of her."

After a moment, he turned to face them. "I'm here looking for Helen Black."

"You're him, aren't you?"

"What do you mean?"

"The city man. The Mayor's son. The guy who chased Helen into bandit country. Her beau."

He didn't know how to answer the mish-mash of truth and romantic gossip.

"It's very important that I find her. She is here?"

"She was. She's gone off on that white horse of hers to fight with the men."

With some questions, he got the story of Helen's unmasking of the bandit spy and their men heading off over the hill to fight the bandits.

As they talked, he noticed details about the camp, with hardly any men to be seen, and the women fearful for their own safety and worried about their men.

Two younger women came up. Both carried knives and had a blue ribbon knotted around their arms. "We have the spy."

He followed them to a smaller group. There were more who wore the blue ribbons. Bound and gagged, he was frantic to catch the man's attention. James couldn't feel anything for the rapist, surrounded by victims of his cult, waving knives.

"We were going to get more information out of him."

James nodded. Then he said, "I don't care what happens to him. I've already got the information I need.

"But I do care about you. Don't stain your souls over the likes of him. He's not worth it."

He turned and went back to the others. Whatever they chose to do, he didn't need to watch.

"I'll be sending City Guards to stand guard over the camp until your men get back.

"But right now, I've got to move some soldiers to go help them in their battle. Keep watch for any bandits that escaped from the slaughter at the bridge and signal if you see them."

He got back on the motorcycle and left before there were too many questions—ones that he didn't want to answer.

...

"Sergeant. It's good to hear your voice." He held the radio to his head, grateful for freshly-recharged batteries. As long as he wasn't in enemy held territory, he'd reserve code for critical information.

"And you, Sir. I need you to get to HQ as soon as possible."

James could hear the urgency in his voice. "Okay. But I have information about bandits crossing near Panorama Ranch. Do you have that on the map?"

"Um. Yes. There it is. Oh, not good for us. No easy way to get reinforcements there."

"Well. It's confirmed information. Likely the attack at Mansfield Dam was a diversion to keep us away from this. Send everything we have."

"Everything? Um. Copy code."

James scribbled down the message. He had been told of the Houston train while in hiding, but it appeared they had begun to spread out and hold several blocks once the City Guard detachment had been recalled to help with the Mansfield Dam attack.

"I repeat." He decided to speak in the clear. The Houston troops likely had the same history as the City Guard. With the same guns, the same tactics, and the same radios. Assuming they had been lucky enough to have stored their old electronics in metal boxes too. He didn't care if they heard him right now.

"Send all available troops. If the Houston soldiers want to walk around in our city, I'm not going to waste strength protecting them. If the bandits break through elsewhere, they're on their own."

. . .

Hek heard the bus arrive and watched as the last of the City Guards boarded and drove off. He wasn't the only one watching.

Across the water, on the roof of the seventy foot tall Hyatt Regency in South Austin, a signal fire was lit. It was on the backside of the little utility structure on the roof that likely held water tanks or elevators or something, but Hek knew it was there, so even if the flames were hidden, he could see the glare.

He growled and picked up the bundle that Maria had been packing. "What is this?"

"It's the laundry. It's almost done."

"Girl, the bandits have given the attack signal. I just saw it right over there. Get started moving, or I'll pick you up and carry you myself!"

She shrunk back from his ferocity. Others sleeping in the camp were peering out of their tents, wondering what the noise was. Hek cared nothing for them. For some crazy reason, he wanted this stupid little girl to be safe, and she hadn't the smarts to move when ordered.

Gabriel smiled sadly at the man. "Hector, if you would be so kind as to help me with this cart, we will be moving right now. Laundry or no laundry."

Hek fumed, his muscles aching to do just what he'd threatened, but instead he nodded, picked up the handles to the cart and glared at the girl.

She grabbed up her laundry bag and moved. He took another step, moving right behind her. Gabriel and Saul carried bundles and helped frightened mother Rebekka with her valuables.

A few others in the nearby tents had watched the show and started hurriedly throwing their things together as well.

...

A guard knocked on the Mayor's office door.

George shook awake. He'd slept in his chair, dozing off as he'd reviewed the endless reports dealing with keeping the refugee camps resupplied.

"Sir?" The guard opened the door.

"Yes, Cecil?"

"I've just gotten word to evacuate the building. The Houston troops have begun to fan out, and there's some fear they may decide to occupy the Driskill. I was told to make sure you were safe."

George sighed. "Yes. I guess that make sense."

After his last encounter with the Houston Ambassador, he'd looked up the history of Angelina Eberly and her cannon and re-read the tale of her defense of the Texas archives from Houston back in the early days of the State.

I could use a cannon myself right now.

Mindful that he might lose any of the documents in his office to Houston, he hurriedly emptied his safe of the most critical items and filled a large file box. Cecil helped carry it down to the ground floor and out to the car. Probably his house wasn't the safest place either, but other than going to Camp Mabry, that was the best he could think of.

No sooner had he gotten into the car than Cecil said. "Oh no!"

George looked, and saw Houston troops moving their way. "Go. Go north."

They pulled out onto the road and drove as fast as they could in the dark.

Brazos Street ended as they reached the Capitol grounds, lit by moonlight. George had an idea.

"Take the Capitol access road."

They turned left and then right at Congress, and into the curved road that looped around the imposing building. "Park behind the Capitol."

"Sir?"

"I need to stop there."

Cecil slid the Mayor's car into one of the parking spots in between vehicles that hadn't moved since the Star. They carried the record box inside.

"Who is there?" Jake Dennison came down the stairwell with a candle in his hand. "Mayor?"

"Hello, Jake. Remember that story you told at the dinner party a couple of years ago about the Legal Library?"

"The Legislature Reference Library? Yes."

"I have an emergency donation, but I'll want it back." He hurriedly described the problem.

Jake nodded. "As a State official, I shouldn't take sides between Austin and Houston, but just this once. Come on." He led the way up to the second floor. "And you'll owe me."

Cecil peered out the window. "I can see troops moving. I don't think we should risk the car."

Jake pushed the record box in among dusty books. "I know all the hiding places. Come on."

...

At 4th and Congress, since the Star put Schlotzsky's out of business, Chester Abraham had been running a little restaurant, making do with whatever supplies he could get at the Farmer's Market. He had his gripes about the city government like everyone else, but Chester's had become a popular place in town. It was his life. And he wasn't about to turn tail and run just because people were afraid the bandits were coming.

In the early morning hours, he was having second thoughts.

First, the Houston troops had moved into place, taking positions all along 4th Street and even moving into the ground floor shops. Three soldiers had positioned themselves in his doorway.

Chester lived just above his restaurant, and he was of mixed minds as he listened, crouched down in his bedroom, to the soldiers talking about how they would break his decoratively painted windows if the order came to fire.

He was ready to go yell at them, but then again, if they were there to keep the bandits away, he could live with broken glass. Better to stay quiet as a mouse.

The Invasion of Austin

Red of the Dragons was in the first wave of Hunters that streamed out of their hiding places in South Austin and rushed the Congress Avenue Bridge. Laughing, shouting hunters pushed aside the feeble barricades that had been set up to hold off an attack. But there were no defenders.

His smile was broad. The plan had worked brilliantly. The two feints in force up on Lake Austin had pulled all the defending troops away from the main city gates. Too bad about the Wolves and Bears that suffered those losses, but getting rid of Samson wasn't a bad call. The Rams and Lions with him today were more reasonable men.

Of course, the Dragons led the charge.

With hardly a slowed pace, they were across the bridge. Screams of farmer sheep waking to find that they'd been conquered again drew some of his men off to taste the fruits of victory. Maybe he'd discipline them later. Maybe not. This far it had been like the fortune teller predicted. None dared stand in his way. They were like a tide.

Glinting in the early dawn, the fabled Capitol building was straight ahead.

This one's different.

Back before the Star, when he wore a floppy beret as part of his uniform, he'd toured Washington D. C. and seen the sights. He hadn't gone into the U.S. Capitol building because it had security gates and it was too much hassle. He was interested in seeing the one before him. Maybe he'd take it as his new castle.

Others in the street with him were feeling the same, because he heard a low chant as they walked, "King Red. King Red."

Then, "Troops!" He focused on the next street up.

There were indeed troops. A line of them positioned out in plain sight with rifles pointing at them. The Dragons began to slow.

Red didn't. He knew nothing could stop him now.

There was a man, right in the center, waving a white flag.

Parley. He wants to talk.

Red kept right on walking, stopping about thirty feet in front of the line. There were more troops, out of sight. Some were positioned in the buidings along the street. More were just hidden by the buildings. The line extended both directions along the cross street.

"You're in my way."

The commander of the troops, in a dark green uniform, stepped forward a few paces. "I'm Captain Nunez representing the Houston Council."

Houston? What are they doing here?

"So what. I've got business up at the pretty little building up ahead."

"Houston does not care who rules Austin. But we do care about the railroads. As long as the rails and bridges and trains are left untouched, Houston will mind its own business."

Red estimated the numbers. His Dragons alone could take them. But this force was well armed, and he was sure he could see a machine gun nest up in the tall building on the right. A quick, decisive charge would overwhelm the uniformed grunts on the ground, but he'd lose many men before he could root out the machine gun.

And it didn't match the prophecy. All troops in Austin would be swept aside.

"I have no interest in your big metal toy train sets. As I said, I've got business up ahead. Get out of my way and I'll tell the boys to ignore you, for now."

Nunez nodded. He signaled to his forces and they stood aside.

Red spoke to Brent at his side. "Pass the word."

His Hunters strode on through, although not without a few sneers at the Houston soldiers as they passed.

. . .

Helen cut another strip from her borrowed white dress and bound the man's arm tightly to stop the bleeding. She'd lost count of how many battle-field dressings she'd made. And she was deeply grateful for the morning light.

The fight had been mixed. With more defenders arriving throughout the battle, it had never seemed likely that they would be overwhelmed by the bandits, but it wasn't a clear victory either. As soon as the bandits realized that the stretch of shoreline that had been their target was too well defended, many had let the current carry them farther downstream.

Some of the farmers moved down with them, and discovered buses unloading soldiers to help down at the WatersEdge houses. Soon, some of the injured came back in her direction, once the word was out that she was treating the wounded.

Farther downstream from that, the shoreline was again free of roads and the ground too steep. The morning fog was making it impossible to see them. Some of the bandits surely came ashore in that undefended terrain, but they had to be scattered out.

I guess it was unrealistic to think we could stop them all.

"Thank you."

"Just stay quiet. Don't move unless you have to, or your wound could break back open. I'll try to get someone to come and move you."

His eyes got wide and he raised his arm.

"No. Please ..."

She was knocked aside and the knife was tugged free of her belt. In a flash, it came down in the farmer's chest.

Helen looked up into her nightmare.

Wolf-headed Samson grinned down at her. "Well if it isn't the little girl with the stinger. I guess I'm fated to take knives away from you."

"You!"

Quickly, his hand slapped her down to the ground. He growled, "I told you. Women don't talk!"

He tore a strip from her skirt and bound a gag around her head, and then with his knee on her back, he bound her wrists behind her.

Too much had happened to her. Terror had come and gone. Pure boiling anger was all that she felt as he lifted her over his shoulder and waded out into the water. He snagged a crude raft left on the shore and they began to drift silently downstream, hidden by the morning fog.

Everything in Helen's head was washed away by the thought, *I will watch you die!*

...

James was torn between wanting to be at the bandit crossing at Lake Austin, and getting back to HQ to pick up the details he hadn't been able to get over the radio.

Sergeant Willowby's urgency swayed him, although he promised he'd get back to make contact with Helen Black as soon as he could. He owed her that much for Rose. He had an apology to make for his casual dismissal of her horses when they first met.

Other than the heavily armed guards at the gate, Camp Mabry seemed nearly deserted. Everyone was out fighting.

"Get in here...Sir." Sergeant waved him in as he stopped the motorcycle.

The man was harassed and dark eyed. He had been on the radio, keeping the battles organized for too many hours to count.

The map he had laid out on the table looked horrible.

"Both the Mansfield Dam and lake crossings were feints. The main force, something over two thousand men, were hidden in South Austin, waiting for us to move out the last of our defenses. They walked right in with hardly a shot fired."

"What about Houston?"

"They lined up, and then let them pass through. No exchange of hostilities, from what we can determine."

James felt sick. He'd misjudged Houson and the bandit commander both. It was his call that triggered this invasion.

"And Sir, no one has seen your father. He was evacuated from the Driskill, but he didn't show up at the house."

"Where are the bandits?"

Willowby showed him on the map. "They're spreading out from their march up Congress Avenue, but the Capitol building appears their main focus. A scout with binoculars on top of the Wells Fargo building reports that the bulk of them are setting up camp on the Capitol grounds. They're butchering the cattle, cutting down some trees and setting up roasting pits. But parties go out at irregular intervals, ransack buildings, and then return."

"So, they're staying put. That's one item in our favor."

"But the Capitol is defensible. If they pulled back inside, we'd have to attack over open ground."

"How much fuel do we have left?"

"We've been draining the tanks keeping the bus shuttling troops around. Not a whole lot left. Not enough, in other words."

"There is a tanker car on the Houston Train. What do you think?"

"Probably diesel, but most of the Houston troops are defending the train. We can't take them with the forces we have left. The only way to get to that oil is to negotiate with them."

James shook his head. "I won't negotiate with snakes. They want Austin to burn. They'll absorb all of our trading partner cities and have clear rail access to the West Texas oil fields.

"By the way, any word from the Lamars?"

"No."

He nodded, dismissing that side trail. It had been a long shot at best, and now that Houston had shown its true colors, a load of crude oil was not going to change anything. The bandits had probably destroyed rail lines and bridges throughout the San Antonio region, and all Houston needed was to keep them from doing the same here.

Would the city have been in better shape if I'd never chased off after them, and gotten myself trapped?

Keep your mind on track! Regrets later.

"Keep a bus running as long as we have fuel to move guards back into the city. Set up a defensive position here." He pointed to Rio Grande Street. "We can move supplies there, even after they discover us. Strength here will focus their attention in that direction."

"Won't that just lead them into the residential sections across Shoal Creek?"

"They'll go that way sooner or later. I saw how they attacked in the Hill Country. They're attracted to fancy homes more than shacks. They'll go west, no doubt about it.

"Now I need to refill the motorcycle and get back to check on the lake crossing. We still don't know how many got through."

"Sir, don't get yourself trapped."

James smiled. "Oh, you'll back me up. You've done a great job while I was gone. Besides, I'll have my radio on. I'll let you know the instant I have trouble. And you let me know the instant you hear anything about my father."

...

Cecil, Jake and George hid in the Speaker's Apartment, praying that the bandits wouldn't notice the relatively hidden room behind the House Chamber. Jake was in torment, as bandits were breaking up priceless wooden antique furniture to use with their bonfires.

Cecil checked the windows carefully. "They're everywhere, but they're ignoring the car. I can see it from here. They think it's just another of the dead ones. If we can get through the window, we might make a dash for it. But it'd be risky."

George shook his head. "If we can ride it out here, eventually the City Guard will bring the fight to them."

...

A few feet away, Red sat in the comfortable Speaker's chair in the House Chamber. He scowled as the reports came back.

"We went all through the hotel. We even found the office the Mayor used, but it had been cleared out in a hurry. It was littered with junk. He must have heard we were coming. The shopkeeper we found hiding in his store said he cleared out just hours ago. But he claimed he didn't know where they went.

"Maybe the Houston troops know. They were all over the place before we got there."

Red shook his head. "We won't get anything from the uniforms.

"Tell me again what the shopkeeper said."

"Um. Just that his car was parked out in front of the hotel overnight, and then it took off, heading north."

"This way? To the Capitol?"

"He didn't say. He sort of broke after awhile."

Red nodded. "Did you get a description of the car?"

"Yep. Rolls Royce. Old style."

Another of the dragons said, "Hey, there's one of them in the parking spaces around the back of the building.

"You don't think he's here, do you?"

Red nodded. "It's fated that we meet, here. Why not? You, check the car. You two, start checking every single room in this monstrosity of a building. I just bet he's holed up like a mouse somewhere."

Red Coronation

James passed the bus on Highway 2222 and waved it down to get the detailed directions to the battle. They were heading to the new defensive position in town. He noted their tired faces and gave them what encouragement he could. He was exhausted as well.

If this were an academic military exercise, I'd be figuring out how to surrender without turning over all the chips.

But he couldn't imagine negotiating with either of his adversaries. *That says something about me, but I'm too tired to figure out what.*

His bike took a wobble on River Place Boulevard, and he started the windy path towards the lake. *And I'm going to have to close my eyes, for at least a few minutes, or I'm going to take myself out of the game.*

...

"Maybe two hundred, three hundred. It was foggy by dawn, so I don't know how many got by us," the big man said, looking off to his side.

"You did a great job. Without your efforts, it could have been a lot worse." James could see that the blacksmith was hiding something. But he couldn't tell what. "I'm sorry I couldn't have gotten more men here sooner, but their spies chose this position carefully. Even with directions, I got lost on the way."

He nodded solemnly. "Helen saw through the spy. We'd have sat there all night arguing around the fire if she hadn't recognized him."

"Helen is here, isn't she? That's what they said at your camp."

He took a deep, slow breath. "We found her horse. The white one."

James frowned. "Snowcap. And Helen?"

He shook his head. "She was doctoring the injured. We found a man she'd bandaged, but with a knife in his chest. No sign of her."

James swallowed, and nodded. The story was clear enough. If she'd left Snowcap, and if the farmers couldn't find her on this narrow strip of shoreline, then she'd been taken away downstream by the bandits.

James said, "She survived before. She's strong. She'll make it through."

"I know."

Neither of them fully believed it.

. . .

James had pulled off the side of the road and stretched out on the lawn chair of a relatively intact, but deserted house. He promised himself a fifteen-minute catnap, but he almost slept through the radio, calling his name.

"What?" He pulled himself upright and shook off a nightmare of gutted bodies and disappointed faces. He brought the radio to his ear.

"Yes. I'm here."

"There's activity at the Capitol building. All the bandits are gathering for something."

"Okay, I'll be back there as soon as I can."

. . .

Hek breathed a sigh of relief as a patrol of Rams were stopped by a runner, and they all turned back north. He slipped his knife back into his belt.

What am I doing? Was I going to fight off my own brothers?

But he had been pushing the Luiz family hard, keeping them out of reach of the hunters who had been taking their pick from the trapped refugees. It was a game with them, making sure they had the numbers to overwhelm any pockets of resistance the refugees might muster. Maria was nearly out of her mind, hearing the screams of girls who hadn't been as quick as she.

But if the patrol had caught up with us, they'd have called my name. She would have known.

. . .

Red smiled at the three captives. "Which of you is the Mayor?"

George stared at him. "That's me."

He looked at Cecil, "And you?"

"Bodyguard."

"Looks like you failed." He made a gesture, and one of Red's favored circle, with him the night of the prophecy, put a knife in him.

As the soldier crumpled, he asked Jake Dennison, "And what's your role in the big scheme of things?"

Jake had a notion that claiming to be the representative of the State of Texas might not be his best choice.

"I'm a historian. I was keeping the building preserved."

"A historian, eh? Good. Watch and record and earn your keep."

. . .

As the bearded men streamed into the Capitol grounds, one figure moved up to the ornate, wrought-iron fence along the west side of the property. He moved along the tree line, looking for a good view of the front steps where the large crowd was gathering. He hesitated, as he got a better look at who was there at the top of the steps, then kept on until he finally chose his spot. He pulled a rifle with a scope from his bag and braced the barrel against the fence. He aimed, centering his scope on the beaming man with red hair that seemed to be the center of attraction.

The knife in his side came as a complete surprise, but the man behind him caught the rifle before it hit the ground.

"Sweet," he said, as he got a good look at the weapon, ignoring the man at his feet. He slung it over his shoulder and walked into the grounds with the other hunters.

. . .

Red waved to the crowd, holding a blade aloft, and a cheer went up. Some started chanting "King Red." But he shook his head.

"No, brothers. I'm not King. Not yet."

The others quieted down.

"Sons of the Hunter follow the natural way. Man and beasts follow the same law. They challenge for leadership."

There was a cheer.

Red grabbed George one handed by the collar and displayed him. Although they were roughly the same size, Red was all muscle.

"Meet the Mayor of Austin, an undisputed King in all but name. He has ruled this city since the Star."

George eyed the faces and straightened up, disdaining being held. There was theater here, and he recognized it. Well, he would play his role, but he'd not show them a craven captive.

Red had the stage. "The Lions roar and claw for supremacy. Rams butt heads.

"But Dragons! Dragons take heads!"

Red swung the blade with all the momentum of his body. The blade had been sharpened daily for this task. George's head fell free with a splash of red as his heart took a moment to realize he was dead.

"Today, I proclaim myself Red, King of the Hill Country!"

The roar of the Hunters was deafening.

...

Helen held her chin up, it was the only way she could breathe. She'd been floating under the dock for an endless time.

Samson of the Wolves had cheerfully explained what he was doing, when he felt all over her body for a concealed knife.

"Predators in the wild sometimes take more than they can use right then. To save the good stuff for later, they'd hide it in the bushes, or like alligators, under a tree branch in the river." He tightened the knots securing her arms behind her back and looping a rope across her chest under her shoulders. He pushed her off the edge of the dock.

She was tightly gagged and could barely breathe. He watched as she kicked helplessly, just making sure she floated on her back with her head above water.

"Assuming they don't forget, or find something even better, they come back later to snack on what they'd saved."

She floated under the dock, out of sight until the rope tugged at her chest ant held her in place.

"So girlie," he'd said, walking away, "assuming I don't get distracted, I'll be back for you later."

The strong current kept her trapped. Gagged, she couldn't call out, even if someone were walking on the dock. The position of the rope made it impossible to get any purchase with her legs against the dock supports.

If I could just move my arms....

But she'd been tied securely. Even if she could bear the pain, she didn't have the strength and leverage to dislocate her shoulder or something like that.

If she dozed, the water would splash over her face and she choked. Sometime in the next few hours, it would happen again and she'd be unable to clear her breathing passages in time.

But she could not wish for Samson's return.

...

Sergeant Willowby was waiting as James pulled up next to HQ.

"You're here." The man's face was grave.

"Sorry I couldn't be quicker. I saw a group of about a dozen bandits near Laguna Gloria. I took a side route, rather than try to challenge them myself. They were heading towards downtown. I suspect they were from the lake-crossing group."

Willowby only nodded.

James frowned. "What's up?"

"I just got a report from the Capitol."

James pulled off his gloves. "Come on. Don't keep me guessing. I've had nothing but bad news. I'm sure this is the same."

"Your father was there."

"Was?"

"The bandit leader...beheaded him, and declared himself King. The scout could hear them from a quarter-mile away."

James felt his guts twist inside him. But part of him was detached, observing his own reaction. His recent experiences had desensitized part of his brain to the brutality of it. But when he took a step, he wobbled.

Willowby was quickly there to steady him.

James pushed him aside. "I'm okay." He waved his hand. "Tell me everything else. I need to know everything. We're running out of options."

Willowby opened the door and they went inside.

The other bad news helped him put his personal tragedy into perspective. The beheading on the Capitol steps told him a lot. The attacks had all been leading up to that point. The bandits were combining the forces of their different clans under one leader, and that leader was using the symbolism of the Capitol and taking the life of the Mayor to elevate his status to the next level, a regional leader, not just one clan boss of many. That he could get away with it told James that the clans wanted more than the simple life of a bandit. Otherwise he wouldn't have gotten the support he needed for the attack on Austin.

It also meant he probably didn't need the Capitol anymore. Up to this point, there had been fringe raids on vulnerable refugees or people who hadn't fled the downtown area, but probably, after a blowout celebration party, he'd turn his men loose to raid and burn the city, just as they'd done in the hills.

"We're out of time, Paul."

"I know. And I'm out of ideas."

James straightened his back. "We've come to the end game time, then? What about sending our guys to every refugee camp and through the neighborhoods and tell everybody to get out. Send everyone north. We could burn the last of our diesel carrying some with the bus. The town is going to burn, but ..."

The telephone rang.

James frowned and picked it up. "Hello?"

"James Fuller?" it was the flat voice of Hodges. "I just wanted you to know that my lookout has seen eight fuel transport trucks entering town from Highway 183."

"Fuel trucks?" He couldn't quite grasp it.

"Yes. The one in the lead appears to be the one that John Lamar and his son took. Sam reports different markings on the others, but he can't make them out from his distance."

"Thank you, Mr. Hodges."

The phone clicked, and James hung it up.

"Fuel trucks?" asked Sergeant Willowby. "What fuel trucks?"

"It appears the Lamars have made friends."

"How...how many?"

James grinned, "Enough."

Object Lesson

School buses started arriving at every refugee camp. Two drove up and parked beside a baseball field at the old Austin High School.

The guard with the bullhorn said, "Time to move! The bus on your right is taking refugees to Georgetown, out of range of the bandits. Get on now. Carry no luggage. We'll bring you back when it's all over.

"If you're ready to fight, get on the bus to your left. We need every man with a will, whether you have a weapon or not. We can use you, and you *will* make a difference."

Down the road in the distance, Hek could see other busses, making the same pitch to a different group of refugees.

He nodded and grabbed Maria's arm. "You're getting on the refugee bus now. All of you. The women have to get out of harm's way."

Maria asked, "What about you?"

"I'm going to the fight. I should have done so before now. I'm not going to wait any longer."

Saul said, "I'm going to fight too."

His mother said, "No!"

Hek shook his head. "Stay with your family. They need your protection."

His father put his hand on his son's arm. "Yes, we need you. Your mother needs you."

Hek pulled away and sprinted toward the fighters' bus. He didn't look back.

The guard at the door of the bus nodded as he stepped inside.

The refugee bus was revving its engines. It was full, and another one drove up to take its place.

Saul was the last one to get on board the fighter bus. He grinned at Hek and wiggled his way through the passengers to get close, but he had to stand and use the hand strap.

As they pulled away from the curb, a short middle-aged man stood up and introduced himself.

"My name is Chester Abraham. I run Chester's Restaurant at Congress and 4th. I want to tell you what I heard."

. . .

Captain Nunez was checking on Ambassador Lloyd's comfort in the first passenger car when he heard a rumble. "Sorry, sir. I need to go check on that."

Several of the men had heard it as well, and were outside when the Sherman battle tank appeared from around the corner and pointed it's cannon at the engine.

Nunez jumped to order the men to seek cover.

A man with a microphone in his hand spoke from the hatchway on the tank.

"Captain Nunez," came the loud voice from a speaker on the tank.

Gunfire rang out and bounced harmlessly off the rounded sides. Machine-gun fire from the tank raked the building to the side where Houston had put its own machine-gun nest. The speaker closed the hatch, but his amplified voice continued. "The rails behind you have already been ripped up. A second tank is taking aim at the other engine, just as I have at this one. Unless you cease fire, your train will be a pile of burning rubble in one minute."

Nunez got on his radio and quickly confirmed the presence of an even larger M60 tank behind them.

Nearly at the time limit, he called a cease fire and walked out with a white flag.

"What do you want?"

James opened the hatch and called out, "Now!"

From behind the buildings on both ends of the train, large numbers of angry men poured out and surrounded the Houston force.

James continued, his voice straining to contain his anger, "Five witnesses observed your deal with the bandits to turn Austin and the refugees over to those savages to rape and kill and burn! Their testimony has been written down for your war crimes trial.

"I make you this one offer. Lay down all your weapons, and all your men, except you and the Ambassador, can board buses that will arrive shortly. They'll be taken to Brenham where they can find their own way back to Houston."

"And the Ambassador and myself?"

"Will be detained until talks can be held with the Houston Council. I suppose your fate depends on whether they claim responsibility for your actions or not."

Nunez waited, and turned to the train where the Ambassador whispered something to him.

"And if we decide to fight?"

James shrugged. "My father has just been *butchered* by the man you made your deal with." He pointed to the ring of men surrounding them. Only a few held weapons, but all looked ready to fight. "We have all had friends raped and killed because of your despicable actions."

He took a deep breath. "Personally, I've spent the last six months getting these tanks in prime working condition and I'd just love the excuse to blast your invasion force into oblivion. Even if the tanks can't get you all, not a one of your men will survive the day.

"Sorry Captain. You can't run. You can't win. I already have you. The word of your betrayal is out. I'm offering your men their lives."

. . .

Sergeant Willowby took a second from his duties getting the final fueling queues set up and running. Against his instincts, he'd accepted the help of nearby residents to manage the traffic, turning more guards loose to drive buses and manage the volunteer fighters.

But he also had to play host to their guests.

The Midland truck drivers weren't soldiers, although they all carried a pistol at their belt, and there were rifles in the cabs. Ruben Franklin said, "We'd like to help. That's why we came."

Willowby smiled and shook his head. "I appreciate it, but you men and the fuel you brought were just the help we needed. And right now, I'm not about to send you back home with injuries, or your trucks with any scrapes. My commander would have my head."

Ruben chuckled. "Commander Fuller looked a bit intense. Are you certain he's the man authorized to make the trade deal?" He was still a little overwhelmed by the way the young man had dictated the five-page document off the top of his head, as if he'd memorized it.

It was a pretty broad agreement, and he'd have to take it back to Boss Richardson for a line by line inspection and approval, but if the Boss wanted the opinion of a simple truck driver, he liked it.

There was the IIS station which would put the MOB in instant contact with cities all over Texas and the world. There was the fuel-for-grain exchange, which had final prices to be negotiated, but he'd offered to pay Houston prices for the good-faith shipment they'd already delivered, and that was five times what they were getting from the northern cities.

Then there was the agreement to restart the Texas Railroad Commission, for the railroads. Austin and the MOB and other governments to be added later would fund the restoration of the rail system in Texas, and Ruben had seen more of those tracks than most men. There were bridges needing repair and places where flash floods had left rails in the air, stretched across a new gap in the terrain. And then there were the ghost trains, those big cross-country trains of a hundred cars or so that had been stranded by the Star. Who knew what was still in all those containers? Certainly the bones of the crew, stranded deep in the desert under the radiation from the sky, weren't telling. All of those would need repair, even if just to move them to a siding out of the way.

But even more than just getting the trains running again, Ruben liked the whole idea of it. It was very MOB-ish, with cities coming together to build something bigger, like it was in the old days.

Even more than all the details in the agreement, Ruben was pleased at what it didn't contain. Boss Richardson had briefed him privately and there were certain things it was too early to discuss, like a mutual defense pact.

Neither Austin, nor the MOB had reason to trust the other. And neither had any real idea of the other's capabilities. It was one reason he'd offered to help. Not to spy, not really. But just to look.

Of course, when all those military tanks wheeled out, that was impressive.

. . .

Hek pulled Saul out of the main group getting instruction on how to use their new weapons.

"Do you know how to use a gun?"

"Yes. I've hunted rabbits and squirrels. Dad and I have gotten deer two seasons now."

"What gun did you use?"

"Dad just called it a deer rifle."

"Bullets bigger than these?"

"Um. Yes."

Hek nodded. "That's what I thought. These Houston rifles are M16's. They look fresh. I still see some cosmoline that hasn't been totally cleaned off. They use a smaller caliber bullet."

He coached Saul through the use of the weapon, sometimes duplicating what was being said to the larger group, but Hek wanted the boy to survive, so he wanted him to know everything.

"It's the ammunition. M16's were great back in the day, when the USA could manufacture tons of bullets and let the grunts spray bullets by the hundreds, by the thousands. But if that crate over there is all the M16 ammo that we've got, these guns could be useless by the time this battle's done.

"Your dad probably got reloaded ammo, and that is probably charged with homemade black powder. That won't work with these M16's, at least not well.

"What I'm saying now is hoard your ammo. Don't use the burst fire settings unless you have to."

Hek showed him how to hold the gun, how to aim. By the time they were loading the bus, he'd done all he could.

He gestured for the boy to lean closer.

He whispered, "Whatever happens. Whatever you see, or hear, I want you to tell your sister this—you saw me get shot in the battle, and then never saw me again."

"What? What do you mean, Hector?"

"I mean I'm not going back when we're done!"

...

"Bravo! Bravo! King Red." He clapped.

Red looked up from the table, where he'd been savoring a large slab of steak.

"Samson?" He narrowed his eyes. "When did you show up?"

He pushed his wolf-hat back slightly. "Oh, I've been here since before you gave your pretty speech and named yourself King." His voice changed, getting choppy and bitter. "I had to stay in the back, since, you know, not all my men had shown up yet."

"But you survived the raft crossing okay?"

"And so did some of my men." Samson raised his voice so everyone could hear him. "And you know something else about my men?"

"What?"

"They are all well armed!"

Samson pulled the rifle with the telescopic sight from his shoulder. "See what I picked up? I took it off a sniper that was ready to put a bullet in your head.

"You see I couldn't have that! It was before you had declared yourself King. It was before the prophecy was complete."

Red nodded, trying to divine what Samson was getting to. More and more of the celebrating hunters were stopping their revelries and turning to watch.

"Sit down, have a steak. Sounds like I owe you one."

"In a minute. I just wanted to tell you what I thought of that prophecy."

Red gestured for him to go on.

"You see, I talked to some of your men. I had the whole story, word for word. It was fascinating stuff. That fortune teller walking into your camp and handing you the keys to the kingdom like that. It'll make a fascinating object lesson for the future, as we sit around the fire."

"Object lesson?"

"Yes, of course." Samson was waving his arms, gesturing as he talked. The rifle was like a part of his arm.

"You see the thing I noticed right off about your prophecy—there was no ending to the thing. No 'happily ever after'. No 'and he lived a long full life and begat many cubs'. Nothing like that."

The rifle fired. Red jerked with a red spot in his chest. He made a sound as he slumped down with his face in a slab of red meat.

All through the crowd, Samson's men revealed their weapons. There was a cry of anger, punctuated with a single shot, and another body collapsed.

Samson smiled broadly at the crowd. "You see! Object lesson. You can't accept great gifts from your enemy! It's not truly yours unless you take it from his dead hand." He snatched up the knife from Red's hand, with a slice of beef still dangling from it. He bit, chewed and swallowed.

"Just so it's clear—I'm Samson, King of the Hill Country!"

King Samson

Jake Dennison, former Texas State Comptroller, now apparently the first historian of the Kingdom of the Hill Country, scribbled furiously on his yellow legal pad, trying to keep up with the speech this new king was giving to solidify his position.

Privately, he wondered if the bandit could make his coup stick. Jake hated Red, not the least for his ruthless murder of the Mayor, but at least all his followers had cheered him on. This new one, from a different clan, the Wolves, made his plea that Red had sacrificed the Bears and most of his Wolves as cannon fodder in the drive to take the city. His audience was paying a lot of attention to those with their guns out.

Samson was praising the Hunter virtues, and Jake had to grit his teeth and copy down the words. His own life was at stake here.

...

April was treating Sam to an apple pie that she and her mother had baked. He griped about being the guinea pig, but the pie did smell very good. April was in a good mood after he had come back down from the roof and told her about Joshua Lamar and the tanker trucks. She had been the one to see the potential in Joshua's IIS offer. It had been her idea to give special consideration to Joshua's request, and she'd been fretting that her action would come back to haunt her.

Seeing it turn out right was a big relief. Sam was happy, since he was really the only one she could share her good spirits with. They were conspirators together, and it was just not something the other girls would understand.

He got one bite into the pie. It was good.

And then the phone chimed.

He jumped up. "I'll go get it." April's mother nodded.

"I'll save your piece."

He ran down the corridor and snatched up the handset.

"Yes, sir?"

"I'll be arriving at the Whiting Building in twenty minutes. At that time, but not before, I will need you to unseal the main entrance and come out to help me with a special task. Can you be ready?"

"Yes. What's the special task?"

. . .

Joshua shifted gears on the flatbed truck, pleased that the training he'd picked up from his father let him make this run on his own.

During the trip to and from West Texas, he'd had long hours to think about his future, and to talk with his father. Even from the beginning, James Fuller had promised that Austin would pay them enough so he wouldn't have to worry about money.

But that was assuming the bandits were defeated and the trade deal with the MOB went through. Still, regardless of what his father made out of the deal for the family, he still had his own concerns.

He wanted to be able to earn a living and support a wife, come what may. If he could keep doing these jobs for James Fuller, he'd be in a much better position to be independent.

He wanted to be someone a girl could fall in love with.

A particular face came to mind.

But then, the distant sound of an explosion shook him out of a pleasant daydream.

. . .

The Capitol grounds were chaos, with the smoking crater where the cooking pits had been. Bodies were scattered across the torn-up lawn.

The more experienced men knew the sound of the incoming round and had reacted, but even the ones who had avoided the blast suddenly found themselves in a hail of small arms fire, some of it clearly automatic. Bodies crumbled all around.

Those that could, hurried into the wide open front entrance of the Capitol building.

And then there was the rumbling sound of tanks, approaching from all directions.

. . .

Jake Dennison grabbed his pad and hurried upstairs. Bandits that had been up there, were now hurrying down to see what was going on. Jake wanted to see too, but he preferred the vantage point of the railing above.

Samson was snarling, stalking around the room, ordering people to the windows. Broken glass was scattered around, some from the blast of the explosion, some from the incoming rounds, and some from bandit defenders seeking to stick their rifles out.

But the hail of bullets quickly faded to an erratic shot from time to time.

The rumbling noise stopped. Jake checked the outside view.

Tanks. I never thought I'd see this day, here at the Capitol.

His personal fears quickly overcame his protective feelings for the building.

Four of them, coming from all directions. I don't like the angle of those big guns.

No one knew he was here. If they even thought about him, they might assume he was already dead.

Waving to the people outside is probably not a good idea either.

He couldn't see any of the small-arms shooters, just the tanks. From the lack of return fire, probably the bandits couldn't see their attackers either.

Down below, Samson was conferring with his staff, at least by the looks of their outfits. They all had a coyote hide costumes.

The light changed, and he checked outside again.

Just clouds. It was a big bank of clouds moving in. *Are the rains coming back?*

. . .

Hek and Saul waited on the roof of a six-story office building, with the Capitol grounds laid out below.

"Just relax, kid. This could take hours—days even. Fuller is trying to keep casualties to a minimum on our side, so he's not wasting lives trying to rush the place. They're stuck inside, probably with little or no food. If I were inside, I'd wait until the middle of the night before staging a mass breakout."

Saul asked, "Would that work?"

"Possibly. At this range, you're not going to be able to hit anything with any accuracy. We got so many of them in the first minute because of surprise and because so many guns were spraying bullets at the same time. But if, say a hundred or so of them raced out the western side of the building all at once, only the shooters on that side would have any chance at all, and the sheer numbers would protect some of them. They'd be in among the buildings and protected before they could be wiped out."

"What about that big gun on the tanks? That would kill many at once."

"Yeah, but how fast can they fire? How fast can they aim?"

. . .

James sat in the tank, watching the activity inside through the heavy glass periscope. It would have been better if they had signaled for a parley first, but their leader was a schemer.

He picked up the radio.

"Sergeant Willowby, how are the refugee evacuations coming?"

"It's dwindling. Right now, we're squabbling with the people who don't want to leave their livestock."

"I need the buses."

"Okay, but try not to get them too shot up."

. . .

"Hek, there's something...."

They peered over the edge of the roof, careful to not present a tempting target. A big string of yellow school buses, all of them spewing black exhaust, were entering the Capitol grounds. Shots came from inside, but it didn't slow or stop the process. All the buses were circling counterclockwise, steering cautiously as their drivers crouched low to avoid being shot. As the first bus completed its loop, it put on the brakes, parked close to the building. Someone tried to make a dash from inside, but a short burst of machine gun fire from the tank put a stop to it.

When the second bus stopped right behind the first one, actually bumping, Hek said, "Ah, he's tightening the noose. The city's got enough buses to make a tight barrier around the building. That mass breakout I mentioned? Can't happen if they have to crawl over or under the buses."

On cue, the four tanks, three of one kind, and one smaller, rumbled forward, moving up like evenly-spaced dark pendants on the growing necklace of yellow.

"Hey, a white flag!"

It didn't stop the process. It took another ten minutes to complete the barricade.

...

Joshua found the Whiting building with his hand-drawn map. As he pulled up, a young teenager waved him around to a loading dock. Backing the flatbed trailer up to the the dock was a lot more difficult that just driving forward, and he had to make several attempts before it came to a slightly bumpy stop.

When he got out, Mr. Hodges was there to greet him. "I'm glad you found the place. Go over and stand with Sam, while I move the station onto the truck.

The youngster waved. "Hi. I saw your trucks on the highway."

"Oh? You were at the IIS station when I visited, weren't you?"

"Yep. I work there."

Hodges was obviously an expert with the fork lift. He lifted the packaged IIS station and deposited it in the center of the flat bed with a minimum of moves.

"It's up to you to secure it."

Sam and Joshua worked together to secure the straps that held it all in place.

After Hodges parked the fork lift, brought down the bay doors and secured their locks, he talked to them.

"I'd advise getting to know each other. I am recommending to James Fuller that you, Joshua, go with the IIS station to Midland and put it into service, with Sam to be your instructor.

"Sam, with your experience, I would have recommended you for the position of IIS station operator, but because of your age, you would have difficulty getting the necessary respect from your new customers. Do you think you can cope with the journey and being gone for a month or so until Joshua is fully trained?"

"Oh, yes! I'd love the chance to see other places. Of course, I'll get flack from April. She doesn't think anyone knows IIS operations better than she does."

Hodges nodded. "But I really don't think her mother would approve of her taking this journey.

"Joshua, what do you think about taking the position of IIS station operator in Midland, away from friends and family for at least a year?"

He looked at the man's shadowed face and had to stop and think. *A responsible position, yes! But away from her?*

· · ·

Helen blinked the stinging sensation from her eye. The last ripple had caught her off guard, and by the time she'd finished coughing, her eyes were watery and raw.

Was that thunder I heard? If it rains, I'm done.

She'd noticed the cloud bank moving in. Other than watching snails crawl on the wet lumber, there was little to keep her entertained.

Lake Austin is supposed to be constant level, but if the streams pour in, adding to the existing current, the water could go higher.

And all it would take would be another inch.

Helen returned to her daydreams. She could visualize it plain as day, when she returned home to take care of her horses. Each horse would need special attention. And she would not waste another day until she started teaching Jenny everything she knew about horses. It was a shame how much she'd neglected her little sister.

It puzzled her, though, how many times she'd seen James Fuller in her dreams.

· · ·

"Are you ready to surrender?"

The man who came out waving the flag looked confused when James addressed him over the speaker.

A second man, more muscular, with a coyote headed hat came out and pushed the first man aside.

"You're talking to me."

"Oh, afraid I'd shoot you?"

"I knifed your sniper that was about to off Red."

"Hmm. So you aren't in charge either?"

"Yes I am. Red is worm food. You're speaking to King Samson!"

"So, high turn-over in that job?"

Samson looked at the speaker, then focused on the periscope. "Are you afraid to come out and face me, man to man?"

"Just cautious, like you were. I see that man in the shadows with a rifle propped up on the table. If you'll kill your own 'brother' at the drop of a hat, I don't think you'd let a white flag stop you."

Samson was having trouble, unable to make eye contact. Frustrated, he said, "What makes you think we'd surrender?"

"The usual. You're vastly outgunned. You have no supplies. And if you've killed the leader of the Dragons, you probably have quite a few enemies inside those walls, just waiting for their opportunity. I don't think you've got much time left."

"You think you can dig us out? It'd be expensive."

James sighed. "You know I'd really hate to bring that magnificent building down on your heads, but I can do it. And I'd rather ring out some old history than risk too many lives. Too many of our lives that is."

Samson grinned. "Red underestimated me and paid the price. I think you underestimate me too."

"Oh? In what way?"

He tapped his forehead. "I don't go into battle without an exit strategy. Unlike my poor, shortsighted predecessor, I didn't come into this city without knowing I could get myself out."

"And how do you propose to do that?"

Samson flicked his fingers and a familiar face was moved, bound and gagged, into the doorway. "I've got hostages."

James knew and liked Jake Dennison, and if he called Samson's bluff, his life would be cut short quickly as an example.

He chuckled. "One hostage? As I do the math, if I let you out, you'll kill dozens, hundreds, before the week is out."

"No, you'll lose hundreds before the *day* is out. Not all my men are inside here with me. I've been in Austin before. I went to school here before the Star. I know where the rich people live. The people that *matter*. And I've got many families locked up in their own houses, just waiting for the signal. Or waiting for sunset. You see, I don't think you've got much time left.

"Oh, and by the way, one of those hostages is that pretty little thing that rides a white horse."

Hostages

Ed held his wife's hand. "Sorry about this. I didn't see it coming."

The pair of bandits had entered the house through the back door, and before Jane could scream out, they'd bound and gagged her and her mother. A moment later they caught Ed and Angela at the top of the stairs. They'd disarmed Ed before he thought to raise the pistol.

They were all kept in the living room, where the dirty blonde-haired one sat in Ed's favorite chair and watched them, bound together in a huddle on the floor.

The other one, short with dark hair and a broad mustache to compliment his beard, rushed in with a worried look on his face. "Explosion at the Capitol building. I think I can hear gunfire as well."

"Calm down. The boss thought something might happen. That's why we're here sitting in luxury, waiting for sundown."

"But what if the word doesn't come?"

"Then we do our business and get back across the water."

Jane started shivering. Her mother held her tightly.

Ed whispered, "Don't worry. I can't tell my fortune, but I checked Jane's a long time ago. She will live a long life."

Leona Gunn tried to laugh, but couldn't. "Good for her, but what about me?"

"I can try to check, if you really want."

She hesitated. Her own life had been a roller-coaster of ups and downs. If she'd have been told her future when she was her daughter's age, what would that have done to her life?

"Okay." She nodded.

Ed leaned close enough to touch her. He smiled.

"I sometimes get just a single image of the future. That's what I got from you."

"What is it?" She was frightened of the possibilities, but she was terrified of her current position, at the mercy of known killers and rapists.

Ed closed his eyes. "I see you, and Jane, and her newborn baby. Her husband was there with her. You were the doting grandma."

The blonde-haired bandit chuckled. He'd been listening. "But what color was the cub's hair?"

Ed's smile faded. "It was black. Just like her husband's."

Jane asked, "What did he look like?"

Ed shrugged. "Not someone I've ever met. About your age."

She smiled.

The bandit with the mustache said, "So you're that fortune teller?"

"You didn't know?"

"No. Samson just pointed out some houses and assigned a couple of us to each of them. You're hostages."

Blonde-hair said, "At least until sundown. Then we can do what we want with you."

Mustache asked, "Can you do that fortune teller trick on me?"

Ed nodded.

He asked his buddy, "How about you?"

Blonde-hair shook his head with disdain.

Ed held up his bound hands and he got close enough to touch, then he sagged back and began laughing.

"What? What is it?"

Ed shook his head. "I'm only going to say, you're the luckiest bandit of them all."

. . .

Willowby voice over the handset said, "I don't know if I could have made that deal."

James walked a few yards farther from the exodus and pushed his talk button. "I'm trying to keep the death count down, for our people."

One by one, the bandits were filing out of the Capitol building, some wide eyed and deeply suspicious of the hundred or so rifles pointed at them. Those with knives could keep them. Those with guns had to surrender them, to be given back on the other side of the Pedernales River. Then they filed into a bus, along with a driver and a pair of riflemen to keep watch. Their mixed bag of weapons was stashed in the luggage bin. Samson watched the whole thing, holding his new rifle and grinning. His smile was especially broad when he saw the look on James Fuller's face.

Distant thunder rumbled, and for an instant, people on both sides flinched.

"It's not going to be popular, you ceding the land north of the Pedernales to the bandits." Willowby said over the radio.

"I didn't give them the land, I gave them a head start. Now, here's some preparations I need you personally to take care of. Copy code."

"Code?"

"Right. 73405 23009 ...."

...

Helen worried when she stopped shivering. The water hadn't been too bad at first, with the sun beating down on the dock above her, but when the clouds came and the lumber cooled, it was just the endless stream of cool water draining the energy out of her.

So I might not drown, at least consciously. Hypothermia will set in and I'll conk out.

It was a less unpleasant way to die, at least.

But she wasn't quite ready to give up. She twisted her body to the right, and then to the left. *Exercise. Anything to keep my body temperature up.*

...

James rode in the empty bus, with just Samson, a pair of guards, and a driver. Two motorcycles followed behind. The other buses were parked on a vacant stretch of Mopac, surrounded by guards on motorcycles and a several trucks, all heavily armed.

The lone bus was given the job to rescue the hostages, or from Samson's perspective, to collect his men.

"No, the girl comes last."

James didn't argue, but he felt another twist on the mental cord that kept his anger under control.

"Turn left here."

Samson was enjoying his role as tour guide, even sending them up dead end streets as a joke.

"Okay. Stop here."

James followed Samson outside, clearly aware of where his pistol was, and just how close he dared to get to the bandit 'king'.

. . .

The blonde-haired bandit was up on his feet, peering out the front window when the bus arrived. He looked around behind him, puzzled.

Ed said, "Your partner shaved his face, stole some of my clothes and escaped out the back fence. You'll never see him again."

Their captor raised his arm to smack him down, but then Samson, out on the street gave a dog-like whine. He watched his leader make some hand signals, then he pulled out a long knife.

"You're lucky this time." He cut the ropes on Ed's hands and walked out and entered the bus.

Ed untied his feet, and even before he freed the others he went to the front door and yelled, "We're all okay!"

. . .

Samson snarled, first when he heard who had been freed, and then again when his underling whispered that his partner was gone.

"Problems?" asked James with a smirk.

"I'd keep that look off your face if you want to see the other hostages!"

"Our people covering the rest of your lot have their guns on full-auto. Hostages work both ways."

They moved on to the next house. Samson's mood had turned. He played no more games, but the look on his face showed plans for revenge churning away.

Eventually, they collected eight more teams. The pair of guards on motorcycles confirmed the hostages were mostly okay.

"Now, Helen Black," James said. He'd been patient. He wasn't anymore.

Samson hesitated, then gave the directions to a lakeside house off Scenic Drive. He didn't bother to get out.

"She's tied under the dock—if she's still alive."

James was out, running down the slope.

"Helen!"

There was no response. He ran out onto the dock. "Helen?"

There was a noise below.

He tossed his gun and radio to the dock and then jumped in.

She was there, a soggy bundle. He cut the rope and carefully pulled her free against the current. When her eyes looked up at him, he felt a wall he'd built, a wall against hurt and disappointment—preemptive grief—collapse and wash away.

He tugged the gag free. She took a deep breath, and said, "James."

. . .

James broke a window in the house and stole a blanket and a dried loaf of bread. "You stay here. I have work to do."

"No." She shook her head. "I'm coming with you."

He explained in a few words about the hostage deal.

"You shouldn't have done it. They're killers, all of them. They will kill again."

"And I won't stop until all of the Hill Country is cleansed of their tainted cult. I traded a head start for lives. Not just yours." He smiled.

"And Samson is up there in the bus?"

"Yes."

"Then give me a gun and I'll kill him myself."

James shook his head. "I can't do that. I've had to deal with faithless, backstabbing 'allies' already. I'll keep my word, to the letter. I'm delivering him and his men to the Pedernales, no matter how distasteful it is. I won't have treachery staining Austin the way it's stained Houston."

"I'm still coming."

. . .

Hek reached over and flipped the slider to full-auto on Saul's gun. Some of the bandits watching laughed. "The cub looks like he's ready to wet his pants."

Hek, seated in the rear-facing seat behind the bus driver, turned back to the bandits packed into the bus. His face was set and his eyes alert. His own weapon was positioned clear to spray the inside of the bus with bullets on an instant.

Toward the middle of the bus, a couple of Rams exchanged looks. When the time came, they'd be ready. Hek was playing his role, but they knew the real score.

The radio squawked and the string of buses started moving.

They took Highway 2222 to 620. Approaching the Mansfield Dam bridge, they slowed to a crawl, as the guards had time to open only one lane.

Saul looked out the window at the piles of corpses and poked Hek to look.

"Keep your eyes on the captives."

But they were all looking out the windows too. As they reached the other side of the bridge and entered the main kill zone, a troop of men and a boy, all with guns, watched from horseback. A tractor with a grader blade had been deployed to push a lane clear of bodies. The air was thick with the smell of death.

...

Helen looked out the window with her hand covering her nose. She waved. James wasn't sure if she was waving at the men, or the horses.

From the rear of the bus, Samson snarled. "It's all that fortune teller's fault. He did this."

James just shook his head. "He only reveals the future; he can't change it."

He snorted in disgust. "Don't tell me that! This is all his doing. The Sons of the Hunter were going to move north around the lakes, bypassing Austin altogether. Then he came in with his prophecy. After that Red was crazy, and the story spread far and wide.

"So in spite of the rains and the high rivers and the lack of preparation, we all raced in to see the great and wondrous city fall to us.

"Red was so intent on becoming king that he burned his brothers like kindling, wasting men so he could rush in and fulfill his prophecy. I had to kill him, to save us all."

James glanced at Helen. Bundled up in the blanket, and having devoured half a loaf of stale bread, her skin had come back to something like its normal color.

In a quiet voice, he said, "Don't pay any attention to him."

She nodded. "I don't. Only...when you kill him, I want to see."

He felt her anger. It was like his own, but he didn't like that part of himself.

"You know, history will call me a monster."

"You? Why? You saved the city."

"Yes, but after that, with the bandits gone, they'll judge me for chasing them down and killing every last one and burning out every hint of their diseased cult."

She was silent for a minute or so. She'd heard him mention that his father had been killed. "You're going to be the new Mayor of Austin?"

He shrugged. "That's the way to bet. I was trained for this. I won't turn it down."

She leaned closer, keeping to a whisper. "The bandits will be in the Hill Country, not, unless they're crazy, back in Austin. Make a formal case that the bandits were criminals—raping and killing. Every last one of them. It was part of their cult. Sentence them to death, and then make the offer to all the surrounding towns. If they call, you'll come and clean out the bandits."

He nodded, thinking it through. "Shared blood guilt. It won't be just me."

"And if, somewhere, a bandit reforms, and his neighbors don't object..."

"Cities of Refuge, like in the Old Testament. Yes, I like it." He smiled at her. He'd have to find a way to visit her on her horse farm from time to time. Even when she griped at him, she made sense.

"What are you two scheming up there?" growled Samson.

James called back, "Just thinking of the day when you're just a bad memory."

The Pedernales Crossing

Shortly after they turned onto Highway 71, the convoy of buses slowed to a stop.

Samson yelled, "What's going on here?"

James shook his head. "Stay put."

He stepped to the door and a motorcyclist pulled up. "Sir! The bridge over the Pedernales River is impassible."

From inside, Samson shouted, "Treachery! I knew I couldn't trust you."

James ignored him. "Halt the convoy here. Drive this bus up as far as we can. I want to see this myself."

James glared at Samson, but as their bus pulled out of the line, they both sat down and rode until they got close to the bridge.

Helen recognized the place. That was where she was shot. That was the house where she was held captive. And...those smoldering ruins marked the place where she had escaped being raped when Red claimed her as a hostage.

Good riddance.

The bus pulled to a stop.

"Samson, you can come with me. The rest of you stay in place."

Sergeant Willowby came running up when he saw James get out of the bus. He eyed the man in the furs with suspicion, but addressed his commander.

"Sir. The bridge is impassible."

It was pretty obvious. A large tanker truck was crashed at an angle, nearly blocking the whole width. It was burning a tall billowing plume of black smoke. The fire even flamed to the railings as if the pavement was burning.

"What happened?"

"Sir. Well I think one of the towns on the other side—maybe Johnson City, sent a fuel truck here to deliberately block the return of the bandits. From the heat of the flames, I'd be worried that the concrete will crumble. Maybe that's what they planned. I don't know how long it'll keep burning."

Samson said, "Well it looks like you'll have to turn us loose on this side, doesn't it?"

James stared back at him, no emotion showing. "That was not the deal. I would escort your men to the Pedernales and let them cross. No more than that. I'm perfectly willing to line the buses up here and send your men across the bridge right now."

Samson stared at the flames. "You can't do that."

"Yes I can. Sergeant Willowby. You'd help me organize that passage wouldn't you?"

"Sending the bandits to flaming hell? You bet. All of us would."

"No! Just because the bridge is out, there are other ways across. There's a road just over that way."

James nodded. "Yes, the Hamilton Pool road crossing. I'm familiar."

"We'll cross that way. The river is well down from its peak."

James considered it for a minute or so.

"Just this one extension. You cross there or the deal's off and we'll toss your bullet-riddled corpses in ourselves."

Samson glanced at the sky, but the sun was obscured by the clouds. It had to be mid-afternoon already. Crossing in the dark would be even harder.

"Let's go."

James radioed to the convoy while Samson listened. Get the buses as close to the river as possible. Unload the bandits. Let them string a guide rope to assist the crossing, but get them moving.

...

The scene was a mess. Too small a road, and no places to park. The road was filled with yellow buses end to end.

A guard rapped on the side of the bus. Hek and Saul stood.

Hek yelled, "Time to move!"

The guards outside held their guns on the bandits as they stepped down. Hek kept them covered from the inside.

As the Rams passed, one of them reached out his hand and grabbed Hek's arm.

"It's time. Let's make our move!"

Hek stuck the muzzle of his M16 into the man's neck. "Get your hands off of me."

"But Hek?"

"I'm not the man you think I am. Now get moving."

Puzzled and angry, the bandit moved down the steps.

Saul watched, confused and disturbed. But he didn't let his aim waver.

...

It was a madhouse, on the verge of chaos. The city forces with their M16s lined both sides of the road, which wound like a children's playground slide down and around the steep grade down to the water level. The pavement was slick with mud from the previous high water. Some of the bandits recovered their guns, and in a couple of instances, there was a brief exchange of fire. Only the overwhelming firepower of the M16s kept it from getting out of hand, which was lucky for both sides. At that close range, the city troops would be shooting each other by accident as often as they'd bring down bandits.

The final bus arrived when more than half of the bandits had made it across.

Samson led his men down to the water, watching as they moved, hand over hand with the rope, through the muddy water.

The rain clouds had grown ominous, and thunder shook the air.

"The water is rising."

James said, "Then you'd better get moving. No more extensions."

Helen put aside her blanket and climbed out. In her tattered dress, torn to strips from her bandage making, she watched passively as the last of the bandits grabbed the rope and started over. Some of the braver troops were chest deep in the water, keeping the bandits moving with the barrels of their guns.

Suddenly, water from a downpour a dozen miles upstream came rushing through. The water surged. One of the city soldiers was swept into the current and most of the bandits were stripped off the rope. The water soon hid even that from sight.

A youngster, one of the refugee volunteers cried out, "Hek!" as his companion vanished into the waters.

Samson, planning to be the the last one across, looked in horror, as across the way, his men who had not left the shoreline were also being caught up in the flash flood. One of the buses came off its wheels and began edging into the current.

"You can't!" screamed Samson.

James pulled out his pistol and aimed it squarely at his head.

Samson grabbed the rope in the water and in panic, started across. The turbulence ripped his grasp free before he was five yards into the current.

"Help!" he had time to gasp. No one made a move.

James said, "'The Hill Country itself will save us.'"

Then he yelled orders. Get uphill. Abandon the buses.

Helen stood watching the current, her arms wrapped across her chest.

"Are you okay?" he asked.

"I guess. I'm tired."

"Me too."

He led her to the top of the hill, where their bus waited. Many of the troops would stay, to pull as many of the buses clear of the water as possible.

Once they were moving, James pulled out his radio.

"Sergeant, how is the bridge?"

The static distorted his voice. Lightning was flickering across the sky. There would be many places flooded tonight.

"Okay. It was in no structural danger. We turned off the flames as soon as you were out of sight. It'll need repaving, but that's it."

"Good. Get the bridge cleared and start sending patrols up toward Johnson City. Be on the lookout for bandit stragglers. There may be as many as fifty to a hundred that made it across."

"Only fifty to a hundred? What happened?"

"Flash flood. Not my hand."

"Thank God."

Helen frowned at him, as he turned off the radio. "So that whole bridge thing was faked?"

"Yes. My plan was to send them across the low water bridge on foot to give us time to send armed patrols ahead of them. I gave them the letter of my deal, but not a comma more. I had to keep the tactical advantage.

"The details were Sergeant Willowby's handiwork. I just told him to make the bridge look impassible."

She leaned against him in the seat. "I'm going to sleep for a week... no I can't I have to find Snowcap and ...."

"Some man named Risk has him. He said he'd keep him safe for you. My soldiers are feeding Nomad."

She calmed down again. "What about you?"

He sighed. "Politics. Getting the refugees back home. I'm going to be needing to make some kind of deal with the East Texas lumber mills to provide shipments of fresh lumber to rebuild the burned out homes.

"And by the way, I'll need more horses. I want to keep a permanent version of the Hill Country Rangers for rural patrols, to compliment my Motorized Guards. Maybe combine them. I don't know."

She watched him. He was beginning to slur his words.

"James, it'll be a while before we get to town. Lean over here and close your eyes."

He was asleep two minutes later.

Succession

Helen woke totally confused. The bed was huge. The sheets were soft and dazzlingly white. The room seemed larger than her house.

"Ah, you're awake!"

"Angela! What are you doing here?"

She giggled. "I'm your chaperone. We can't have you spending the night at James Fuller's house without one, now can we?"

"I'm a little confused."

"I don't doubt it. When the bus arrived, both you and James were fast asleep. He went off to do army things, but you were like the dead. I heard you were trapped in the river? Did you eat at all yesterday?"

"Yes, a little. But now that you mention it, I'm famished."

She nodded and pulled a bell strap. "They'll bring something up soon. Now get up. We have to get you dressed."

Angela had brought a selection of dresses.

"Um. Angela, these aren't your size."

She chuckled. "No. I suspected you'd be needing them eventually, so when we went shopping, I ah... placed a few orders."

"You're still playing matchmaker, aren't you? You know, it seems like everyone thought James and I had something going on. I don't know where that came from."

Angela just smiled. "I have to do something to keep myself occupied. My maid resigned and I'm not ready to deal with hiring a new one yet."

"Oh, Jane?"

"Yes, your young man Joshua came by and proposed, and she said 'yes'."

"Joshua! I can't think of him as that old."

After Helen found one she liked—not too fancy, she asked, "Do you know where my old clothes are?"

"Those rags?"

"Yes. I need something."

When the food arrived, Helen ate heartily. Angela tracked down the old clothes.

Rags they were, but the staff had washed them.

Helen picked up the blue strip and tied it around the sleeve of her fancy white dress.

"What's that for?"

"Memory. Remembering all the women who bear scars."

...

James drove up close to mid-day. She almost didn't recognize him clean-shaven.

"I like your uniform."

He smiled, "And I like your dress. Have you eaten?"

"Yes. But if you..."

"No. It's just that I've been summoned to the City Council chamber, and I was asked to bring you along."

"Me? Why?"

Angela hopped up. "I'll get my shawl. Don't leave without me."

Helen sighed. "My self-appointed chaperone."

"That's fine."

"Did you get any sleep?"

He grinned. "Actually, I did. Several hours, in fact."

On the way, he asked about the blue ribbon. She explained how it happened.

He looked off into memory. "She was a fierce warrior. Probably unhealthily so, but I wouldn't have stopped her. She had scars."

"There are a lot of women with scars—scars of all kinds. I don't know what I can do for them."

He sighed. "That's a problem no man can solve. Your ribbon is a good first step."

Helen looked at him in the eyes. "James. In nine months, there will be another problem."

He sighed. "I know."

She said, "I heard them laugh. Cubs, they called them. Every place they destroyed, they'd leave behind their cubs.

"And when the time comes, families will have to cope. Some will accept the child with no complaint. Others will become scapegoats."

He sighed, "I'll have to do something. The 'cubs' are innocent in all this."

Helen nodded, "That's it! 'The cubs are innocent.' We'll have to start soon, so everyone will have heard it."

"But it will take more than a catch phrase."

"I know. But I'm happy you're thinking about it."

Angela stared out the window, pretending she wasn't listening, but she had to dab some moisture from her eyes.

...

The same woman who barricaded her access to the Driskill that first day was there to lead them, all smiles, to the Council chamber. Helen had no illusion that she was the source of the pleasant greeting.

The room was crowded.

"Have a seat, James. You too, Miss Black."

James tried to identify the people. There were three of the original Austin City Council–Nelson, Johnson, and Gonzalez. There was Jake Dennison.

He met Jake's eyes and nodded. The man nodded back.

He'd ignored Jake's life when he'd been treated as a hostage. Would there be problems down the line with him? They would have to talk.

There were also two of the men he had seen during the fighting from the refugee camps, but there were four others he couldn't place.

William Nelson spoke, "The City of Austin has been left with a crisis due to the death of George Fuller. Let's be honest and acknowledge that while we have maintained the illusion of a representative government, neither Austin, nor the State of Texas has had an election since the Star.

"So we must either restart that process, or choose an alternate method of governmental succession."

Nelson nodded to Jake. He rose and addressed the group.

"As you know, I was trapped in the Capitol building with the bandits during the ill-fated 'reign' of Red the Dragon, and then the bloody succession to Samson the Wolf. In a bid to save my life, I became the historian and observed the process.

"I must say, even as barbarians, they made their case for their claims to power in a very clear way. Red killed the Mayor. Then Samson killed Red.

"When subsequent historians look at this time, they may suggest that the claims for kingship were valid, based on conquest, just as they were done in the thousands of years of our history." He sat down.

Nelson took over, "Which brings us back to our problem. If we just declare a new Mayor and pretend that everything is just as it was, what happens if some bandit somewhere, or some descendant of Red or Samson, declares that he has the right to the kingship."

James looked at the assembled faces. There were no objections, no complaints at the stretches of logic. *They talked this all out before. They're just re-hashing it for me.*

"James, no one here disagrees that you defeated the Houston attack and also defeated the bandits. From all reports, you were the one who killed Samson, by forcing him into the water at gunpoint to be drowned.

"It's cleanest all the way around to just abandon the illusion of the office of Mayor and declare you King."

There was silence. James tapped the desk. He looked at Helen, who seemed enormously amused by his predicament.

"Will the people accept it? This is America, after all. We did away with kings."

Gonzalez spoke. "And Americans followed all the pagentry and scandals of the British royals before the Star. We weren't that disconnected. And when was the last time anyone...anyone heard a complaint about the lack of an election? Even before the Star, voter participation was down. People felt disenfranchised. Since then, everyone knows that things have changed, and that every institution is up for grabs. We print our own money. We have cities acting like independent states.

"And the people love you, James. If I tried to put on a crown, they'd have my head. But not you. The people will accept it."

"But not everyone is happy." The new voice was one of those he recognized from the fight. "It's all fine for Austin to have their king. But what about us in Dripping Springs? What about everyone from Llano to Kerrville? The bandits claimed 'King of the Hill Country'.

"As cleverly as Mr. Fuller here trapped the Houston troops to get their guns to wipe out the bandits, we suffered a month of bandit attacks before Austin did anything. It was only at the last minute that Austin even let us across the Colorado River.

"No, if there's going to be a king. It needs to be a 'King of the Hill Country', just like the bandits' prophecy said. And we don't really trust Austin to act in our interests any more."

The big man, Derek Risk, spoke quietly. "There is a compromise. I think we'd agree to a Kingdom of the Hill Country, if certain conditions are met.

"One, James Fuller would have to live elsewhere. He has strong ties to Austin, but he needs to grow broader roots.

"Two, if someone the Hill Country community trusts, someone like Helen Black, were to become queen, then I think we could make this happen."

Nelson said, "Austin could agree to that. The King would be responsible for the broader scope of problems, like that trade agreement with the MOB, negotiations with larger city states or regional governments, and the defense of the people.

"City details would be left to the council, although we'll probably change our titles. I rather fancy 'Duke Nelson', myself. And maybe add some fresher blood."

James looked at Helen, eyes blazing, her arms crossed.

She thought it was funny when they were running my life.

He mentioned, while the moment was ripe, "I might suggest to the Council, that they could do worse than to elevate Sergeant Paul Willowby."

He turned to his side. "By the way, Helen, what do you think about their plan?"

She took a breath, ready to lay into them all, then looked him in the eyes.

She froze for a moment, her eyes showing a mind churning in thought.

"Ah...I might like to have some time to think about it?"

Nelson nodded, "Certainly. But we'll need to move quickly. The people will need to be assured that everything is going to be okay."

. . .

Helen sat on the desk in James Fuller's office. He sat beside her. They were alone.

"I have one condition."

He held her hand. "What's that?"

She looked him in the eyes. "There will come the question, 'Was I raped by the bandits?' You will need to 'neither confirm nor deny'."

"What? Why? Samson assured me he never got the chance."

She nodded. "That's for you and me to know. No one else."

"Okay. I agree. Why?"

Helen stared at the wall. "If I'm going to be 'queen'—I can barely say the word. But if I am going to be someone in that position. I want to be there for all the women who suffered. There's a lot of healing needed. There will be a lot of women who won't want to answer that question either, and if they have me as an example...."

He nodded. "Makes sense. It's nobody's business. Official policy."

"But now I have something, too."

"What?" she asked.

"If I turn the down the offer to be king, and go be a horse farmer, will you marry me?"

Epilogue

Ed was dressed in a crisp gray suit, tailored before the Star in Italy and preserved like jewels by the shopkeeper who realized he could charge a fortune for it when the right time came. Angela, clasping his hand, was no less resplendent.

"I told you."

"Yes you did, My Lord."

"Shall we find our seat, Countess?"

. . .

The castle with its high, white stone-work towers crowned the ridge. They could see Inks Lake off in the distance. The actual ceremony would be held indoors, but the pageantry leading up to it was worth watching.

The newspaper tried to turn the cost of the fancy uniforms of the Rangers into a minor scandal, but nobody really minded. The mounted soldiers, looking almost like knights from the middle ages in their white tunics, marked with a crest showing a rearing horse, lined the entranceway leading up through the surrounding walls. Third from the end, dressed almost the same, was a woman wearing a blue band on her shoulder. According to the news, Tammy Wilson was making quite a name for herself in the Rangers, and she had no end of fans among the young women.

There were deep blue canopies spread around the garden, just in case it rained, but nothing was going to stop this day.

On a dais, James stood, watching as Helen rode up on her white stallion.

Kingdom of the Hill Country

One of the attendants riding with her was little April Jensen, on her new horse Sterling. It had been a gift from James, after a quiet suggestion by Mr. Hodges. From all reports, April was becoming quite popular with her friends.

Helen dismounted, and walked the steps up to join the King. Her dress was white, and sparkled in the sunlight. There were no sleeves, as was Helen's custom, and the scar from her battle wound was plainly visible, just below the blue band she always wore. In the months leading up to the wedding, everyone in the Kingdom had come to know her. People appreciated her heartfelt outspokenness, proclaiming time and time again, "The women of the Kingdom have a voice."

Sprinkled throughout the crowd, among the well-dressed new royalty, and among the merely wealthy, there were a few blue bands as well. On the surrounding roads where the couple would ride shortly, there were blue bands in abundance among the thousands of well-wishers.

But all eyes were focused now on one place.

James took her hand, and the joy on her face shone strong and clear across all time and space.

The PROJECT Saga

Star Time

Kingdom of the Hill Country

and coming soon

Iron War

But what about Abe and Sharon?

The heroes of **Star Time** and their adventures on the world of the Cerik will be coming in a companion volume —
Tales of the U'tanse

Can't wait for it to appear? Check for short fiction in: **Henry's Stories**, the on-line magazine.
http://HenrysStories.blogspot.com

Small Towns, Big Ideas

A collection of science-fiction tales where high school aged adventureres take that extra step into the unknown.

Emperor Dad

Roswell or Bust

Extreme Makeover

Lighter Than Air

Falling Bakward

Golden Girl

Follow That Mouse

Bearing Northeast

The Copper Room

.

CPSIA information can be obtained at www.ICGtesting.com
Printed in the USA
LVOW130006240512

283080LV00002B/5/P

9 781935 236368